Lily Dunn is a writer and mentor. She is the author of a novel, *Shadowing the Sun* (Portobello Books, 2008), and a memoir of her father and the legacy of his addictions, due from Weidenfeld & Nicolson in 2022. Her creative non-fiction has been published by *Granta*, *Aeon* and *Litro*. She co-runs London Lit Lab with fellow writer and friend Zoe Gilbert.

Zoe Gilbert is the author of two novels, *Folk* (Bloomsbury, 2018) and *Mischief Acts* (Bloomsbury, 2022). Her short stories have been broadcast on BBC Radio and published internationally, and have won prizes including the Costa Short Story Award. She is the co-director of London Lit Lab, where she teaches and mentors creative writers.

T0266741

A WILD AND PRECIOUS LIFE

A Recovery Anthology

Edited by Lily Dunn and Zoe Gilbert

unbound

First published in 2021

Unbound
Level 1, Devonshire House, One Mayfair Place, London W1J 8AJ
www.unbound.com
All rights reserved

'She Will Be My Joy' by Jamie Guiney first appeared in
The Wooden Hill (époque press, 2018)

'Are You Intoxicated?' and 'End of an Episode' by Rob True first appeared in
Gospel of Aberration (Burning House Press, 2019)

'I May, I Might, I Must' by Marianne Moore from *New Collected Poems of
Marianne Moore* reproduced by permission of Faber and Faber Ltd

Text design by PDQ Digital Media Solutions Ltd

A CIP record for this book is available from the British Library

ISBN 978-1-78352-964-3 (trade pbk)
ISBN 978-1-78352-966-7 (ebook)
ISBN 978-1-78352-965-0 (limited edition)

Printed in Great Britain by Clays Ltd, Elcograf S.p.A

1 3 5 7 9 8 6 4 2

Supported using public funding by
ARTS COUNCIL
ENGLAND
LOTTERY FUNDED

If you will tell me why the fen
appears impassable, I then
will tell you why I think that I
can get across it if I try.

Marianne Moore, 'I May, I Might, I Must'

Contents

FOREWORD

WILL SELF

I've always had my suspicions about the well-trodden trope that 'the road of excess leads to the palace of wisdom'. For a start, William Blake certainly wasn't referring to any sort of drink- or drug-induced state, and nor was he evoking any sort of higher understanding – one borne out of the lower psychic depths; rather, his was the proto-typical Romantic sensibility: he saw the world in a grain of sand quite as much as understanding that this world is but a grain of sand in the great maelstrom of creation.

The first few experiences someone has with intoxication can indeed be revelatory, but what the thousandth LSD trip, shot of whisky or line of cocaine add to the individual human psyche seems at best nugatory, and at worst highly destructive. And anyway, most people reading this will be familiar with the way those great glittering epiphanies gifted by intoxication turn back into dross once you regain sobriety.

The literature of intoxication is also condemned – so to speak – out of its own mouth: the better it invokes this state, the more transitory its own insights are likely to be. But by the same token, there's also a literature of recovery that seems to be voided in its own enactment. 'I used to be a junkie/alcoholic/compulsive eater or shopper,' legions of memoirs and *romans-á-clef* assert, 'but I'm all right now!' This isn't really literature at all – but a complex sort of virtue signalling, whereby fragile psyches seek one another out.

Even when writing by those who are self-consciously recovering from addictive malaises doesn't perform this function (really a virtual version of group therapy), it can still get off to a dreadful start when its writers believe they're engaged in some sort of cathartic act. Fine, write for catharsis if you like – but once again: this isn't literature. Catharsis can be a by-product of literature, but never its reason for existing.

Of course, I've written plenty of stories – and even entire novels – about addictive illness. I've flouted everything I've written above – and worse: I've published reams of stuff that doesn't just describe alcohol- and drug-induced mental states, but positively revels in them. But to quote William Burroughs, one of my literary mentors – and a man who himself died on a maintenance methadone scrip – 'Wouldn't you?'

By which I mean: wouldn't you, if drugs and alcohol had been such a major part of your life? I'm a member of that generation of heroin addicts that sprang into being following the Iranian revolution of 1978 and the mass importation of heroin to Britain from the so-called 'Golden Crescent' that followed. In a few short years, Britain went from having a few hundred safely registered opiate addicts to many thousands of feral ones: it's this background of moral panic and an exploding culture of intoxication that's informed both my life and my work.

So, write about what you know – there's nothing wrong with that.

Of course, worse even than the types of drugged writing I limn above are what I term 'drug pornography': description of scenes of abandonment, ecstasy and attendant moral dereliction that give straight-going readers a little thrill of schadenfreude. Not good. So, with these preliminary remarks dealt with, I hope you enjoy this collection of writings inspired by addictive illness and recovery from it. Have these writers managed to avoid the pitfalls? It's for you to discover.

INTRODUCTION

LILY DUNN

A Wild and Precious Life sprang from my own recovery from my father's premature death due to alcoholism in 2005. Eight years later, and still suffering from grief (though I wasn't really aware of it at the time), I found myself phoning around recovery services in Hackney, east London, volunteering to teach creative writing to those trying to forge a life beyond their addiction to drugs and alcohol. It didn't take long before I was given a job at Hackney Recovery Service, affiliated with St Mungo's, a charity that helps homeless people, where they'd been keen to find someone to set up a regular group. Its ease felt fortuitous.

At the time Hackney Recovery Service was in a building just off Mare Street, with a series of treatment rooms and a busy reception; plastic chairs nailed to the floor, a mix of clientele waiting to meet their key workers or to get their prescriptions. Many used it for safe needles and prescription drugs, but regulars were also those who had been through treatment – the reduced drinking or abstinence programmes – and were facing a life that is clean. Alex, my supervisor, took me into the various groups to publicise our plans for the new creative-writing class, and there was a lot of interest. But, he warned, many of the recovery service users had chaotic lives, and so retention was a challenge. I went into it with low expectations.

The first class was a surprise. So many people streamed in that we had to get extra chairs from the adjoining room. That week we had a young grandmother who rapped for us; we had

1

an ex-crack addict; an Irish guy who was a natural poet, and a woman who, months later, would come back crying, telling me how the group had changed her life. We had fourteen that day.

What all these people had in common was that they all wrote. Some on the back of napkins or receipts when they were sitting in the park with their friends; in those empty spaces, they imagined themselves into other people's lives. Some wrote down their anger, or confusion, or pain, and had quickly realised how much clearer they felt as a result. Some wrote songs and performed them; others just quietly made notes on the movements of their day.

During that initial six weeks, we built a tight group of people who came regularly, wrote, discussed and read out their writing. I was struck by their openness and softness of heart, a readiness to gather around the table and to share. They were in a trusted environment. They had key workers. They'd been through various therapeutic courses. They were used to facing pain and difficult feelings, being honest with themselves, and sharing their stories.

My most loyal student, Susie, would bring her big notebooks to class with pages and pages of scrawl and tell us how she often scrapped what she had written in reaction to crippling self-doubt. When she read out the work she produced in class, I'd drop my head and close my eyes, clasping my hands. I barely took a breath, not wanting to miss a beat; it was so heartfelt and beautiful. When she'd finished, I'd glance up at Alex and we'd both smile in acknowledgement.

Six weeks turned into three months, and the group was so successful that my supervisor asked if I could stay, and so I applied to the Arts Council for a grant. We were successful, which meant I could bring my teaching partner Zoe Gilbert in to help. After nine months of teaching, we did a nationwide callout for recovery stories. We chose the best and most varied, and this book is the result.

I'd got my hands on an anthology of poetry called *Beyond Bedlam*, in which famous poets' work was mixed with writing by patients from Maudsley Hospital. I was growing increasingly interested in the correlation between mental health and creativity, struck by the talent in my group, not only their openness and willingness to go straight to what mattered, to touch on their truth, but also, generally, how easy this was for them. I reflected on how difficult I had found it as a beginner writer to find my voice, and to cut through the layers of self-consciousness. I questioned whether there were other routes to 'writing well' than the obvious technique-focused graduation programmes, which, in some cases and with some students, might even be counterproductive. It felt as if I had touched on something new: the idea that good writing, which would compel the attention of others, can also come from a place of knowing yourself.

I walked away from my time teaching this group humbled by the power of writing, by what can be learned once you're ready, and where it can lead. We write to transcend the harsh or mundane realities of our world, just as we drink and take drugs to do the same. But writing also helps us reflect and think and understand situations from all perspectives. It opens the mind and heart not only to what's inside, but also to what's out there. It forces you to wake up.

When teaching creative writing, I always tell my students to look around them, to notice the detail, to recognise the stories in the everyday. Just this simple act, if practised, can help turn off the unhelpful warring voices in the head. We can be caught in the turbulence of our lives, or we can choose to try to understand. Crafting our experience helps us do this: adopting a persona, a narrator, a tone, a particular stance, separates that experience from us.

But I also left knowing more about addiction. I had wanted to understand it better to protect myself from my own propensity for fantasy, delusion even, and how close at times I had stood on the edge. But more, to understand my father. Teaching this group, reading the varied work, being present at the events we've done since, has helped me shine a light on this slighted world, so that those who turn away or shake their heads in disapproval might stop and reconsider.

Much like renowned addiction specialist Dr Gabor Maté, my supervisor at Hackney Recovery Service believed that most of his clients had been through some kind of trauma. What interests me is that drugs then act not to repress those difficult feelings, but instead help bring a person back to life. 'The addict's reliance on the drug to reawaken her dulled feelings is no adolescent caprice,' writes Maté in his book *In the Realm of Hungry Ghosts*. 'The dullness itself a consequence of an emotional malfunction not of her making: the internal shutdown of vulnerability.' Vulnerability has evolved from the Latin word *vulnerare* 'to wound'. As Dr Brené Brown states, in order to be vulnerable 'we have to allow ourselves to be seen, really seen.' What Alex and the key workers at Hackney Recovery Service were doing was helping their clients reconnect with their true selves.

This book is filled with this wounded vulnerability, painful, raw and wild. It has evolved from difficult experience, but also from strength and curiosity, and has developed into something that I hope will be an inspiration to many.

ABOUT ADDICTION

ALEX GOSTWICK

My job at Hackney Recovery Service was to engage the people who came to our project in meaningful activities to help them break the cycle of addiction. Through this work I came to understand addiction as a very common human affliction that does not discriminate based on age, race, creed or gender. Addicts who wish to break the cycle face the task of navigating the murky underworlds of both their fractured psyche and modern society, where collective shaming, criminalisation and stereotyping further burden them with the symptoms of a profoundly sick culture.

If this seems overstated, I invite you to consider whether our trashing of life-sustaining ecosystems is entirely isolated from countless people's spiralling alcoholism or descent into drug abuse.

The clue might be in our separation: from family lineage and culture; from the natural world and a sense of how to make meaning out of the modern one; from a sense of home and place; from neighbours; from older and younger generations; and from the nourishment an interdependent community can bring us.

The addict often bears their psychological traumas alone, seeking home in a fractured and self-obsessed culture but finding only false order and precarious opportunities. This is not to diminish individual sovereignty and the choices we make; rather, it is to say that addiction is both a solitary and a collective phenomenon that requires all of us to practise a

5

broader compassion. By this, I mean a kind of compassion that understands the symptoms and roots of addiction, and does not rush hastily to 'fix' them but tries instead to salve these wounds and rewrite the addiction narrative.

This is precisely why creative writing has a place in an addiction support service. With the right guidance and support, writing is a healing tool. It offers insights, perspective, escape and community, and a means of expression for the soul.

The sessions we ran were a cauldron of creativity. A right bunch of characters crammed into a room in a Victorian townhouse, led by our facilitator Lily through exercises in self-authorship, poetry, meditation, and the form and structure of fiction. Our writers brought ragged and tender attempts at poetry, spoken word, short stories and autobiography. Raw talent came calling as sure as day, and there were moments of true inspiration.

Over many months, faces came and went, but a core group remained, and in this group grew the fragile stirrings of resilience. For those writers featured here, what developed was a commitment to do the writer's work; to learn to rewrite their stories and deliver to us a piece of beauty.

THE ANTHOLOGY

ZOE GILBERT

It was not at all obvious that compiling and editing an anthology around the theme of recovery would be a joyous experience. The delight and pleasure that mounted as Lily and I read through submissions from authors for this book was a wonderful surprise. I often laughed, and delighted in that laughter. Here was so much humour, so much skill, and above all, so much honesty. All kinds of writing can make the writer feel vulnerable, but in these pieces, vulnerability was tempered by control, those deep and vital decisions the author makes about the shape they will give their story.

This is true for pieces here that are autobiographical, as well as those that are fictional. All have an urgency, a message that might be communicated with a wry slant, a direct sadness, a punch of fury or from a place of contentment. All these authors have a self-knowledge that shines through their writing, and yet each reveals that knowledge in an original way. It was easy to recognise that shine, to know that every piece we chose for this anthology can be trusted by both its writer and its reader. And that's important when we're talking about recovery.

What we mean by recovery, though, might be many things, and we don't have to reach a consensus. Recovery might be a stage, a process, a task, a state. It might be one that can be left behind, or that never really ends. It might be safe or precarious, hard-won or inevitable, tinged with regret or alight with relief. It's not straightforward: does recovery ever really happen? These ways of thinking about recovery are some of the reasons why we chose the title *A Wild and Precious Life*.

At Hackney Recovery Service, Lily, Alex and I were talking about the anthology long before it existed. We wondered what to call it; we didn't want to evoke solemnity, or sanctimony, or imply that its contents might be a melancholic tour of human difficulty – because the writing we had already witnessed in the group at Hackney was anything but that. We wanted to encapsulate the whole gamut of emotion and experience that recovery provokes, but also to acknowledge that the life lived before it, whether shaped by addiction or other challenges, is just as real and full and important. Lily remembered a poem, 'The Summer Day' by Mary Oliver. The poem's characterisation of life as wild and precious grabbed us: this was what it felt like when we sat with the writers at the recovery service and heard the words that captured their experiences. Recovery is precious, but life in all its wildness is precious too. It is everything we do, not just recovering, that makes us who we are.

So we decided that this anthology would include work not just by those experiencing recovery as they wrote, and not only explorations of recovery from addiction. Illness, whether mental or physical, does not discriminate any more than addiction does. Depression, disordered eating, post-traumatic stress, life-threatening or long-term physical illness, loss: these affect so many of us at some time, and we wanted to recognise that. Human beings are so often recovering – we are a community that has this in common – but no two human stories are the same. We hope that this collection of writing, from the exuberant to the thoughtful, the furious to the hilarious, will move you as it has us. It is full of life: all of it wild, all of it precious.

JOY

SCRIPT

MAGGIE SAWKINS

Lily's swigging spirits with Bikini Girl in Lightship Inn. Slim Jim's spiking it with mystic pills. Nitwit Nick sips his Pimm's. Bikini Girl's dissing it. Finds shrimp-pink lipstick. Slicks Nick's lips with it. Winks. Nick's livid. Lifts his fist. Lily sits tight. Mind's spinning. Misfits, mimics, bigwigs, dimwits imbibing it, sniffing it. Slim Jim flips. Nick's slinging it. Bikini Girl's high. Bigwig's winging it. Lily's thigh. Kissing, licking it. Bikini Girl sighs. Lily sips Tixylix. Pinpricks. Prickly skin. Itching, fixing it. Things shift. Spirits fly. I'm scripting it. Thrilling, isn't it.

ARE YOU INTOXICATED?

ROB TRUE

Theron stood on the kerb, shouting at a bus stop.

He had been walking down Church Street, concerned with the blue car that had gone past three times. Theron rubbernecked as it made a fourth pass, then cursed himself for making it obvious. He didn't want them to know he knew.

It's definitely the same car.

As he looked back round, he was startled by the bus stop. It stood stark against the grey street, strange. Horror bloomed in his gut, like an explosion. Hollow and twisted at the core. He stood still. A screaming whine crashed through his ears from far off and then stopped. The bus stop watched him, mocking, knowing. It was part of the plan. An enemy.

Not that way, the bus stop said.

Fuck off. I know what you're trying to do, Theron said back.

People gave him a wide berth as they walked around him. He looked up at the sky, shouting at the clouds. A police car pulled up, flashing lights. Two officers got out and approached Theron on the pavement.

We've had reports of menacing behaviour by a man of your description.

Theron grinned.

Are you intoxicated?

Theron said nothing, staring straight through the officer.

We're going to search you. Have you got anything on you, you shouldn't have?

Theron just stared, but they were already down his pockets. Out came the shiv, followed by a piece of hashish.

Down the station, they searched him again. He stripped down, one item of clothing at a time. Theron watched as they patted down his jacket.

Whatever's left of an ounce of cocaine in the lining of that jacket, like a hard fist.

Theron had bumped some idiot for the dough and got the coke to sell to buy heroin. Instead he started injecting it and couldn't stop. The copper with his jacket passed it back to him. They hadn't found it.

How did they miss that? It's fuckin' solid.

They took Theron to a cell, locked him in and left him to stew a bit. He lay back and stared at the wall. Flaked paint through graffiti. Strange worlds through layers. The faces. The worm at the controls, changing time. Eye seeing inwards, outwards, upside-down-wards. Theron lay smiling. He had a lump of pure cocaine in his jacket lining. He knew he would see a doctor soon. Diazepam and methadone. Lie down on a bench. *Que sera sera.*

OFF YOUR TROLLEY

JULIA BELL

I was with you that weekend in Wales
when the wheels came off.
And we flew down the hill
hard and fast and thrilling,
dragging the world and its strangeness
into the autumn with its barriers and No Parking.
Into the acceptance of death,
or was it the death of acceptance in the way we screamed?

The leaves left us and still we kept flying. Soon.
Now. Over the edge, too fast to think.
All that I worried about irrelevant:
my desire, my inability to provoke desire, my displacement.
That dark night in Birmingham when I said yes when I meant no.

All of these things and so much more forgotten
in the head rush of the ride without the fairground.
Just me and you and your bleak longing.
And the long road speeding ahead of us,
lost and potholed, so far away from home.

MORE IN COMMON

ANGELA JAMESON

The questions on the dental-health form throw me.

'Do you smoke? Have you ever smoked?'

I came in for a check-up, a paltry effort to take care of my health. And straight away I feel challenged. It's a straightforward question, but I know the implications and the judgement.

It may as well say: 'Have you ever sinned?'

I confess: I have.

I don't repent.

Smoking kills, I don't dispute it. But I think back to that first cigarette and the fact that a part of me was slowly dying a long time before I took my first drag. And I'm grateful to the girl who gave it to me.

It was my first term at secondary school. Three miles away from my home. It wasn't my choice, but that's where my older brothers and sisters had gone, and, if it was good enough for them, it was good enough for me. That's how things were decided when you had seven kids, apparently. To make it fair, we all got the same. Never mind that when Mum and Dad chose the school for them it was a grammar school and now it was a comprehensive, with little to differentiate it from the local school where all my mates went.

I caught the bus from the bottom of our road to the school lay-by. A double-decker, often packed by the time it got to my stop. But if you took the back seat the lads at the next bus stop would glower at you until you moved. And then you'd stand, jolted about amid sneers and jeers. I tried to steer clear of the fag-smoke cloud and hacking laughter. For a couple of months, at least.

I got into a habit of just missing that bus so I'd catch one going into town and walk down Mowbray Drive – a long, dreary dirge of a walk devoid of trees or grass, with only tarmac and concrete, lined with low-rise, flat-roofed, industrial-estate grey. I doubt my parents ever walked up there. Kids who lived locally walked that way: boys' sports bags slamming their thighs on every other step; girls clutching bags to their chests like comforters, or maybe like shields, as I soon understood.

Life would have felt very different if I could've shut myself off with headphones and music. But this was the early eighties and the personal stereo had only recently been launched on *Tomorrow's World*. So I walked, senses exposed and under assault. Visual misery of grey and beige, of tarmac and concrete; and tarmac and concrete is broken with blasts of red or yellow for double glazing, tools and paint set to a backing track of hiss and slur of traffic, spattered with the tawdry cajoling of lads in their gangs, usually on the other side of the road.

'Show us your tits!'

'Excuse me, will you suck my cock?'

All I could do was cringe and keep walking. *Just ignore them: they'll soon give up.* They'd have got as much titillation out of seeing each other's nipples as seeing mine – I was so far off showing signs of puberty. But that wasn't the point of their shouts. Ritual humiliation of all vulnerable-looking girls was their game.

The instant beetroot of my complexion didn't help much. It only piqued their interest, and requests to lift my skirt and get in my knickers would ensue. I fixed my gaze on the pavement and quickened my pace until the end of the road.

Hugging my schoolbag didn't seem like an effective long-term solution.

One of those pale grey mornings, I was stopped by some boys from a couple of years above. They walked in front of me, getting slower and slower, not letting me pass.

'You're in first year, aren't you?'

'Yeah.'

'He fancies you.'

Beetroot.

'Can I finger you?'

I tensed.

'What about him?'

One of the boys put his hand over his fly and rubbed vigorously.

'You're making me hard.'

'Will you give him a blow job?'

'No.'

They didn't touch me. I didn't think they would harm me. But they didn't let me pass, either.

I wondered how I was going to get out of this when Louise yelled in her husky roar: 'Oi, Robbo! You got a stiffy?'

The boys looked past me and one of them blushed crimson.

'Let's see it, then!'

The boys nudged one another to back off.

Louise's thatch of strawberry blonde came into my peripheral vision. A glowing fag butt was tossed to the floor and she twisted it out with her pixie boot.

'What's the matter, Robbie? Can't you get it up?'

She gave a coarse chuckle and shoved her hand through the

crook in my arm. The boys stood aside, silent now and watching as Louise and I walked off, laughing.

That was the beginning of my friendship with Louise.

It was a while before I asked her if I could try a cigarette. School had finished. We'd probably been to netball or something and some of us were walking down Mowbray Drive to get the bus.

Louise sparked up, lit a second off the first and passed it to Julie.

Louise always played centre, Julie goal attack. I was usually wing attack.

'Can I have a drag?'

Louise looked at me, surprised.

'Do you want one? You can have one. But if you have one, you'll want another, and that's it then – you'll be addicted.'

'What? I don't think so! Not from just one.'

'She will, won't she, Julie?'

Julie nodded slowly, pouting her lips to make smoke rings.

'You don't want to get addicted. But here, have it.'

And she lit another fag and passed it to me.

Some people seem to think all addicts are clearly stupid. After all, if you choose to take something you know is bad for you, then you must be stupid. Or brought up badly.

I was neither.

Other people think you do it to look cool. Really? The smokers I saw weren't cool: like crows, they crouched, cold, cowering in a scuzzy nest of fag butts round the back of the gym.

*

I took a cigarette because I wanted to. I wanted something more in common with Louise – the only person in a while to get my back when I needed it.

If I close my eyes, I can still see her face. I can hear her brassy voice bright with laughter.

'Hiya!' she called across the main street to me one day when I was in town with my mum. I cringed inwardly.

'Hiya!' she called more loudly and waved her lit cigarette at me.

I waved back and watched wistfully as she and my other friends tottered off to Top Shop in full make-up and heels, tossing their heads and laughing together.

'Who was that?' Mum asked.

'Friend from school.'

'In your year? Smoking?'

'Yeah.'

'She looks common.'

The questions on the dental-health form still challenge me.

I know the implications and the judgement.

CASHMERE OVERCOAT, 50P, WHITECHAPEL MISSION

LANE SHIPSEY

You swing the barrier; the train guard takes his cue. 'Young man, young man, come back and pay your fare.' Seeing 'man' thanks to your black hat, shaved hair and ankle-length man's overcoat. Too big for you, but the throw-outs of some grand-bellied Tory will do to warm the icy Victorian house you share with students, workers and others in the spiky-haired housing co-op crew. East London, old school, where proper tea is theft, and the coffee is instant, where dinner's mostly from the local takeaway – twenty pence a veggie samosa, twenty-five for meat. Quickly over the barrier is how it went: you didn't have the tube fare anyway, and the hop, swing, jump was swift and sweet.

LOVE

SPOONS

(after Philip Larkin)

MICHAEL LOVEDAY

If I were called in
to construct a psych ward
I should make use of spoons.

Tools for obligatory chicken soup
(that friend for our yellowing,
yearning bellies).

Spoonerisms:
lame for giving
a language that's betrayed

us. And, every nightfall,
patients should bed down
together: the body in curved embrace,
infinite bliss of our huggable selves.

TELLING BLUE

ASTRA BLOOM

'When you are mine I will call you Blue.' I tell him that from the start.

Baby boy is in the air. His colour is blue. I'm not allowed near. 'Shoo. Go on, *shoo!*' We, the pack, are scared away. She thinks us feral. But it's two o'clock and she hasn't fed us, and it's her that's showing her teeth.

This start of a boy comes from our mother, that's what they say; but less you think a bird comes from a tree, or first light comes from a window – you know that's a lie. I've known his coming. And though they say newborns see-think upside-down, and are dumb, I don't believe it. I think there are things this baby's tiny ears could catch and start drinking; I think of buttercups open to summer rain, light as lacy curtains, balls of yellow water-light wobbling, balancing. I see a big sister's words should be like raindrops; I realise I must start watering this wee thing.

'Now, Blue,' I tell him, 'there's a block of brown flats at the bend of our road by the pub, Sprout, you come from taller than that. There's this huge sky – always morphing – white as an albino rabbit, flower-blue, school-blue, bruise-grey, witch-black – and in it you get these miracle things called *stars* (which you'll *sing* about, yep, Blue, you will, you *must*). And there's this moon like a big lick of cream – *so* bright... And above all of that – now, you won't remember your height – but *you*, baby

– before here – you were Aloft. Beyond. Highest of all. And very mighty happy in this place called The Sure Place, or The Palace of Friends. We'll go back there one day. Even God and his angels can only visit Sundays. No one's ever alone there; it's filled with beauties: people and children in pink and blue and green. They never stop kissing and laughing and singing. Very, very high, like birds...'

Other times, it's important I give my baby brother the skinny. And I can see he brightly likes me being honest. I tell Blue about when he was birthed:

'Now, let me see... Yep. I was on my back beneath the bay window in my bedroom. I'd pulled my socks off, put my eyes out to rest on the blue spring sky; I was flexing my bare toes, though it was cold. The bay's a cold cave, it's true, I used to go there to catch my death some days... But on this day I was following the long white scar line from an aeroplane (it was pointing me *so* high) when I rolled onto a pinched-from-school-drawing pin. It was that exact same second, little boy, that you came in. I was pierced in my climbing-spine between my wing bones; right where the cap on my flying heart goes, when you were born, Blue. I heard you, a screaming fat fish swimming up thighs, bashing into air. And I've never got that pricking out. Sharp and rust are in me. If you lick me, I taste of clockwork.

Blue likes this; his mouth turns to a wiggly pink rain-worm.

Course, I don't, *I can't* say: 'Well, you've come to our land now, little-mite-thing. In the street, to people, you are a big, "Ooh, *number six*!" But, Blue, really, *What will we do?* You are not cress in the cupboard. You need much more than my school seeds in their Stork marg tub. Blue, how're you gonna survive in this family's dark little club?'

So, I'm not saying lots. And the day Blue was born I started up a new cough. I can't shake it off. I think it's my words all tangled in snot.

'So, you have a new baby brother?' The Miss in our school is so nice.

'Yes. He— He's... I—' Vic's vapour won't rub this up. And a div is what I sound like.

But what can I tell? Outside thinks, *Oh, she's in her shell, she's a little shy girl:* I'm not. I'm a fury with blinding pinhole-eyes and a tongue of blue fire. But I can't, I can't string all the phlegming words together. I can't tell anyone: *I'm in shock – it's shock I'm in, not a shell.*

In the blue paddle boat of our minds, Blue and I rock together; he hears me whisper: 'Dear Blue, the love you receive comes strained through the thick black curtains of grief. It's bogey-nosed-pig-eyed. It is weak. Drip a little, drip, it weeps... And who can I tell? I don't know who, Blue. And it's not this Miss. Her nice proper face fed on proper dinners, you can tell from her mash-potato-cheeks and her brown-liver-eyes, her nice-proper-smile would drop off her chin in surprise, if I said:

'My brother, Miss – I worry – he's alone in that stuff-pit-room, twisting his squealing neck off looking for her while she's out buying black bras. The hand that rocks him, Miss, it needs some steadying. The heart he searches for, Miss, it's a mess, all cut up and bleeding.'

No, I can't go telling. What? Am I gonna go moaning – '*Oh, Miss, his pink ribbon tongue's tearing in shreds from his screaming... Oh, Miss, inside of his gob looks like the rats have been in...*' ? No. Then I really would be a whinging brat. A little-bitch-snitch; the kind of snivelling wimp who'd like to bury her booing face in the Miss's fat-flower-dress... (Such a pretty dress. It's called linen. When she wasn't looking, I felt it.)

No. I just keep coughing. It's a ram-sham-wrack cough and it's really not pretty. And, *'If-you're-beautiful...'* She, our mother, always says, but I'm certainly not. I've got fourteen warts on my fingers, and the littlest one is bleeding, its flower head is popping ripe seeds, *it's bloody well breeding.* 'Want a plaster for that?' the Miss says. I do, I do, I do. Yes. I nod. And she's not even angry though I've bled on her dress. And the way she's looking at me – it makes me wonder if my coughing is a language – or if it's that my eyes are whispering to her and I should just shut them. But seeing as God sends me no answer when I ask him—

'Am I spluttering my beans without even trying?' I even dare to treat myself to imagining squealing:

'It's the baby boy, Miss. When he's mine I'll call him Blue. I hear him crying. In the night. But our mother's gone out and I'm tied in: her tights round the doorknob and looped through the stair railing opposite (or sometimes she uses Nan-who's-gone's knitting – doubled-up sheep wool is quite strong for tying things). Miss, I am a stupid girl who never said Goodbye. Never say the things I need to say. Instead, you know what I actually said, Miss? On Nan's death day? *Are we still going to the zoo, for Becca's birthday?* What a terrible girl. It was a terrible dark day. Miss, these are terrible dark days. And I'd like to take your flower-dress and bury my face...'

Now I must check, I must quiet-think, *make sure that I am not actually, really, telling any of this.* No, I can't be, I wouldn't be. But, how-come-is-it-then – that my Miss is staring at me? Because. Because – *no:* no, this is how it goes in my daydreams, no, it's only in my imaginings that my Miss is saying—

'Why does your mother tie the door shut? Can you explain to me what happens when she does this?'

And inside my mind and from the top of a tree, I watch

myself. I can hear me mentioning The Danger of Escape, and Big Roads Outside, and House Fires is why our mother leaves us trapped inside; and it sounds wrong, wrong, wrong; it makes me look like the fattest-idiot-liar. And I feel sick picturing my mother pulling the secret man's fine-checked trousers down in the back of the same white car I caught her getting into from my upstairs window. So I change the picture to me trying to explain things, trying to please the Miss with some good and not-sickening descriptions:

'It's all woven—' I'm sticking up my two hands, slapping them together like men do when they win things, clubbing something together with my dirty little fingers. The Miss's eyebrows come over her fogsome glasses, questioning, so I carry on with my best explaining: 'It's like a web, Miss. I mean, like a spider's gone mad. But I can only glimpse the tying through the crack 'cos it's on the outside of my bedroom door. That's why I can't get out to see to Blue's racket.'

'Of course.' I picture the Miss understanding with some medium-strength nodding.

'When night comes, and he – our dad – has gone on his shift, Miss, our mother's always sneak enough to get herself out, but the problem is, Miss: I get trapped-in and my heart's flapping to run to the little baby...'

Phew, it's OK to just imagine this telling, but it's a bloody good job I didn't really go on to that Miss. No: I know, I definitely wouldn't have blabbed any of that. Never happened in real. I was just thinking and thinking's not bad. I'm not a daughter who mouths off, tell-tales or stabs backs.

No, I'm not stupid. There can't be no telling. I work it through in my head – what I must do is give this baby every drop of my listening instead. I tell Blue, 'I'll send my best hearing through the wall to lie in that chill-cot next to you. My listening will be my arms and my shush.'

Then, each night my longing for sleep is love's greatest enemy.

Still, when we're free, and it's still day, after school, I can creep around Blue's little-haunty-plot; me, little warty, little witchy, justlikeyourfatherspoilsportmisery. I can see my brother's heart through his babygro; it's rose-pink glass and it's running slow. So. Now. I send gold. I'm a one for sending colours, so for him I send gold, saying, 'Blue, look, it's covering you, you can breathe it up through that cutest nose. To you, Blue, I send gold.' And it's not such a wait, before lo and behold, like a magic beanstalk, I see him grow. The precious is in his skin, little Blue is a ripey apricot thing.

'*Oh, you are warm, your heart is pump-pumping, yes it is!*' I coo happy-nonsense stuff at him.

Then, some grey days later, he, the headmaster, is taking me home in his car. We don't have days off, and we are not sick. I won't dare tell him any of this. His car is the colour of peas. I'm killing myself. The seats are checked. She won't be happy. He's a man who reads love from the Bible. He talks of Our Lord. My Blue won't be happy. This suit and this jacket. This kind man. With all his Blessed Children. He'll never in a million understand. Not what he sees. *What if he sees?*

Today I coughed up the class, they wouldn't keep me, I was bending and barking, though I tried to squash it. Now I sit and whisper madly into the thicket of my coughing, 'But the good is, Blue, I might pop in and hold you while she's gone out shopping.'

He, the headmaster, drops me, watches me ring the bell.

'Oh, Mum's getting the baby to sleep, I'll go round the back,' I say. And I dash upstairs, watch him drive that green, hunchback car away.

I see Blue has screamed his little-rat-self to sleep, the red remainder is round his eyes and his fists are frost-stiff. And none of our mother is home. Not one sodding bit. I find me standing there like a wilting flag, a useless piece of shit. Three rings round his cot and still he's still. I reach in a hand: Blue is stone cold and soaking wet. I taste blood in my mouth, in my forehead someone shoots bullets.

Suddenly I'm a young girl who is Fit To Kill; don't really know what killing is, but I warn God – 'I tell you this: if my Blue is dead, I'll tear her up with my teeth. I promise you this, I'll rip the woman to bitching-shreds.'

Then, I manage to wake him. Blue is sag but alive; I thank God in case it was Him got off his lazy arse, did something for once. I get the baby's milk in him, and I trussel him up in something dry. I find I'm holding him in my puny arms, turning around and around like it's a dance. I look at the window, I look at the door; there's no answer anywhere, and, also, *What the bleeding hell am I searching for?* Then there's her roar.

'I'll take you away,' I whisper to my Blue. But where could I go? *Come on.* 'Who would want *you*?' Hasn't she already quite thoroughly explained.

When we're at school this house is our mother's, so now I'm a criminal who's let myself in. I tell her about the headmaster – it wasn't my fault, he made me come here, come now. But it's the seeing of the baby in my arms – not left where she herself left him, her property in her home – that's the thing that means I now need to run. Today, this woman who is our mother, she is so fast. She seems even more juiced up than usual, I think, wherever she's been it's made her thighs even stronger.

'No,' I scream. 'No!' Then a stupid thing leaks from me: '*Please! Please! Stop, I am God's little daughter!*'

And soon, both my Blue and me are crying as inside of my head I yell, *If all children are God's, then why then? Why then?*

All of our life is a tremble. Her shopping bag spills, and there's not food stuff, just something silk.

I'm God's little daughter and I'll eat crackers for tea. I'm God's little daughter and you can hit me. I'm God's little daughter, and I will love that baby.

Then. No. Course I don't say any of that. 'Cos I'm a bending snowdrop in a dark wood, one cockleshell on an empty beach. I'm a flame of fish beneath the ice. And don't be fucking stupid, none of these things have bleedin' eyes to see this life – or mouths to speak the truth or lies. (*Or mouths to make them filthy liars.*) They're tough and brittle and plant and white and caked in ice; they don't have skin, they don't feel pain; they will not snap, their hearts won't break. They do not die, they *will not* die. Even when the squeeze of a mother is sharp and whirl and flip-you-high, even if she's a giant mince grinder in a giant tornado. No.

I remind myself, I remind myself, *They do not die.*

So. There is a storm, like there are storms, and I am a small loose fly. Most probably I am how it is to be lost in the Bermuda Triangle. While she. She has sixteen boots on sixteen legs. She has screaming arms and screaming hair. She has great hands like strangling rags. They whip-cut and choke the world. Then gallop off fast-blur-devil-hares.

And then – No. No, she don't spit me deaf with, 'I don't care if you're the daughter of *Old Fucking Nick*!' Nope. She don't. She never said that. *'Cos I don't have ears.*

And still, and anyway, in the after, we can gently rock. In the blue paddle boat of our minds, I can still call my brother Blue. Because she can't stop me. Not son of a long-tit-wolf. My Blue. Son of God. Still, that's what he is to me.

Some growing later, when he goes humpbacked along the hard carpet floor, I kneel in the baby's world. I touch his sticky little fingers. 'Oh, Blue,' I tell him:

'When you're mine, I'll wrap you in a best blanket. We'll go where the good ladies go. It'll have clean marble stairs, don't ask me how I know, and white snow nets, and a pink bed, and suitcases on a wardrobe. There'll be hot soup and a fast-running pram. And red booties and rice pudding with real sprinkled cinnamon like they use in France. And we'll walk down the street with my handbag over your pram handlebars. And people will smile, as they pass us a polished apple, or a knit grown off their best grandson. With 50ps I'll buy you books. Books, Blue! You'll see. And if people see her coming they'll all close in, saying "There's that Sally, she don't fool us." They'll shoo her off 'cos they like us.'

Another time Blue's alone – he's always alone – straps, pushchair this time, packet of crisps to stuff up his tearworks – I go to him. His colour is blue, it lives nice and fresh with the gold I transported. Now he has sea-wish eyes and his skin is sunbloom. And in comes his hair, and it's bright-glory-straw like picture-scarecrows.

'Your hair has power, you better not forget it,' I tell him. 'See? It blows in the wind from my sneeze, like strands of spaghetti?

That means you are a something that must live on a beach,' I promise him.

And then suddenly at two years old Blue will not eat. I tell him about the magic in yogurt with strawberry bits. I sing about the strength in Marmite. Blue lives on these two with slices of white. He only eats small, small bread squares. I know this is because of those early screaming tears; I guess they ribbed down from his tongue, down his throat to his lungs; and now his heart is dry-sore, and he only wants crumbs.

I pay Blue 5p, now he is three, I try to bribe him to eat; by the time it's crept to 10p, the in of his mouth is raw and lumpy. He's a plummy apricot with bruises. Ulcers in clumps are taking his speaking, which has only done its starting. It's only done its starting.

Awful thing is I know the speak's stopped because of what it has to watch. I am the watcher and I wish he didn't need to see. But, problem is, he's there, isn't he? When our mother's chasing me. And when I'm ended on the floor beneath her, the little mite's watching above me. Like the lunchtime sun. In his high chair, or rolled on the settee or the bed, or on her storming hip clutching the skin on her hell-bent neck.

'Be my sun! Blue, give me strength!' Silently at those times I plead with him, and it's wrong, because he's a baby, and I can never need him. He goes so horror-eyed, poor little scratchit, he just boos and boos. And so when it's all over and she's burned off some hate; when I am free and the world's back up straight, I have to tell Blue boy something before it's too late:

'Listen, Blue. One day. We'll live in a high-up hut on a cliffy-beach, or if not, at the top of a churchyard yew tree. You'll have me, and your own proper new-spanking-speak; and maybe we'll buy one of those dinosaurs that make you so toothy-grin-pleased. You can eat cakes made of crisps and crisps made of cake. And we'll spit all the crumbs down on the people we hate.'

But... first, before One Day, as Blue somehow knew, there were more dark years for him. That school across two bony cow fields, grey roads and grey skies, it was the second most bastard of all places... And when the day came that Blue was called a man, but felt nothing like one, and sat on the pine stool in my kitchen, but was really falling, not sitting – I didn't, or I couldn't, hide my telling from him.

'Brother of mine, it's when you reached eleven that I finally guessed that *God was an idiot lickarse git*. Just like our mother's other friends,' I spat. 'Because, first, I begged her not to send you to that secondary school – but when that plea failed – only buried like a tick in her fury, selfish forgettingness – *I prayed*. I prayed to the God who sent you down here. Please, I prayed, don't now send him *there*. I'm tougher, I'm near the end of my sentence, me and the four others, we're bigger, we've warred it; but not him, too, *not* the baby of us, this last lonely son. Why would anyone choose to put a kid through such a chair-to-the-head education?'

Then, I probably – I really shouldn't have told him any more – but I know I did. I didn't stop, I gave it all to him. It *is* true that I said:

'And, so, Blue, that's when I really got it – God is just some old headmaster duffer's wank in a world of loser gits and liars. All the chances God, "Our Father" was given *and He stopped nothing. (And, no, I don't know why our real father on his shift work all the time meant nothing in the Kind Saviour department – meant little but money at the end of the week...*

I judged that she wouldn't let him into our life, let him near us, but – also, wasn't he a boiling pot of confusion and loss, more like a child than any of us? Anyway – it was always God we were told would be the one to help us...) Blue, I watched you forcing one foot in front of another every day, I saw you come home from school, wilting in that hard white shirt – that scrawny little-boy-body, that neck dragged by that horrible old tie of yours. You were a punched sack. (*But, please know, you were **my** Blessed child.*) That neck still a babe's, too thin in that shirt – which hung out somehow, showing all of the love that you had lacked (*and I felt so sick because I couldn't fucking stuff it back*).

'What do you expect?' she, our mother, said, when your days got slower and slower, your gold leaked too much, no matter that I'd switched it to a bubular thing, tried my best to send it moating round your skin; I sent you off with the best protection I could muster, plus Marmite sarnies each shitting morning. But *still* you went bruised and limp. Your lights were fading. You had those marks on your arms like old bananas. (Remember you told me one day about the teacher with the mullet hair who liked to throw his stapler at you, who made you wear your PE shorts that kid cut holes in? That was bad, but I knew there were even worse things that you weren't telling me.)

And, though Blue said nothing to all of this, I noticed his chin came up and his shoulders went east; he had ears, yeah, he was listening. Head leant back on my kitchen tiles, beneath his closed purple lids his eyeballs were pacing.

So I thought 'Fuckit' to the max then. I undid all the locks, freed my chest from a century of coughs, and I said to him:

'So, Blue, d'you remember I came bothering you again? I crept around you carefully, maybe a bit sly (you were like an animal caught in a trap). When things were bad, remember, Blue? Can you bear to look back? It was your reading we (OK *I*, and at first yeah, it was bit like force-feeding) began to spoon in. Then a little writing. We did homework. Remember? Drop by drop. Things went in. One day, you gave me a story you'd written. Your writing was scruff, your spelling was *paw*, but you had a king, and a dragon. And a wizard, and a sword. And *my life*. I lay down that night, thinking, *Phew, OK. My Blue has some lovely hiding inside of him.*'

Now his eyes came open, sky-pink rimmed and so tired; but blue – his eyes were so sea-blue, and broad and full. They swept over me, so warm, so gently seeing me that my mouth went wide like wings. It loosed its words like a

yellow

bird

sings.

'So, then, Blue, what I did was, I spread it out thick, gave you all my pulp, and had to spin up more, remember? I told of black pigs, four-tongue dogs, poison hills, spotted frogs, wickeds, dark holes, aliens, blood seas, and deathbed secrets. Vile rabbits fighting kind rats. Puddings, and so many other things that could talk. Robbers of souls and home planets you'd fallen allllll the way from. I told and I told you, you odd little plum.'

Here, I stopped my trilling. I looked up to find that dear Blue was smiling. My sun was shining. Yes, I saw that it – *he* – had been there always, behind the clouds, making me brave enough. Quietly, secretly, brightly living for the pair of us.

So then I rang out my last:

'And I'm telling you now, Blue, you better hear it; we'll do what it takes, Blue, to help you get through, we'll heal this...'

But:

'No,' Blue suddenly said. And out fell his soul: 'Netta. *Please.* No. Don't.'

Really, he said, *he didn't want to live. Really,* he said, *he wanted none of this.*

'No. You can't, it's so-too early to go back... Blue, you know, *I lied...* About The Sure Place... The Palace of Friends, and all that—' In front of my eyes my tales were backfiring, while Blue just sat there, his eyes sad but his mouth smiling.

'Nett! Course I know that; you were always lyin'. You were bloody good, *you lied about everything!*'

That's what he said.

And I must tell you what happened then:

me and Blue rocked.

We just rocked together.

And our ears were so big, so strong,

we heard one thing,

so loud. A pin. It dropped.

After all these years, from the

dead-white-skin of my back

and

for a song time at least

our pain, our pain was gone.

We looked with our giant-starve-eyes,

and the water beneath the rocking of our mind,

was *so* clear. Gold fishes like signs

told us: You are here. Fuckit. You. Got. Here.

And at last, it came to me, slipping from the Bible cherished by my headmaster, like an ancient pressed pansy flower, nothing like the words I'd heard preached in assemblies and on Sundays:

'I get it, Blue—' I had to tell him, though it seemed it might
be too much too late.
'I got it first in my bay window on your birth day.
It's Love, Blue. It's Love that is Great.'

Little fishes swimming beneath our paddles,
like gold letters spelling one word that swam in our veins.
For my brother and I that word, so shimmering, so fine,
     it was *Saved.*

THE LAST SUMMER

SUSANNAH VERNON-HUNT

It was not, as they say, a 'cry for help'.
In attic room with ladder left behind.
The unlocked bathroom door, pills spilled.
In place familiar, people, somewhat near.
'Please please find me. Scoop me up in this, my bleakest hour'.
It was not that. It was those three parched weeks in that endless
    dry July.

As we wait, my mother turns to skeletal ghost woman.
My father, brim, full of the living, is now bent over, silent.
I hold on to my big brother.
I feel our hearts quake.

The police with their indifferent caring.
The helicopter blading, circling over and over where your bike
    was found by the park.
Your friends say you must have gone to the music festival.
But you did not come home, and nobody could find you.

I remember you giving the sofa cushion to the car-smashed fox.
I remember the wing-crushed sparrow fed worms with tweezers
    by you.
Both died, and you boy-swiped away your tears.

And then three youngsters playing kick-about footie in the desert-dry park. The ball flying high and far away, landing into the deepest thicket of bramble and thorn bush. It must have been such an adventure for them, running so fast to home. Mum! Dad! Lost our ball! Found a dead body! Even now, I suppose they sometimes mention it, a pub story. A tale to tell.

And me, those arid twenty-one days. Simply catching a bus to somewhere. Twenty B&H from the corner shop, striking a match. No tale here.

You.
Gone.
Here in your bedroom
As I read these words, they seem to bleach to nothing.
My beloved one, my baby brother.
Such pointlessness to the endlessness of this missing,
Your ears stopped up with soil.

Perhaps better,
More true,
To sit dumb.

PROTECT ME FROM WHAT I WANT

ANGIE KENNY

He sat on a wooden folding chair next to the wall, legs splayed so that people were forced to step over them. An unlit cigarette hung from his mouth. He was unconscious or close to it. A leather boy in pants too tight for his girth grabbed the back of the chair and dumped him onto the floor. He remained prone and still as the asshole stepped over him. My cue to do the white-knight thing.

He was young like me and of average height like me, but thin and pale. He had ink-black hair that touched his shoulders and hung around his face in choppy angles. Black eyeliner smudged the delicate skin below his eyes like a bruise. I considered calling the leather hulk a motherfucker. But I wasn't a fighter. I decided it would be just as gallant to help this sweet prince off the floor and allow us both to get out of there alive. I pulled him to his feet. He leaned heavily on me. A trip to the men's room to throw some cold water on his face might make getting him home easier.

I got him into the toilet and sat him on the filthy floor. I soaked a wad of paper towels in cool water and began pressing it against his face, which was heart-shaped with high cheekbones and full lips. A guy at the urinal glanced at my efforts.

'I know him. He's always in here with his boyfriend and they're always wasted.' He turned around, not bothering to zip up. 'He's so out of it, we could both fuck him and he'd never know.'

When I spoke the words seemed random, but together they made some kind of sense.

'What the fuck, dude, we got married today. This is our wedding night.'

He eyed me suspiciously. 'Fuck you. Where are your rings?'

I glanced at our hands – at the bands of silver we both wore on our left thumbs. Bitter fate is sometimes so amusingly sweet. I showed him mine and at the same time raised the hand of my stuporous new friend.

'So he's not with the other guy any more?'

'Obviously not.'

The guy shrugged as he retreated. So the prince already had a knight. I'd still take him back to my place. In his current state, he might forget the inconvenient boyfriend. I felt a brief pang of guilt. Was that any better than using his unconscious body in the toilet? Ah, but he was so fucking cute.

Half carrying, half dragging him, we finally made it outside. The cool night air seemed to revive him. He stood on his own as I pulled out my cell. I kept one hand on his slender shoulder as I used the other to scroll through my apps, looking for Uber.

'Gotta cigarette?' he asked, his words slurring together.

The unlit one had fallen from his mouth somewhere along the way. I released him long enough to tap a cigarette from my pack. I placed it in my own mouth, lit it and handed it to him. I loved the intimacy of that.

'Thanks. Where we going?' He took a long drag and exhaled. As I watched him suck the smoke back up his nose, my dick expanded two inches down my leg.

'My place? I can get an Uber.'

'Why don't we just go to my place?' he asked, handing me the cigarette. His voice was deeper than I expected.

I took a puff and handed it back. 'Where do you live?'

He stumbled around in a circle on the sidewalk until he was

facing the door we'd just come out of. He pulled the cigarette from his mouth and used it to point to a second-floor window above the bar.

'Right up there.'

Well, that was convenient. Wouldn't need a car to go there. 'What about your boyfriend?'

For the first time I saw a spark of life in his bleary eyes. He shook his head and threw the cigarette on the pavement. 'Don't have a boyfriend.'

It wasn't so much an apartment as a room. There was a separate bath, but no kitchen – just a small fridge and a microwave. The only sink was in the bathroom. The place wasn't as messy as I would have expected. Wasn't as messy as mine. In fact, it smelled amazing. I suppose from all the burning candles.

'Man, you really shouldn't go off and leave candles lit. Gonna burn the place down.'

He didn't say anything as he fell back onto the bed. I stood over him and watched as a shadow passed over his beautiful face. He'd invited me in. I wasn't trespassing. Still, I felt like a peeping Tom peering through a billowing curtain – catching glimpses.

His eyes were a pale blue-green and wide. Tears pooled at their edges and spilled down his cheeks. His mouth was slightly open. His bottom lip was particularly lush, fuller than the top one. When finally he looked at me, his expression seemed to beg, 'Please.'

He raised up on his elbows as I sat next to him on the bed. I touched the side of his face, letting my fingers slip into his hair. I tucked a loose strand behind his ear. I imagined we were around the same age, but at that moment he looked impossibly young. As he stared back, he began swallowing and nodding his head.

'You OK?' I asked. He responded by grabbing the hand that wasn't laced into his hair and pulling me down beside him. He kissed me with an anxious, hungry mouth. His tongue pushed against mine. It was soft and amiable and he tasted like sex. Sometimes guys taste like booze or cigarettes or whatever they had for dinner or nothing at all. Maybe this guy tasted like all these things in a perfect combination. But since it made me want to fuck him, it tasted like sex to me.

I had no interest in quick, pants-around-the-knees fucking. We were on his bed, candles lit all around us. I wanted to take my time. Mostly I wanted to get him naked. I recognised the track marks the minute I pulled the leather jacket off him. His arms were thin and the muscles long and stringy. Some of the marks were old and some were fresh. I cupped his elbow in my hands and stared down at him. He looked up at me and smiled a crooked smile that was like a dare. Like he was saying, 'Yep, that's what I am. Take it or leave it.'

I'm not sentimental. I'm not romantic. But I knew already this song was going to get stuck in my head. I fused my gaze with his and, never breaking it, leaned down and gently kissed his sores. A little bubble of sound escaped his lips – like a laugh and a sigh and a sob.

I pulled off his boots and removed the rest of his clothes. That is, a pair of torn blue jeans riding low on his slender hips. His head lolled back against the pillow. He was like a rag doll, conforming to my will. Besides the red and black needle pricks, his skin was smooth and warm. He seduced me without one bit of effort.

I knelt on the floor between his legs, placing my palms lightly on his knees. I ran my hands up his thighs and over his hips, his abdomen and finally rested them on his chest. I wanted him so much, but he seemed too vulnerable – too completely under my control.

'You sure?' I couldn't get the rapist in the bathroom out of my mind. He stared at the ceiling. He didn't even look at me.

'Shut up and fuck me.' He did not have to ask twice.

I pulled off my clothes and knelt again between his legs. I dove headfirst into the pool, but nothing I did got him hard.

'Don't waste your time, man. I'm too fucked up.' I didn't stop. Instead, I reached up to play with his nipples, pinching them hard.

He sighed and muttered sarcastically, 'Yeah, that'll work.'

Finally he pushed my hand away. 'Forget it. Just let me get you off.'

I crawled back onto the bed beside him. I was wrong. Without the boots, he was at least two inches shorter than me. I kissed the corner of his mouth. 'Nope. It's all for one and one for all, or none for anybody.'

He studied me with wet, bruised eyes. Finally, he turned his back and muttered, 'Whatever, man.'

I stared at that back. I wanted to press my lips against his skin, but I didn't. I noticed his breaths were getting sharper and heavier until he was practically gasping. The gasps became sobs. I touched his shoulder, but he jerked away from me and fell out of the bed.

'Whoa, what is it?'

He didn't respond. Instead, he crawled across the floor into the bathroom, kicking the door shut. I didn't know what to do. Should I leave? See if he was OK? I didn't want to leave. I wanted to spend the night. I knocked lightly on the door.

'Hey man, you OK in there?' I leaned close, but all I could hear was his jagged sobbing. I tried the door and it wasn't locked. I found him wedged in the little space between the tub and the toilet. I squatted in front of him, my heels pressed against my nut sack. I reached for his hand and he let me hold it without any resistance.

With my other hand I gently brushed aside the hair that veiled his eyes. His lips were pink against his pale skin as if they'd been chewed. 'What's up, lover? You want me to go?'

He pulled me towards him. 'No. Don't go.'

'Good, 'cause I want to stay.' I leaned forward to kiss him. Our clenched hands dropped into his lap.

'Come back to bed. We can sleep.' My tone was that of a negotiator trying to talk a jumper off the ledge. 'Maybe make love in the morning.'

He let go of my hand and covered his eyes with his palms. The black polish on his nails was faded and chipped.

'Only if you feel like it,' I added. 'Sweet and slow.'

He moaned – open-mouthed and full of pain. 'I'm such a fucker. I'm such a total shit.'

'You? No way.'

He dropped his hands. His eyes were rimmed red and streaming tears like a faucet that wouldn't shut off. 'My boyfriend died yesterday. He's in the fucking morgue looking exactly like he did when he was alive and I was going to let you fuck me.'

It was a sucker punch to the gut and it knocked me on my ass. 'Shit.'

'That's right. I'm a fucking piece of shit.'

'No, that's not what I meant.' I shook my head to clear it. 'Look, it's grief. You didn't want to be alone.' I shrugged. 'It's OK.'

He was nodding and catching his breath like a child coming out of a tantrum. 'I don't want to be alone. I don't. It's just he and I were, like, overcome.' He looked directly at me. 'You know what I mean? When you're so overcome by another person?'

I nodded. I actually didn't know. I wanted to know.

'Come back to bed, baby.'

For the third time that night, I helped him off the floor. I got us both into bed and held him. He curled himself around me and buried his face against my neck. I smiled to myself and stroked his soft hair. It smelled like shampoo and cigarettes. Everything about him was so perfect and so beautiful. Except maybe the scars that tattooed his veins.

He didn't say anything for a long time. His eyes were closed. I thought he'd fallen asleep and then, 'It was an overdose.'

Not all that surprising, I thought, but didn't say out loud. And then he read my mind.

'It was actually weird 'cause we were both on the methadone. And when we did shoot junk, we always did it together. But he was alone and I don't even know how he got the stuff. How did he buy it? He didn't have any money. That's why I'd gone down to the Western Union to get some cash my grandma wired me for my birthday. I wanted him to go with me, but he was too tired. He wanted to sleep 'cause we'd been fucking around all night. So I let him sleep and I stayed out all day. I saw a friend outside the Western Union office and I went back to his place to smoke some weed. He said he'd drive me home. Better than taking the bus.'

He wiped his wet face on me. 'I wish it had been like a car accident or a plane crash. Then there wouldn't be all this fucking "I told you so" from fucking everybody.'

'I know,' I said as I continued to pet him. I only had generic comforts to offer.

'You know, man, you've been really cool. I mean, I know you just wanted to get laid. But you didn't have to be so nice.'

I wanted to laugh or maybe cry.

'Well, you know, just lying here with you isn't exactly a hardship. And we don't have to do anything tomorrow, or ever if you don't want to. We can be friends – see what happens. I wouldn't mind that.' I was such a fucking liar.

He turned his head away from me. I couldn't see his face. I started to say something, but before I could, he said, 'God, I wish he was here.'

This time I didn't say, 'I know.'

'Do you ever wish for things?' he asked.

'Sure.'

'Like what?'

'I don't know – to be rich and famous, I guess. To be able to get anyone I want into bed. Stay healthy. Be happy.' I shrugged.

'Are you any of those things now?'

'I'm not rich or famous. But I'm healthy and I'm pretty happy. And technically, I did get you into bed.'

'So then you have the most important things already. I mean, if you got sick – you wouldn't still be wishing to be famous, would you? You'd be wishing to be healthy, which you already are.'

I rolled over on my side, cradling his head on my arm, and stared down into his face. 'That's pretty fucking wise.'

'For a junkie.'

'For anybody. The guys in my band talk about which comic-book characters are fags. They talk about what their imaginary porn names would be.'

He laughed. I made him laugh. I felt like Superman. Superman is a fag.

'Well, H fucks you up, but it also gives you time to think. Trick is remembering all the brilliant ideas you get when you're wasted. You gotta band?'

'Yeah. We're called Stained Sheets.'

'No way. We saw you in San Francisco. You were great. Wow, you're the singer, right? You look kinda different.'

'Yeah, no facial hair then.' I rubbed my face for emphasis. 'We're less punk now. I'm even trying to write something like a ballad. We'd love to sell out.' I laughed, but he nodded like he understood exactly what I was saying and everything between the lines.

'We had a band,' he said. 'Called ourselves Horse. Everyone thought it was 'cause of our particular fondness for heroin. But it was really about his particular hugeness. I wanted to change the name to Hung. It would have been less confusing.'

Yeah, as much as I loved talking about his dead boyfriend's big dick, I changed the subject back to music. 'I don't think I ever saw you guys.'

He shrugged. 'They know us around here, but we never toured or anything. We taped one of our shows once. I can show you sometime, if you want.'

'Definitely. That would be cool.'

'We weren't doing much lately.' He looked at me through that tousled mop of hair. 'We were shooting too much shit. Kept missing gigs.'

He leaned across me, rooting through a shoebox on a small table next to the bed. He came up with a Polaroid photo. It was of the somewhat faded face of a grinning man. His bleached blond hair showed a couple of inches of black roots. His tattooed arm was around the man who was in my arms now.

'I'm afraid some day I'll forget what he looked like. I'm gonna look at his picture every day so I don't forget. Smack makes you forget. That's kind of the point. But I don't want to.'

'How'd you get started?'

'With heroin? At Berkeley. Well, not at Berkeley exactly. But maybe because of it.'

'You went to Berkeley?'

He rubbed my face. 'I like your pointy sideburns.' And then after a minute, 'Yeah, I did. For a while anyway. I got kicked out of the dorms for letting him stay with me. He wasn't in school. So after that, I decided to really lay it on my folks and I came out to them. They kinda disowned me. Refused to pay for school as long as I was with him. Well, fuck 'em. That wasn't a choice. So we were on our own.'

The sun was coming up. I took the picture from him and put it back in the box. 'You should sleep if you can,' I said.

'You too.' And then after a few minutes of silence, 'Hey man, I'm sorry. I don't remember how we met, but I'm glad we did.'

I hugged him closer and kissed his forehead. 'Me too. Now go to sleep.'

After a few minutes, his steady breathing told me he was dreaming. It wasn't long before I followed.

It's like the stories of people meeting on blind dates and running off the same night to Vegas to get married. I was sharing a place with my band. I told them the next day I was moving out. They were immediately suspicious of his intentions. It was never his fault. I dragged him to every rehearsal, every band meeting, every gig. I never wanted him out of my sight. I wasn't about to go to the Western Union office, or anywhere without him.

One night as we lay in the bath together, washing off the day, he told me about our next-door neighbour. I'd seen him in the hall a few times, exchanged pleasantries. He was a surfer dude with shoulder-length blond hair and an easy-going warmth. The ladies loved him and he had a string of them in and out of his place.

But this was a once-upon-a-time story when my boyfriend belonged to someone else. When his name would have meant nothing to me.

He sat between my legs, smoking a cigarette. I washed his hair, shielding his face with my hand as I used a cup to pour water through the black silkiness. I watched it trail down his back to the curve of his beautiful ass. He took long draws off the cigarette, pulling the smoke deep into his lungs, and speaking on the exhales. It turned out the story was a romantic one. I knew he didn't share it to hurt me. It was just part of the process of remembering – of not forgetting.

'It was Valentine's night. We'd just made love among the Chinese take-out cartons. We were just settling in for some long, deep kisses, when we heard pounding on the neighbour's door and a woman's voice yelling, "I know you've got a girl in there!"'

He said they wasted no time crowding the peephole to get a look at a swaying brunette as she continued to pound and bellow. They returned to the warmth of their cosy bed, only a few feet from the action. After a while she quieted down and they returned to cuddling and kissing, assuming she'd given up and staggered home.

'If he was in there, no way was he opening that door. It took a couple of notes before we realised what we were hearing – the forlorn singing of Whitney Houston. Except it wasn't Whitney. "And IIIIIIIIIII will always love youuuuuuuu!"' he wailed, imitating the drunk girl.

'We took one look at each other in the darkness and began to roll with laughter. It was evil, but we laughed anyway.'

They laughed until their sides hurt. Laughed until the police took her away.

'I could always make him smile... could even end a fight with a few bars of "I Will Always Love You",' he said.

'It's a nice memory,' I said as I pressed my mouth against his shoulder and began to suck his pale, wet skin. It would be red there tomorrow. You're mine now, the mark said.

'Yeah, that was a good summer. We were trying to clean up our act. Shared a lot of sugary Cokes at the Greek restaurant down the street,' he said.

I knew the one he meant.

'The man behind the counter would always glare at us when we took advantage of the free drink refills.' He laughed at the memory. '*That's free refill for you. Not you and all your friends!*'

It was a perfect imitation of the large, hairy man behind the counter.

'We could go there for dinner later,' I suggested.

'Nah,' he said and stubbed out the cigarette.

As days melted into weeks and we were still together, my confidence grew. I made sure he visited the methadone clinic daily. And every time we made love, I kissed his arms and legs, secretly searching for new track marks. Maybe not so secretly, 'cause I'm sure he knew what was up. He was just too played out to protest.

He got sick a few times. I don't know if it was a bad or weak dose from the clinic. Maybe he was sneaking an occasional fix. Junkies are sneaky even when they're beautiful and sweet. And sometimes he wasn't sweet. Sometimes he was a petulant little bitch. He'd lock himself in the bathroom now and then. What was I supposed to do – kick the door down? I tried.

Whatever was making him sick, I took care of him. I bathed his face with cool rags. I held his head while he threw up – usually on me. I fed him, loved him and felt for the first time in my life that something outside myself was important. Maybe it was crazy. I was crazy. But the heart wants what it wants, as they say. And my heart was as sure as the lipstick stains he left on my cock when he blew me.

One morning I awoke to discover he'd made a shrine of the dead boyfriend's remaining effects. Incense and candles deified black sunglasses, a lighter, a guitar pick and the Polaroid.

I sighed. 'You're not getting rid of me that easily.'

He looked up at me with eyes like bee stings. Back then he still cried himself to sleep every night.

'What did you say?' he asked.

'I wasn't talking to you, baby,' I said.

It was a week or so later when he screamed, 'You don't love me. You just want to fucking control me. You want me to forget him. Well, fuck you. It'll never happen!'

I'd taken the lighter from the shrine. He noticed it was missing. I realised I had lost it. I got in his face and for a brief moment, he looked startled. I wasn't going to hit him. I rarely raised my voice to him. But I was pissed.

'Don't tell me I don't love you. You have no right to say that. You can say I'm controlling. You can say I want you to forget the bastard 'cause I'd give my right nut for you to. You can even say I'm fucking delusional to think it will ever work between us, but don't say I don't love you.'

I stormed out and went downstairs for a beer. I was halfway through my second one when he appeared beside me. He touched my hand, but neither of us apologised. We just sat silently drinking and holding hands. That's when I knew I was in real trouble. I'm addicted to this man, I thought, as surely as he's addicted to drugs and death.

'What if these feelings are impossible to part with?' he asked finally, as he wrapped and unwrapped his hand from mine.

'Feelings for him or for me?'

'Yes.'

I can't remember now if that was a good day or a bad one. There were definitely more good days. I was happy to wake up to him in the morning. He was happy to have me next to him at night. I was his current life preserver. He was my new Achilles heel.

We stayed together. We lived. We haunted record stores looking for obscure things to amaze each other with. We danced in clubs. We drank in bars. We fucked and made love every chance we got. We were happy in torn jeans and leather jackets, dirty fingernails and weird hair. But we were happy and relatively healthy. Wanting anything more would have been greedy. We carried on like this until we did get greedy – each in our own way.

One night he asked if I thought the dead boyfriend had killed himself. I was in a bad mood and tired of hearing his fucking name.

'I don't think it matters. Dead is dead. And you know, baby, I don't fucking care. The bastard scarred you for life. I think he's a total prick.'

I expected him to walk out or to at least not talk to me for a week. But he just said, 'Yeah, you're right. It doesn't matter.'

So I guess it doesn't matter why or how my baby bought a fix. Or why he ended up dumped unconscious outside an emergency room. Thank God for whoever dumped him there. That was twenty-one days ago. He's been in court-ordered rehab ever since. He gets out today.

We weren't allowed to talk on the phone or see each other. I wrote to him. I don't know if he was allowed to read my emails.

I know he didn't write back. In the last note I told him about our show tonight. He could come if he wanted to. We could live together again. I still stay in his room. I've kept up with the rent.

I'm on stage when I see him walk in. He sits at the bar and I catch his eye. We're between songs so I wave. He smiles but doesn't wave back. I tell my band the song we're going to play. I've been waiting 'til he showed – praying he would show. The music swells and as I sing, I can't take my eyes off him.

If pain had eyes, would they look like his? If lust had a face, would it be mine? His touch is fire, yet I feel so cold.

How can I stay? How can I go? How can I stay? How can I go?

I know I'm lost. I know I'm beat. When I hear his sigh and it's enough to keep me with him one more night. Every day it's one more night.

He's my affliction, my addiction. Fuck you if you don't understand. We want affliction, live for addiction. He's mine. What's yours? He's mine. What's yours?

If desire had a mouth, would it taste like his? If love had a heart, could it be mine? My touch is fire, yet he feels so cold. I beg please stay. Please don't go. I beg please stay. Please don't go.

I know he's lost. I know he's beat. When he hears me sigh, is it enough to keep him with me one more night? Every day it's one more night.

He's my affliction, my addiction. Fuck you if you don't understand. We want affliction, live for addiction. He's mine. What's yours? He's mine. What's yours? He's mine. He's mine. He's mine. What's yours?

As I watch him watch me sing, I wonder where this all will end. After the set, I meet him at the bar. We kiss awkwardly. He's gained a little weight. I tell him he looks good. He does. He tells me he's clean. I say I'm glad. He says he can't promise it will stick. I say I know. He tells me he still may not have gone as low as he can go. I tell him if he falls, I will pick him up. He tries to say he's sorry, but I won't let him. He says he missed me and I listen. I can't tell him how much I missed him. There aren't any words. Or maybe I already told him. That's what I meant to do.

'I like the song. It's about me.' It's a statement, not a question, so I don't have to say yes. 'It's about addiction so it must be about me, eh?' He laughs nervously and swallows hard.

I take his hand and like that first night, he lets me. 'Baby, it's not about your addiction. It's about mine.'

He nods and kisses me lightly on the lips. 'I know. Let's go home.' And again I don't have to say yes.

SHE WILL BE MY JOY

JAMIE GUINEY

I take an orange from the bowl on the table and head outside. She will be home soon, pushing over the tall hill with cherry in her cheeks and freshness upon her skin, through her hair. It is still only spring, yet warmer than normal. I sit down on the low wall, in a space that gets the sun, and start into the peel with my thumb. She is the only person I've ever seen that can remove the entire rind in one spiralling piece. Mine is a shred-job, bits and juice all over the place before I even release the first segment.

The air smells like grass with a smidgeon of berries – maybe the farmer has cut the field. The iron gate needs some paint, and I think I'll have the energy, but know by the time I put on old clothes, find some brushes and a tin of paint, bring them outside and kneel down to begin, it won't be as simple as that, because it never is. The old flakes will probably need to be scraped away, the metal stripped down to a workable surface. There will probably be something wrong with a hinge. I'll go back through the house and out to the leaning shed to look for a wire brush or a screwdriver and when I make it back to the gate, I will be exhausted and in pain and have to go indoors to lie down.

And so, my life these days has become a series of calculations. Sitting on this low wall, estimating how many steps it might take just to walk across to the field, stop by its gate and stroke the old horse or check for pyramidal rows of fresh-cut grass – or try to work out how I can clean all the windows of the house, how many days it will take and how much energy it will use up. I sit here eating this orange and try not to think about how it has already used up some of my reserves just peeling it.

She will have left the city by now. The high-rises shrinking slowly into old stone buildings – then there will be nothing but thatched roofs, concrete yards and patchwork fields. Not long until she is here beside me – sitting, talking... being.

I am cold all of the time. It is like winter has crawled inside me and decided to rest out the other three seasons until its time has once again come around to prosper. On days when it rains, I sit by the window wishing it would stop, that she could get home without the soaking. Sometimes I feel brave and take the black umbrella to meet her off the bus, but by the time I get down the hill and out to the end of the road, I have no energy to get all the way back up again. Though it's worth it, that pain – to see her a little earlier, to lessen her rain.

Today I will wait. Apple and cherry blossoms have begun to sprout in their familiar whites and pinks. Wild daffodils poke out from hedgerows across the way and lean towards the sun to enrich their stems, brighten their yellow. I gather the leathery pieces of rind into a loose pile beside me on the warm stone and close my eyes to rest. My head feels like I'm moving on a slow-chugging boat, cutting its sluggish path through the sea like scissors through a sheet of material. My breaths fall shallow and the pain starts to pound up through the back of my neck and I must try to open my eyes again, for these moments feel like they can only end in sharp blackness.

And she will come. Pushing over the crest and a little out of breath, with a tiny ball of crimson in each of her cheeks. She will catch me sitting there and her head will fall to the side to tell me that she is tired – but she will still smile. As she walks, the sun will drench her body in its golden beams and she will stop by the wall and embrace me or kiss my forehead. I will hear her voice, smell her hair and her skin and all of her that comes with it, and she will be my joy.

ORBIT

POLLY HALL

I want to reach you. I'm the lonely satellite orbiting helplessly around your pain year after year. These cycles fill with more obstacles to avoid, the space junk left by anniversaries, time deadened by the emptiness you leave. What happened in the galaxy of your experience to shut out that light I loved? If it were just an eclipse, a passing phase, a once-in-a-lifetime blip on the radar, maybe the darkness would seem mysterious or exciting. I miss your beaming smile, the echo of your laugh tumbling through the stratosphere. I miss the fire and threat of adolescence, your spirit. I wish I could steer my trajectory into those stinking grey asteroids that threaten you with crushing oblivion. I wish I could beam back a better view or fly backwards like Superman to alter time itself. If only I could show you the distances you are capable of travelling, that you are not alone. If only you realised you are the centre of not just my universe, and that none of that other stuff matters.

HOW TO COLD TURKEY IN TWENTY-FIVE EASY STEPS

RUBY D. JONES

The Week Before

1. First you must forget. Forget how bad it was last time and the time before and all the times before that. Fortunately, making you forget is one of opioids' many superpowers. It's one of the reasons you love them. Wonder whether this forgetting is like how women allegedly forget the pain of childbirth, an evolutionary trick to encourage them to do it again. Except you will have nothing to show for this but your quivering, newborn self. It will have to be enough.

2. Gather your instruments. All addicts are amateur pharmacists: a foundation of this, a middle layer of that, a top note of the other; whatever concoction will make you feel perfect – which is to say, feel nothing. These are transferable skills. Find a recipe for the first six weeks of opioid withdrawal in a book your therapist recommends. Turn your nose up at the inclusion of pain pills in the heroin chapter – you're not a *junkie*, for Chrissakes. Spend your drug money on the supplements the book recommends anyway. When you see the number of pills you're meant to take each day, try to quench your excitement.

3. Plan the first few days for when your girlfriend is away. She's seen you through enough withdrawals, missed enough

of her own life to watch you sweating and shaking and terrified, withheld judgement when you inevitably relapsed. She will offer to stay, of course, because she is an actual angel who you don't even almost deserve. Insist that she goes.

Day One

4. In the morning, think: *This isn't so bad.* That's because the drugs aren't out of your system yet. Have a spurt of energy and no idea what to do with it. Act like a crazed *Hausfrau*. Clean the kitchen. Wipe down the cupboards, throw out ancient condiments, wash down the fridge, anything to expend some of the energy scratching at your veins demanding you do something, do something, do fucking anything, *now*. Decide you'll need some healthy food. Make a lasagne from scratch. Make spicy chickpeas. Make two trays of granola, hating yourself for becoming the kind of dickhead who not only *eats* granola but actually *makes their own*. Boil chicken and rice for your dogs and watch them wolf it down while you tremble, surrounded by nourishing food, hungry only for your poison.

5. Check the clock. Two hours have limped past. The rest of the day yawns blackly, a bottomless cave.

6. Walk your dogs. Cut the walk short because you keep breaking out in hot sweats, then shivering under your drenched shirt, and your legs are starting to burn. Go home and run a bath with a whole bag of Epsom salts. Marinate in the too-hot water on a crunchy layer of grit. The salts feel like hot coals, but that's nothing compared to the

muscle-ripping ache of dry land. Stay in the bath all day, refilling it until the hot water runs out.

7. You will not sleep. Some bastard has replaced your blood with fire ants. It is impossible to lie still. It is also impossible to sit up, stand, or walk around; to read, write, or watch television; to exist in the furnace of your flesh. Even the dogs slope off your bed in the early hours, sick of your writhing and sweating, your whimpering and shaking. Drop off for half an hour. Dream about your dead friends.

Day Two

8. Wake up crying. Ransack the house looking for drugs, as if you'd forget about a secret stash. Hate yourself for deleting your dealers' numbers.

9. Pray to all the gods you've never believed in. Bargain: *I'll put up with the rest of it for twice as long if you just take away this clanging migraine/searing backache/burning leg muscles/bone-deep need to rip off these layers of traitorous flesh and their putrid desires.* Desire, fucking desire, always too much and for the wrong thing.

10. Measure time by the gradual lightening of the sky, the shadows of clouds dragging along the walls, the uneaten lasagne growing crusty in the fridge.

Day Three

11. Wake up from another drug dream feeling like you're not on fire. Your body is empty and hurting, but nothing burns. You can move – so do. You haven't eaten in three days. Make

yourself a smoothie: kale, spinach, berries, coconut water, fucking *chia seeds*. Drink half of it and spend the next half-hour shitting through the eye of a needle. This will last a few days. Take some anti-diarrhoea pills. Try to drink water. Don't stray far from the bathroom.

Day Four

12. You'll have focused so hard on getting through the physical agony that you forgot about the emotional side of withdrawal – again. When it comes, you'll miss the shakes and the sweats and the aches and the writhing. Worst is the loneliness, the gnawing, all-consuming, foul-breathed yawn of loneliness, starting in your stomach then expanding like a dark balloon around your ribcage; the need to be touched, to be held, cocooned from this hell of your own making.

13. All of a sudden you'll miss everyone. All the people you cut off so you could be alone with your drugs; all the friends and family you left in another country; your girlfriend still abroad. All of a sudden your terribly human needs – love, companionship, friendship, community – will bite you, hard, on the arse. It will feel like being skinned and dowsed in acid. The pills were your lover, your best friend, your family. You wanted for nothing; now you need for everything.

14. Make yourself ask for help, even though there's nothing you despise more than vulnerability. Text your girlfriend. Call your mum just to hear the voice of someone who loves you. Tell her you have the flu. Hate yourself for lying. Email your friends, the ones who've been where you are, and accept

their support. Change your plea bargain: *I'll take a month of Day Two pain if you take away this panic/loneliness/despair/bottomless need.* Wonder if this ravenous need is your new normality, if the drugs were just the salve for this original wound.

15. Cry. Cry at the lost years, your sped-away youth, your stupid decisions. Cry because you miss home but you're not sure where that is. Cry because your dogs are crying because you are crying. When you stop crying because the world is so unbearably awful and start crying because it is so unbearably beautiful, recognise this for what it is: progress.

Day Five

16. Your ability to read will return. You'll never have been so grateful for anything in your tiny little life. Re-read your favourite books. Remember lines you read years ago. Anne Michaels on learning to tolerate images rising like bruises within you. Jenny Holzer's plea: *Protect me from what I want.* T. S. Eliot's promise that another moment one day will pierce you with painful joy. These words will become mantras, if you were the kind of person who believed in mantras, which the uneaten granola suggests you're in danger of becoming. Cut the sarcasm. These words are the thread that will string together the dull jewels of you. Let them.

17. But do not, under any circumstances, read the news. The world's drab machinery can self-destruct just fine without you. Knowing so many people are so much worse off than you will only make everything immeasurably worse. Try to believe this: there is no hierarchy of pain.

Day Six

18. Wake at 6 a.m., vibrating with energy, to the bluest skies seeping in around the curtains. Feel horny for the first time in years. Masturbate. It will take approximately one minute. Every old, dead nerve ending is fizzing, pulsing, thawing, reforming.

19. Rush out into the shimmering morning. Feel the bliss of sun on skin, grass under bare feet. Sit in the sun-crumbled dust under a tree and look at the sea, the sea, the cauldron of deep-blue sea, the sea that never did desert you despite your best efforts. Feel all that gorgeous life coursing through your veins. You think you can't take it all in at once, but your heart is a muscle; it will stretch to encompass whatever you choose to fill it with. Choose wisely.

20. This is the world when you're not numb. Guzzle it down. Be grateful.

Day Seven

21. Put the radio on while making your morning smoothie. A song will come on from a band you were obsessed with as a teenager. Sing and dance around your kitchen while your dogs yelp and wag at your feet. Belt it out. Download all their old albums to your phone and embarrass your dogs by singing along as you walk them.

22. Lie in the garden all afternoon with your headphones on, blissed out on sun and music and the worlds unfolding behind your ribcage. Your skin will prickle with an almost unbearable generalised empathy, and for once you won't

want to block it out. Remember being a teenager with this music, experiencing every chord change, every big, huge emotion, with an overwhelming physicality. Remember feeling like your emotions were pummelling you, feeling too much and of the wrong thing. Remember the relief of finding pills that could block them out, dumb them down, let you control how much or little you felt. Remember what this feels like.

23. Realise you no longer want to be a shell. Realise you just want to be one tiny cell in this huge, pulsating mess of humanity, however painful sometimes, however messy and confusing and overwhelming. Realise you can't just turn off the *bad* feelings; you can only turn off all of them or none of them. Choose none.

24. Your girlfriend will arrive home, suntanned and mosquito-bitten. Hold the everything of her body in your arms, the everything you've denied yourself from feeling, the everything you turned away from in favour of numbness. Walk your dogs together through sand and mud and silt. Eat ice cream and play computer games in bed. Feel the gentle twitching of her hand on your breast as she falls asleep behind you, the dogs warming your feet, blood-warm soul-buoyant love pounding from your soft animal bodies.

25. Know this: you don't have another one of these weeks left in you. Act accordingly.

TIME TICKS

TORY CREYTON

The evening fizzes up in bubbles from dizzying drinks as we waltz like Matilda under laser beams. Heady anticipations precipitate and pop; we've jumped hoops and skipped beats to get to this time of the week again. The Friday feeling writhes. All good things are coming and all things are good under the mirrored image of a glitter ball. We've waited all week for this day, sifting away hours living in unheard music. As night calls time on day, this night closes up another working week.

The rebellion starts, all the joy comes out at once as white noise eats up the ticks and tocks of office clocks. There's no space for anything else but now, just this minute, in this moment, inside this now. Again and again and again we spin in a relentlessly, whirlpooling merry-go-round. Keep topping it up, we all are, for this moment, keep topping it up; it's running out.

A wincing searchlight flickers through a waiting room; tomorrow's painful gathering of the scattered is on its way. But our smouldered feet still glow a smirk to the world from where we've tumbled onto a floor and stretched out into splintered comfort. It was good, a glittered palace with embers that still mumble on, but they're almost out.

A few vacant eyes and conversations patter along the walls as present drifts into past. There's nothing left to play with here. 'Say farewell and be quick,' sleep whispers through our limbs, along the carriages of our spent carcases. Will it bring with it a kind repose or malignant one, I wonder as I curl gratefully into its arms. In with it will creep tomorrow, where I will wake alone and set the searchlights out for drink, as a tick burrows its head into my skin.

THE BIG THINGS

ANDY MOORE

It wasn't in the big things,
Not the love-gorged sentiments carved with intention,
It was in you bleeding on my leg while you slept, not knowing
The animal of us,
All beauty and the sweet brutality
Not the poetry,
It's where we grew, bruised and unaware,
Are you awake?
Of joy?
Who ties you?
It was primal,
pure.

SURRENDER

YOU'RE NOT AN ALCOHOLIC

SCOTT MANLEY HADLEY

You're not an alcoholic.

You've never crashed a car.

You've never been arrested.

You're not an alcoholic because you go most of the day without a drink. Not all of it, but most of it.

You're not an alcoholic because you don't drink in the morning.

You're not an alcoholic because you're not doing things drunk you should be doing sober.

You're not an alcoholic because you can stop drinking: you went a whole month without drinking recently, and if you were an alcoholic you wouldn't be able to do that.

You're not an alcoholic because you don't drink and drive.

You're not an alcoholic because you don't start drinking as soon as you think about it, and you think about it all day and deny yourself a drink even though it's there, in the cupboard, in the fridge, under the stairs, in the shops, in other people's houses.

You're not an alcoholic because sometimes you talk about other things.

You read the news.

You go to work.

You get things done.

You're not an alcoholic because even though you wake up on the floor in different parts of the house once a week or so, that's normal; you've been doing that for *ages* and everyone does that from time to time, right?

You're not an alcoholic because when you're drinking you appear to be sober, no matter, until all of a sudden you—

You're not an alcoholic because you *can* still get drunk, right? If you were an alcoholic you could drink a bottle of vodka and go to work fine.

You're not an alcoholic because you can still get an erection.

You've never collapsed.

You've never lost a job or pulled a sickie because of drinking.

You're not an alcoholic because alcoholics are in treatment, alcoholics see doctors, alcoholics get help.

You're not an alcoholic because you're still drinking, and alcoholics DON'T DRINK.

You're not an alcoholic because you're not trying to give it up.

You're not an alcoholic.

So, have another drink.

PORTRAIT OF A PISS ARTIST AS A MIDDLE-AGED WOMAN

MICHELE KIRSCH

I wake up in a Valium stupor, in a room that used to be the cold storage for a butcher's shop, now converted into the cheapest bedsit in Hackney. I can see my breath condense in the cold air, so I know I am alive, and freezing. For a moment I think it's smoke. Fall asleep smoking and you will die a cliché. Don't let chips fry unattended and don't smoke in bed. Don't light up several gothic-style candles to give your stinking room some atmosphere. Most importantly, don't become a drug addict and wake up in a drug-addled stupor. Then you can avoid the other things.

What happened the day before? And the day before that? I reach for my overcoat, which is also my bathrobe, to stagger the few feet to the wardrobe. I feel for the bottle under the heap of stuff: clothes ruined by damp, boxes of pills, photos of my children, photos of my dead best friend, and a crumpled-up bridesmaid's dress for the wedding of a friend from church. Lavender, long, silk-feel, expensive, and no, you can never wear it again. The big lie of bridesmaid's dresses: shorten it and you can wear it again; it cost over £100. That's fifty miniature bottles of vodka. That's two scrips of Valium. Enough to keep me sedated for a week.

I couldn't wear it again. I could barely wear it for the wedding. Where we had to drink Shloer and listen to speeches, as I prayed not for their happiness but for it all to be over so I could get back to my bedsit to drink and do drugs; and for my dress to not fall from my shrunken frame as I staggered behind the bride-to-be. The dress was a cruel reminder that I became a devout Christian and raging drug and alcohol addict at roughly the same time. The spirits and the spiritual vying for my soul. Bible study every Tuesday night, where Smirnoff and Valium penetrated my eroding stomach lining with Swiss-watch precision. It will kick in fully by the time we are at Chapter One, Verse Four of Ecclesiastes. It's lovely to study the Bible when drunk, though hard to say 'verily' when the tongue is finding it difficult to reach the roof of the mouth: verlery, velvelty, verity, aw, you know whaddi mean, folks, just truly…

When was that? When did I go to church, stopping off in the offie on the way for those aeroplane bottles of Smirnoff, downing three before I got to the top of the road. Then, nicely loaded, singing 'Glory to God in the highest…' Because, yes, I was high.

When was that? I can't remember.

These days I can't even remember the sentence I said two sentences ago, until someone tells me, 'You just said that. And you said it before that, too.' Because they want to tell me how boring I am since my life became so very small: bedsit, pills, drink, internet shop, repeat 'til passed out drunk. I am trying to remember what my grand plan was. I think it was to leave my husband and children for a while to get clean. To become a nice wife and mother again. I think at some point I realised that the plan was not going according to plan.

I find the bottle. I am a morning drinker because time no longer holds me in chains: I don't have to take the kids to school. I don't have to go to work. I just need to go to the corner shop, the off-licence, the dirty doctor off Mare Street who prescribes me what I want, for a fee. His patients, private, are a strange mixture of crack whores, junkies, and those pony sort of girls who grew up in the Shires and need jabs for a gap year in India, to help, like, poor people. The pony girls are in rude health, with high ponytails, clear skin, and they talk about 'doing' countries. 'Last year I did Cambodia but rally, it's so touristy now... but it was very spiritual, and it totally changed my perspective?' The crack girls examine their nail extensions for imperfections, and shout at people on their mobile phones. They look lacquered, not just the nails, but with heavy make-up to disguise the hollowed cheeks and premature lines. Their leggings are so tight around their emaciated frames you can see (if you look, I try not to) the outline of their labia.

The first time I see the doctor, who works in the back of the chemist's shop, he looks at me quizzically. I don't look like the crack girls. I don't look like the pony girls from the Shires. Maybe he worked for the NHS but decided this was a more interesting gig.

'Why are you here?'

'I'm trying to do a Valium taper. I looked it up on the web. I'm on thirty milligrams a day right now and need to come off by two milligrams every two weeks. Can you help me?'

He sighs. 'Oh the taper story. Tell me another. No, just tell me what you need and then I can see my next patient.' He looks at me again. 'Oh, I understand. Housewife. Valium housewife. I don't see too many these days.' I don't bother to elaborate that I am no longer a housewife. It was getting in the way of my death style. Ten or so months previously I told my husband I needed some space. Was I that trite? I think I left it to him to tell the children. The plan was to shut myself away and get clean. That was the plan. Oh, yes I've mentioned that.

I go to the newsagent, where I used to buy the newspaper and comics for my kids. Hamdy asks, how are the children? He always does. 'Fine,' I lie, before buying a pen and notebook to copy down the phone number on the index card in the window that reads 'Room to let'.

'They grow up so fast,' says Hamdy, who used to provide them with lurid-coloured ice slushies, and magazines with toys, stickers or nail varnish stapled to the front. I temporarily forget what he's talking about. Hamdy is famous for not stocking porno mags. He doesn't know there are different types of pornography. Mine consists of websites of pharmacies in India, which provide often bogus supplies of Valium for 'you, for you madam, very good price. Our favourite customer.'

I am lost in a fog, as usual, and just say to Hamdy, 'Yes, they do,' hoping this is the correct response. The weather is terrible. Yes, it is. The council is useless. Yes, it is. Children grow up so fast. Yes, they do.

I buy a roll of extra-strong mints and copy the phone number from the card. It is the only card in the window without a glaring spelling or grammatical mistake. I leave the shop, ring the number and go straight there. A young man shows me the room. A bed sinking in the middle, mattress stained with the nocturnal explosions of other sad cases like me. A small sink, a small fridge, a huge wardrobe and bars on the windows. I love the bars. I can pretend I am in rehab, or prison. He tells me the rent is £60 a week. It is 2010. Nothing is that cheap in Stoke Newington. I give him a cash deposit, and go back home to pack a case.

I keep forgetting exactly why I am leaving my husband. We've been together twenty or so years and had kids a few years into our relationship, and even got married at some point, a sort of blurry afterthought. He's not been a bastard. He's not cheated on me. He's a great father and a loving husband. My children are teenagers. I write letters to a childhood pal in Liverpool and go to great lengths to say that my husband is my rock. What I don't tell her is I am the thing that crawled from under it. I don't tell her I've left him... them. Mothers don't do stuff like that.

And of course, the plan does not work. Living alone means I can drink and do drugs in peace. Occasionally I try to cut down, hiding the bottles of drink and pills from myself, like, on top of the wardrobe, or underneath the bed; given the rough dimensions of the room, ten feet by eight, there is nowhere to hide anything. Sticking a bottle deep into the mound of clothes at the bottom of the wardrobe, it rolls a bit and the neck sticks out, the red top begging to be unscrewed, so I can pour the liquid down my neck. I decide to ignore it. It reminds me of my children hiding behind the curtains, their feet sticking out from underneath, the fabric juddering with their badly stifled giggles as I called out in mock consternation, 'Now where, oh where could they be? I'll never find them at this rate. I guess I'll have to bake those brownies all by myself...' and they would leap out of the curtains, shouting, 'Here we are! Here we are!' Mothers do stuff like that. The hide-and-seek and brownie-baking years. I must have been good at some point.

I get a routine going. First, I throw on an item of clothing from my floordrobe, count out my pound coins and go to the corner shop. The transaction has become wordless. I put the coins on the counter, he passes me the bottle, and I pretty much run back to the bedsit to pour some into my pound-shop mug that reads 'I (heart) Mum'. I bought four, and made all my family drink from them. When I moved out I took one, and suspect they gave the others to a charity shop. Mum left. Everything drunk from that cup will taste bitter.

When the shaking stops, when the stomach settles enough for a cup of Nescafé with little granules of dried Marvel milk floating around the top, I make my second trip outside. I cut through the estate, watching the children spin each other on the two broken swings, twisting the chains that hold the seat until they can twist no more, and the swing unravels, sending them into a whirling seated pirouette. They stagger about, laughing, their dizzy eyes sending them careening in all directions before falling to the asphalt. I realise this is the kid version of getting drunk. The grown-up version, you still unravel, but bring everyone down around you.

I go to the Somalian internet shop to use the computer, putting a pound coin on the counter and fifty pence in the Somalian relief-aid box. Mustafa, as usual, is watching a harrowing video of the famine in his mother country. They are all variations on the same theme: a widowed woman, her starving child, crossing a barren land, digging up inedible roots and sucking on them. The kid dies. She buries him in the sand. Flies all round her face; she's too beaten down to brush them off.

Mustafa stops looking at the film and greets me warmly, if erroneously. 'Michelle Obama!' It is a running joke that long since ran out on me; another American lady called Michele, only she is First Lady. There's a broken fridge stocked with lukewarm orange fizzy drinks. The shop smells like old rice and people who don't bathe.

'How is Barak?' he asks, jovially.

'Oh, you know, running the country and stuff.'

'Have you told him what's going on in Somalia? Will he help?'

'He's working on it.'

It's easier to play along to get it over with, to get to my little cubicle and swallow some pills and take sly sips out of my flat bottle. I am working on a long piece about becoming an alcoholic, but I never get to the end, because I am still in it. I have sent sections to a publisher, who says she does not want to publish it because she does not know how it will end, and that I will regret writing, in a book, the feelings I had around my family, the one I left. She seems to suggest that one day I will regret writing these things down, and she's not wrong.

I type a few lines, and take a few sips when Mustafa prepares for one of his five daily prayers. He asks me to mind the shop when he goes to the toilet for his ablutions. These include washing his nostrils out with water, so he emerges from the loo with a dripping nose.

I say, 'Don't shit me, Mustafa, you're doing lines of coke back there.'

And he looks confused and says he would never put Coca-Cola up his nose.

Today I type fast because I have an appointment with the addiction nurse in Mare Street. I have a skin complaint, an all-over itch that is impossible to scratch. At first they thought it was my liver, a sort of pre-jaundice condition, but when I arrive at the clinic and take off my clothes to show her the rash, she peers closely at it, tracing lines with her gloved fingers and then removing the gloves to write notes on her computer.

She says, with a brisk efficiency and slight unprofessional weariness, that I have a double problem: scabies and bedbugs. The first she can treat, or I can treat, with lotions, applied to every part of my head and body. The bedbugs, she says, are an increasing menace in rented accommodation. Can I have a word with my landlord? The room itself needs to be treated, the mattress thrown out. For that itching she can only give me antihistamines, but best not to drink with them because they...

and here she sighs. I didn't stop drinking for my family. I'm probably not going to stop for the bugs.

She shows me a diagram about how to apply the lotion, and she really does mean everywhere. She says she'll watch me put it on so she knows I am getting it right. It's chalky, and it has a strong chemical smell. It stings the bits I've scratched raw. There is a bit at the back I cannot reach, dead centre of my back, my spine sticking out, reptilian, every bump covered by a thin layer of raw skin. I used to take the kids to the Natural History Museum to look at the dinosaur skeletons. We went through their gift-shop loot on the long Tube ride home: pencils, erasers, colouring books. I was a good mum, once. When was that? When they were too young to remember. They won't remember that bit. They'll remember this bit, the bit when I left.

She puts the gloves back on and gently rubs the lotion into the area I cannot reach. Tears spring up in my eyes. I start sobbing. She stops. 'Am I hurting you?'

I say no. This is the only time another human being has touched me in about a year. I had forgotten what it feels like. In this case, it's painful, every nerve ending rattling as the chemicals sink into my pores.

I have another appointment. I try to space them out so I have somewhere to go each day, but today it is impossible. I run the short walk between the clinic and the town hall, stopping off in Wetherspoon's to down a double vodka.

At the town hall, those who sit next to me wrinkle their nose and move to a different seat. I have a ticket with a number on it, and when my number flashes on the screen, and a soothing female voice intones over the loudspeaker, I get up, gingerly, to walk slowly to the right room. My body is on fire. I am afraid I am having an allergic reaction to the delousing lotion.

The woman behind the desk taps away at her keyboard as she gestures for me to take a seat. We have met before. The council is trying to decide if I am a worthy candidate for council-sponsored rehab.

She looks at me and says, 'I see people go in, and they get well, and they come back to the area and they're using again. But not all. Some get well and stay well. You… I don't know. I can't tell with you. What do you think?'

'I don't know. I've never been to rehab.'

She shows me some leaflets of the rehabs the council endorses. It appears I have a choice. There are photos of the countryside, and the beach, and neatly made up beds in small but tidy rooms. Photos of smiling people, all races and ages, and information on the 'comprehensive' care package on offer. I see one in Bournemouth, and it reminds me of a summer holiday with the kids, in the rougher part of town where the holiday flats were cheaper. Amidst all the fat lobster-red sunbathers, and white sunblock-painted children making sandcastles, a Martin Parr tableau, I saw thin, pale people roaming the beach in groups of three. They were fully dressed, often in black, with pale skin poking out from under hoodies, and large sunglasses. I remember laughing with my husband, 'Look at all the goths! I didn't think they came out during the day.' One was sitting apart from the others, eating a melting Cornetto under the shade of the lifeguard chair. I wondered about his story.

The woman in the council office says, 'What do you think?'

I say I like the one in Bournemouth. I was there once. It was nice.

'What? The rehab?'

'No, the beach.'

She looks stern over her spectacles. 'This is not an all-inclusive beach holiday. This is a treatment centre.'

I say I know that, and that I am grateful that the council is, or might be, willing to support my recovery.

A few weeks later the woman phones me. She tells me to pack my things to be ready to leave the next morning. I mutter thank you and haul my suitcase down from the top of the wardrobe. I chuck some things in – jumpers, pants, a crucifix, my stash of drugs, a Bible, some CDs and photos of my children – then drink a bottle of vodka. I fall asleep on the edge of the bed, roll over and, ribcage first, fall onto the hard edge of my suitcase, before landing in the suitcase itself. When I take a breath, an enormous pain wracks my body. Something is wrong. I ring my best friend, who comes straight over and phones an ambulance. When they find me curled up in my own suitcase, one says jovially, 'Michele, you were meant to pack your things, not yourself.' One of the paramedics tells me I have broken two ribs, and nothing can fix them but time.

The next morning, my friend takes me to the station in a taxi. She carries my case, and helps me onto the train.

As we pull out of the station, I hold my breath; for a moment it eases the pain. My friend waves, a sad, mechanical wave, and I wave back, a fresh wave of pain shooting through my body. Our children, toddlers, had been at playgroup together, messing about with blocks, sand and paint. My daughter, as a birthday treat aged three, read a story about a monster to her playgroup friends, with pop-out pictures. She read it so convincingly, pausing for effect in all the right places, as I'd done when reading it to her, that she scared the shit out of all of them. Several cried. Some were too traumatised to eat the Morrison's shop-brand Sweetie Mountain Cake.

Soon I would join the pale ghosts on the beach, hiding from the sun, from the jolly families, from the memories of my own family, and from the future memories I had, at one happier time, planned to make for them. I get drunk on the train – everyone who goes to rehab has one last use-up – and fall into a head-lolling, dreamless sleep. A guard wakes me at Bournemouth, shaking my already shaking broken body.

When I tell the cab driver the address, he peers at me through the rear-view mirror. I can tell he is trying to work out if I'm going to throw up.

'No offence like, but lots of people going there, they, well, you know. I've got to take the car out of service and get it cleaned, costs the earth, and it's you what has to pay it. So, you know, if you want me to pull over, tell me quick.'

'Just try not to go over any potholes or bumps,' I croak.

I arrive at the treatment centre and nod off in a chair. I am appointed a peer minder, a beautiful girl. If I ever get lost I just need to find the tall girl with the long red hair.

One week into treatment and it turns out the flat we are staying in is infested with bedbugs. I have come up in deep red welts, as before, in triangular patterns of three: breakfast, lunch and dinner. There are six of us, and we are all kicking something, some further down the line than others in terms of being clean. We are in various states of unwell. Me, I can barely breathe: every cell, every nucleus and cytoplasm of every cell begging me for Valium.

One of the counsellors comes to tell us we are to be moved to a B & B, but that we must try to look 'normal'. 'And for goodness' sake don't tell them where you're from.' We check into the B & B, standing close together, some of us shaking. 'We're on holiday,' I say loudly, unconvincingly.

The next day, an Indian summer in late September, we make a trip down to the beach, the same beach I went to with my children all those years ago. I am pale, thin, wearing black clothes stained with pinky, chalky calamine lotion. I sit with my group. Someone is playing techno music on a phone. I hear the crash of the waves, the shouts of the children, the strange, muted sounds of other people's conversations. It is too hot. I go to sit under the lifeguard chair, like that boy with the Cornetto. I now understand who he was, why he was here.

A few months later, the weather has changed. We have skipped autumn and are straight into winter. I am walking with my housemates to an AA meeting. It is long and boring. Some guy, some gal, used to drink. Lost everything. Then they found AA. Now they have a life beyond their wildest dreams. I am still shaking. I am still almost surgically attached to the red-haired girl. On the way home my friend and I pause to look into a terraced house. We can see the Christmas-tree lights, a flat-screen telly playing *EastEnders*, and a chubby, merry family of four squeezed onto the sofa. They sit wordlessly, passing a huge tin of Quality Street back and forth. The others in our group are going home to heat up Cup-a-Soup or a past-its-sell-by-date ready meal. My friend and I stand transfixed by this scene of pre-Christmas normality. This is like telly to us. So far removed from our normal that we can't move for curiosity. Which sweet will they choose? When will the children have to go to bed? Suddenly I turn to my friend and say, 'I'm not one of you, not really. I'm one of them. I should be home, eating sweets, watching telly with my kids.'

He looks at me and says, 'No, you're the wrong shape.'

'What, for normal life, or for this family?'

'Both.'

We bundle up our jackets and half speed-walk, half run, to catch up with the others. A sleet is descending. The sharp, cold air stings my lungs. I feel strangely renewed. I know I am the wrong shape for some version of normal life. But maybe, just maybe, I can find a new normal, fresh as the white snow drifting in crescents on my windowsill.

BRICKSKIN

CLAIRE DEAN

We met when our kids were little. I used to see her on the school run. Her daughter was in the year above mine and she had a younger son who was always fighting to get out of his buggy. We never acknowledged each other, although we shared the same pavements every day. I kept my head down in the playground too – everyone else seemed to be friends.

Her skin was reddish-brown and cracked. I thought it must be some kind of eczema. Glancing at the scabs on her hands made me want to cradle my own. She lived on one of the streets that led to the prom – where all the old B & Bs have been turned into flats. I'd see her struggle to get the buggy in up the steps and think I should try to help.

I didn't intend to follow her that day. Her son was yelling and she was motionless, blocking the pavement in front of her door, and then she slowly turned the buggy towards the prom and pushed on. It looked like she was forcing the wheels through sand.

People don't go all the way out to the end of the pier. It's longer than it looks and there's nothing there. The boarded-up lighthouse has been a café at various times over the years – there are layers of ice-lolly posters on the walls – but it always closes down after a season. Crude bird statues are waymarkers along the railings. My kids used to be terrified of them.

She'd sat down on the bench. Her hood was shadowing her

face but she seemed to be staring at the hills across the bay. With the tide way out, the mud was apocalyptic. Apart from the odd skein of bladder wrack and plastic, there was no sign that water ever touched the broken seabed.

I knew I had to speak to her. I couldn't pretend it was an accident that I'd found myself out there too. Her son had fallen asleep in his buggy. A tatty bit of blanket hung from the corner of his mouth. She was so still it looked like she wasn't breathing. At the neckline of her t-shirt, her skin broke into rows of tiny red bricks. They encased her neck. Her jaw was rigid, eyes glassy. I wondered if she could actually see me.

'Must think I'm awful,' she said.

'No, I'm sorry, no of course not, I...'

'Keep wondering...' It looked like it was painful for her to speak. The skin around her mouth was pitted and red-raw. The heaviness of her tongue made her words slow. 'Keep wondering why kids... haven't noticed. Maybe have and don't say. They can add it to long list... things I did wrong when they were...'

I didn't know how to reply, so I sat down beside her. Seagulls tore through the sky above us and we sat for ages watching them claw at the wind. Her son's blanket fell to the floor and she flinched as he began to gripe in his sleep. I replaced it as gently as I could without waking him.

'It's too hard sometimes, being a parent,' I said. 'People don't say it, but they should.'

'When I've got them to bed... Can't stop thinking. More... I... think... worse it... gets. Think every bit. Every room. Marks on wallpaper. Books on shelves. Spider behind TV. Crumbs in carpet... chocolate cake. If don't think it'll all disappear and... I'm scared I will too... Kids'll wake up. I'll be gone. Not there. Not able to look after them. They need me. I'm all... they've got.'

You're just trying to keep them safe, I thought, but I didn't say it.

'Longer I spend... inside, more it shows. Know what you must think. I'm going to stop.'

I didn't know what to say. Suggesting she went to the doctor's seemed patronising, ridiculous. I didn't want to say the wrong thing.

She coughed and it sounded like her lungs were splintering. 'Sorry. Sound like my Grandad... Without forty a day.'

'I tried smoking at school,' I said, 'but I was rubbish at it.'

'Me too,' she said and she tried to smile. 'It's damp... In my lungs. Can't escape it. Worry what it's doing to kids. Flat we're in. Used to be cellar. All windows halved. No light. It started... I was thinking... About more rooms. Trying to get higher.' She stopped to get her breath and I noticed how the cuffs of her sleeves were stained red with either brick dust or crusted blood, or both. She was constantly trying to pull them down to cover her hands.

'Walls thin. Damp gets in. Mildew on curtains. Puddles... windowsill. Can hear drunks outside shop across road. I keep thinking – *up*. So many staircases and hallways now. Worry I'll get lost... Walls thicker higher up. Rooms smaller. Like a... lighthouse. Used to see sea from windows. Now glass smeared. Or boarded up. Lying down, can't escape footsteps on pavement. Up the stairs. Can't sleep... Sorry. Shouldn't have... I'm OK. Not a nutter. Honest. Sorry. Need to get the shopping done before he wakes up. Look at him... sweetheart... Like a little pug when he sleeps.'

I knew what she was doing. I wonder if most of us have something we don't talk about. A thing we don't tell anyone, because doing that would make it real. And if we do find a way to talk about it, we worry we won't be believed because how could someone be OK and smile when they have this thing going on. To fight off shock or pity we lighten our tone, change the subject, say we're OK, but then we're left with the thing that telling woke up.

She was using the buggy handles to heave herself up. I didn't know how to help her, but I didn't want to leave her alone with what she'd told me. 'When I was little I always tried to get through the back of the wardrobe,' I said.

'Did too. Favourite book... At school.'

'I still reach right to the back of every wardrobe, just in case. My daughter's got an obsession with finding rabbit holes to fall down.'

'Ellie was Alice... World Book Day,' she said. 'My... Nanna had pop-up book. House of cards collapsed... Terrifying.' Her almost-smile was fixed into a gash.

'I always got really annoyed that she woke up and it was all just a dream,' I said.

'Would be good to wake up.'

I wanted to say things would be OK, but I didn't, because how could I know if things would be OK? Her son started to whimper in his sleep.

'Better go,' she said. 'Th... thanks.'

I watched until she was a sliver back on the prom. She moved like a ninety-year-old. She was so thin I wondered if she went without food to make sure her kids had enough. Maybe the bricks were all that was keeping her upright.

The following week I passed her near Lidl. I asked how she was, if there was anything I could do to help. 'Am fine,' she said. 'Thank you.' Her eyes were glazed. It didn't feel like she was looking at me. After that she avoided my smile whenever we passed. I'd see her in the distance or hear her son's cries. Then she disappeared.

*

It was after the school holidays that I saw her for the first time in months. Her son was toddling ahead, straining at his polka-dotted reins. She moved faster. She seemed lighter. I saw her crouch to point a seagull out to him and they laughed as it fought its way into a packet of crisps. When I walked behind her I noticed she was trailing dust along the pavement. The wind made shifting patterns with it. She half-smiled at me by the school gates.

Just before Christmas, I found her unmoving outside her front door. Just like she had been the day we talked on the pier. Her son was belly-down on the pavement, screaming. Her teeth were gritted and there were tears in her eyes. 'It's the wind,' she said. 'I can't bear the feel of it on my skin. I pulled it all down. I had to. I thought I'd feel better, I thought I could do it, but now I don't know.'

I stood beside her to shore her up.

WAKING UP

FRANCESCA BAKER

A bell rings out. I blearily reach out to press snooze. But it's not my usual alarm. Opening my eyes, I slowly come to consciousness. The light stings my eyes, and there is an uncomfortable warmth moistening the small of my back. This quilt sweats.

I look around the room. Beige walls, stark. Terracotta curtains, uniform. A wipe-clean floor. Rounded corners for safety. A tainted aluminium sink to my left, like in run-down public toilets in faded seaside towns. The tap does not work; nothing can be washed away. Bolted-shut windows make for a warm, stuffy fug. There's an extra bar to ensure that if we do force them open, we can't slip through. The bar is only three inches off the surface of the glass. None of us are that thin. It all blurs into a sense of bland immobility.

A lady bursts in carrying a tray. 'Breakfastttt!' she shrieks.

I'm here. It's happened.

Yesterday had been hard: a strange whirl of relief, validation, fear, anger and worry in my veins.

'There is a bed available for you,' Dr Thompson had said again. 'You must be admitted.'

I had felt a heart-clamping jolt and ache of hurt as I fell to the floor. The pathetically dim strip lighting seemed to bruise into my soul. Two emotions, simultaneous but indiscriminate; unsure whether the tears in the shadowy valleys of my eye sockets were those of relief at the prospect of change, a way out of this mess, or deep proof of utter failure at life.

'And if I refuse?' I asked.

'We would need to look into making an assessment.'

'You mean section me?'

Dr Elfaki simply stared. Maybe nodded, but it was barely perceptible.

'You think I'm crazy?'

'You are very ill and a time bomb of danger to yourself and others. You are unsafe to be out in the community. If I let you go, I don't know that you will make it much longer.' Her gaze did not flicker.

I sat, my head inclined slightly forward, staring blankly.

My life didn't flash before my eyes, but I had a sense of bombardment. Of moments and feelings being thrown at me. Infiltrating, like a soundless coup, the realisation of what was happening bled into my mind. Tugging my hair, I let out the cry of a wounded animal, and rocked, sobbing to myself as I tried to think clearly, rationally, to get a grasp on all this.

Why? How I have ended up in this state? A loved, bright, capable girl who loves food and hates being thin. Why is this so hard? I have potential. I am not one of these girls. Except I am. I feel painful realisation that I am another tormented creature stupidly starving myself. I curse those vicious voices every moment of every day. The constant self-flagellation that pulls me back from who I am, and tells me I should be 'better'. Let me tell you, there's no achievement from being emaciated. Just a weak and broken body.

The guilt is overwhelming.

So that's why I'm here. A life being stripped down to the essentials – essentials defined by the hospital. I've been up here before, to take a visit. I know the vacant looks. The pacing shuffle. The anxious shiver and the potent tang of bleach. It was hard seeing Mum and Dad yesterday; it was all new for them. I could see them trembling. Dad was trying to be strong, and I love him for it, but I knew that this was breaking him. For twenty-six years now they had been making things better, my physical and emotional plasters on wounds, but they can't save me from this malicious illness. I want to scream out, 'They didn't do anything wrong. They loved me. They still love me!'

'You might need to be here now,' Mummy had said as I clung tightly to her, while she tried not to flinch at the feeling of my protruding bones, 'but you don't belong here.'

If I don't belong here, and I sure as hell can't seem to cope out there, then where? Just where is my place in the world?

The hospital grounds are quiet and desolate. Brick buildings fashioned through the early half of the last century stand beside prefabricated and shoddy structures, their decay echoed in the scent of the large, overflowing green bins. This is the kind of place where people could easily be forgotten. It is still, isolated, not like any hospital I have been to before. I think of the frantic rush of an ordinary hospital, where accident and emergency teems with people and a sense of urgency. Here there is no speed, no urgency, no one seems compelled to do anything. On the way in I noted a vending machine, lop-sided and ageing, empty, bar one bottle of water with a fading label. 'Even the vending machine is anorexic,' I laughed to myself.

As I sit eating my sodden Weetabix, I wonder what belonging in a mental hospital looks like. Are there certain behaviours expected of me? Should I start crying over my cereal? Why is the nurse staring intently? I run my fingers through my hair. I had brushed it quickly when waking, but am now not sure whether it looks a mess or is too tidy. Are crazy people meant to bother with their appearance? Not that I am bothering, looking down to my dishevelled pyjamas and the screwed-up bed linen upon which I sit.

The battered plastic tray and carefully measured portions, labelled with scrawled biro on shreds of yellow Post-it notes, remind me of Grandfather's nursing home. I am now no different from him. All adult responsibilities removed, and to be observed while eating, peeing, washing and not allowed to leave my room. They even confiscated my tweezers, presumably concerned I will pluck myself to oblivion.

When the final crumbs and drops of my breakfast have been consumed I look up. 'So what happens now?' I ask.

'You wait,' says the nurse.

'Wait?' I feel like I'm being told to sit in my room and think about what I have done. I bloody well know what I've done and I want to fix it. This, this is pure punishment. For fucking up my life.

I don't want to wait. I want to recover. I want my life back.

SILENCE

T. K. SAEED

The pool of silence liquidates with the first drop of noise.

Whick whick whirr. (Rhythmic movements overlaid with the faintest metallic screech.)

The smell hits me, as it always does, ferociously, burning through nasal hairs and fine tissue.

I hate its invasiveness, its pungency – the brassy, accusing signature of its existence lingering long after actual death by cremation.

I remember golden fields of mustard and corn, flashing by in a blinding stream of colour on heavy summer days, interwoven with that same insidious scent that slips, serpentine, into clothing and hair and skin; and sinks into the epidermis of the car, so that hours, days and weeks later, the smell rushes out, unwanted intimacy, on opening the door.

I have scrubbed those seats. (No Marigolds – latex allergy to blame; alternatives keep tearing.)

Buckets of bleach and soap and tepid water, and an old dishrag. Wrinkled fingers wearing away at the sturdy cloth, time and again, with lukewarm results. The smell merges with musty bleach and soap.

Whick whick whirrrr.

Crushed pockets of pale green leaves. The quiet crinkle of tissue-thin slips of paper, moistened by tongue. The click of a lighter. A puddle of ash, and a rain of grey dust, erupted from a slender molten volcano, releasing toxic fumes that choke and scar.

His clothes are all disfigured; ash-holes burned into tracksuit legs and t-shirt hems. Black holes in seat upholstery and carpet pile and curtain voile. Silver embers on application forms, ammonia-scrubbed shelves and windowsills, and melded with the dregs in endless cups of espresso-strong tea.

Whick whick whirrrr. (Inhale. Exhale.)

In the bathroom, taking a shower, I smell it. It's sunk so deep, it pervades places he hasn't been: the airing cupboard, the garden shed, freshly laundered towels hot and damp from the washing machine.

Our aspiration was the suburban statistic – one point eight children and a slick car in the driveway. Before shades of debt and infertility; before a back broken by long nights labouring in rain, snow and sleet, on minimum wage. Before smashed phones and wracking sobs, issued from bodies curled in foetal memory.

Whick whick whirrrrr.

And those intense eyes that melt with love, now red-rimmed and bloodshot, spidered and vague, desperately gazing into me (through me), searching for impossible answers. All the while jabbing and stabbing with words fuelled by hyped-up adrenaline, until some time later (and hoarse, competing voices and banging doors), he falls into bed, begging for forgiveness, pleading with me not to leave him alone.

And I don't.

I hate the ash, and musty bleach, spidery eyes and black holes. I hate the crinkle of tissue and clouds of stench. I hate the bitter, paranoia-filled accusations and flashpoint rage, the dropped jobs, meagre pennies and empty fridges. I resent having to hate. I long for white picket fences and white Scandinavian minimalism; immaculate clothes untainted by the miasma of decay. I long for intimacy unmarred by suspicion and regret, and a life controlled by chemicals out of control.

And so the silence grows.

MARIONETTE

TORY CREYTON

Foul fuel rumbles along rusting pipes, onwards to an engine room where a resting battery is housed. It's a suspended generator nestled underneath an unmade bed of dust. On top of this unsettled blanket is a hastily scribbled wish that spells 'please do not disturb'. Soon though, it will be choked back into motion. Cheap liquid cinders spit, drip and seep their way towards the tank to fill it up. Their fumes stretch out like yearning arms begging to be met by the form of their other half, and they will be soon, because this evening an old play is now setting up the stage to retell its tale.

As a well-versed audience member, I sit and sigh, silently bored, same as I had been an hour ago, when the scenery was different. I'd been watching time tick through the middle of a date, one that was going like all the others. It'd looked better in my head than the flesh of the real thing, so I was biding away moments into minutes till it was polite enough to leave. Was I ever interested in this one, in any of them? Or were they all the same route to someplace else? Who did I really dress up to meet tonight? While sitting opposite a stranger, both of us fastened up in our best behaviour, with the first drink drunk, I knew I'd be going home to an old routine. Quick as the flick of a lighter, the boy in front of me disappeared and I was sitting next to my Old Blue Flame.

I left the bar without that boy, the one who had brought us back together, warmed up with the anticipation of Old Blue. Outside, an off-licence lamp twitches and I float towards it, where

I'll find him waiting for me, where I'll place his long-necked palm in my pocket and with intimate silence we'll make our way home. As we slip along the streets towards the scene of our next crime, the cogs of a distant fairground ride rumble and creak.

Soon enough I'm poured into pirouettes, curtains drawn, lights dim, latch down. I'd reached for the clean glass that lives on the dusty shelf and started the alchemy to summon up our secret. I sink, he pulls me to my feet; I drink, he wants to dance. He's holding the rhythms and the strings and is playing with his sugared-up plum fairy, who's nodding along to his maddening song. He covers me in a coat of his arms, a spider and a wrapped-up, muting little fly. Locking my fingers to his wrist, he makes me feel for our deadening pulse.

We move among the dark, sunken deep inside the night's dirtied laundry. Weary, I reach around for a centrepiece, but he's been quietly turning the tables. While dizzied up and blind in kaleidoscopic whirling, he's been snipping at my cords and fastening new strings, silently making himself a puppet. We're stuck together now, twisted hinges of a rupturing carousel. I'm blurry and spun, wrenching and recoiled, pushed down inside the carnival. With leashes round my limbs, relinquishing to noise, I'm held up inside this dance for old time's sake.

Once upon a time we were partners in crime: he would whisper pretty little melodies and I licked up all the ditties, ignoring bridges as they blazed. Now I dance less and less for the chance of some rest. Pinned to the bottom of his collector's box. Dusted in salts, wings outspread and slowly setting, he watches down from the closing lid. The four walls seep, and light flickers and is snuffed out. I face the dark and he faces me right back and now we look exactly the same.

TAIL OF THE DONKEY

FORD DAGENHAM

So I was cutting down, wasn't I? Then stop o'clock for me in maybe ten days. Cos of the blackness it was, the screaming nerves and the loss of buzz.

So in the daytime supermarket, wasn't I? With the fishwives and lonely men in their mum-hemmed jeans.

So I had a basket of steak and onions and those little wines, cos I was cutting down PROPERLY wasn't I? Like the doctor said to. No dangerous plummet to nothing, all sudden like. Tail off, the doctor said, like I was the donkey in that kids' game.

But my hands did stuff without me, didn't they? Gone and got some whisky too, hadn't they?

And at the checkout the orange woman with pencilled-in eyebrows was bleeping barcodes super slow, wasn't she? Cos of her Disney-painted nails.

So I had time to, if I *wanted to*, if I *could*, cos the booze aisle was right close, but I wasn't *about to*, was I? Put it back, I mean. Have some last hurrah, couldn't I?

So it was whisky with red wine chasers that night, wasn't it? And, all pleased with myself, I christened it the Fuckbrain Hurricane.

I suffered blackness, screaming nerves and a raging howling anti-buzz that became the clearest Moment of Clarity I had ever ever known.

EVERYTHING was fine. Had always BEEN fine and always WILL be fine. A world in order. Beautiful it was. So stopping would be fine too, wouldn't it? It would. It would. It WOULD.

A REACH OF ARMS

ROBIN MUKHERJEE

That the rocky shore, the immutable plinth
Of the promontory reflects in our eyes
Does not make us the rocky shore, the plinth or promontory.
We are flecks at most,
Thrown by the waves to cavort, spinning
For a day. And to lose or win,
To lose, or win, has no meaning anyway.

Have I the reach of arms to embrace
The grey nothing of the vasty sky?
I dare not look at you,
In case you've seen it too,
And we should both stand there bewildered
Asking why.

So do we lie to every child?
Sweets and toys and treats
For happy girls and boys?
When even the dust under our nails
Is the empty ocean, wild.

Old men talking. Beware.
They like to spill their crusty beans
Upon the senseless air.

SURVIVAL

WHAT A LAUGH

KERRY HUDSON

Head back, curve of the neck exposed, mouth wide, roaring. We all have this laugh: the family on my mum's side, me and my father. My childhood was filled with this sound and, eventually, my adulthood was punctuated by my own booming 'HAHAHA'. I was proud of it, that familial laugh. We might have been neds or chavs or scavs, but look how free we were. Look how loud our joy was despite the council estates, drug dealers, late giro cheques, boyfriends who liked to slap about a bit, heroin, breakdowns and the terrible childhoods that left their stain. Look how our desire to be happy still triumphed, and so loudly too.

Like many Scottish families, ours was full of drinking stories. Too drunk didn't exist in my world. Any story, no matter if it involved pissing or shitting yourself, rowing with someone never to be spoken to again, ending up in the polis station or with a carpet burn down the front of your face, was accompanied by that laugh. HAHAHA. 'What a laugh,' we'd roar.

At thirteen I started to add my own stories: I pulled down my trousers at a party so a group of boys could assess my pubic hair; I went out drinking one afternoon in the city centre of Norwich and woke up alone in a room with a window that showed only fields as far as the eye could see; I came home at 3 a.m. with one of the legs of my suede trousers missing and no idea why. And all before I was seventeen. HAHAHA. I learned to roll those stories into something bouncing and dynamic. I learned, had been taught, that there was no such thing as too much drink. Drinking meant drunk; drunk meant mortal; blacking out was hilarious. What a laugh.

My dad was absent for much of this. He left me to my mum and council estates and B & Bs while he took his American army pension out drinking with 'bohemian types' (Mum's words) in London, Mexico, Dublin, I was never sure where exactly. Occasionally I'd get a scrawled postcard sent from somewhere with bright stamps and an insane gift: a vintage violin, a tome of poetry, a woollen cape. These items sat unused in our council flat with its stained mattresses and carpets and dank, empty fridge. I'd circle warily around those presents in my shoes that were held together by Blu-Tack, wearing school trousers three inches too short, my shirt greying except for the yellow patches at the armpits until eventually we'd try and pawn them or Mum would chuck them in drunken fury.

The first time I understood the word 'addiction' beyond *Grange Hill* was when I visited my father for a summer holiday in London when I was eleven or twelve. I remember little of the holiday except him reacting like a wounded, savage animal to my pre-pubescent demands and fragilities. I remember his expression: tight, mildly revolted, like I was a bad taste in his mouth. He was a big man and I remember how he towered over me in fury, raised his hand and lowered it again and then proudly said he'd never hit his own child. I remember he sat and told me, searching my face, that he was 'a Valium addict', that he'd gone 'cold turkey', that he didn't like the 'twelve steps'. He wanted something from me. I can't say how I responded but I'm sure I disappointed him by simply shrugging and saying something like, 'All right. Are we going ice-skating or not, then?'

I had never been exposed to the idea of excess. He hadn't

taught me. The concept that the need for something above all else was harmful didn't exist.

A few years later, when I was around fifteen, he would tell me he was an alcoholic. I listened, but I knew he didn't drink all the time. I knew that he went for long periods where he drank nothing. I drank more than him. He tried to explain how he was bingeing; how he'd been mugged in Paris and Mexico and had to get the American Embassy to bail him out; how he'd once invited all the panhandlers under a bridge to dinner and spent his last penny; how he woke up in the street covered in blood; how he ruined his chances at love. We were the same. But I drank more; kept drinking. I think I might have laughed.

I left school at fifteen with no qualifications. I worked as a waitress and went out every night in the seaside town I lived in, and drank, danced and fucked. Every day while carrying plates of egg and chips and fish-finger kiddies' meals, I dreamed of my first drink: a double vodka, lime and soda followed by shots, if my tips were good that day.

Aged seventeen a drunken night went badly, brutally wrong. I hope I can be forgiven for not offering more to you here; I'm simply not ready. After that night, the seed my father planted rooted down somewhere. His ashamed expression, fearfulness, the need etched on his face. I knew at last there was such a thing as too much. There was no way to tell that story, though I did try for many years to shape it into something less terrifying. There was no way to throw my head back, show my neck and laugh at that black gaping hole, no way to pretend. And so I stopped laughing.

I worked like a dog, I pierced ears, pulled pints, gave out darts on the pier so people could win cuddly toys; saved every penny and went to work at a summer camp in America. I couldn't legally drink there, but I was found drinking a raspberry-wine cooler in the woods, was hauled into the director's office and asked if I had a drinking problem. I definitely laughed then.

I returned to college and decided I had to get to university if I wanted a life bigger than Friday-night fucks and family brawls. At university I met my first partner of ten years, who barely drank at all. My fiancé now can only have a single drink before he starts to weave across the floor. I love him for this.

I didn't always stop myself in time. I've often given in to that tidal pull and allowed myself a fourth drink after the third, which I know will tilt a night on its axis. I've done bad things, I've put myself in danger. I've had a lot of fun.

I wasn't an alcoholic. I'd never presume to try to understand the terror of knowing you're eroding the last good thing you have with booze, reaching for the glass anyway and being so fucking glad for that first taste. But I watched it happen to people around me: I watched it soak in; I watched them crumble. And because of this I was able to resist that tidal pull – just. I was able to stop HAHAHAing at horrors. I did not have the life of my lonely father, or of my gentle great-uncle, who got fatally hit by a car one Christmas Eve, or the life of my grandma, who died of liver disease, and right to the end refused to eat but begged for her Lambrini and fags.

It's true, though, that I often think of that need, so strong on both sides of my family, pure genetics, coursing under my skin like I'm lit up. It's true I'm still angry at the world that was created around me, which told me that there was never too drunk, that drinking meant drunk, drunk meant mortal, blackouts were hilarious. Though there's no blame. I think of them, my family. I imagine not being able to refuse that third drink that will become the fourth that will tilt a night on its axis. I imagine giving in to the slow-moving creatures that lie under the surface of every day, waiting to be fed, giving in to that pull, that itch under the skin, and I am grateful for my father naming it, telling me that not everything is a laugh. I'm even glad for the night I learned that myself. These things were my lifeboat. I sailed away on the sea of everyone else's booze: Lambrini, Buckfast, vodka, Brandy Alexanders, whisky and Guinness. Off I went. Knowing it was lethal to swim. Learning it was dangerous to even dip a toe in. Such a laugh.

BEGGING FOR CHANGE

GARY BRYAN

I was often drawn to that desperate place:
It mirrored how I felt inside.
I was always in a rush to get there after buying my gear.

The stink of stale piss and booze,
Used dirty needles crushed into the cracks of the concrete.
I smoked roll-ups made from butts scavenged off the pavement
    and injected heroin and crack into the hole in my groin.

Further up under the train tracks it was dark and quiet. I'd hide
    sometimes to use, alone.
Years of practice; I could cook up and get out within a couple
    of minutes, already back off begging while others were
    still struggling to find a vein.

Sat leaning against a bin facing the door of Tesco, asking for
    change, with head hung low and back slouched,
Sometimes I'd see an old neighbour or someone I knew.
Pretending I was retrieving something from my bag behind me,
I'd try and hide my face.
I still had some pride.
Even the sex work was better than this.

Rain starts, collecting in between those concrete pavement slabs
    and slowly working its way towards me and my cardboard seat,

112

Soaking into my jeans until I can bear it no longer and have to
   leave, whether I have my money up or not.
People darting into Tesco, wet, dripping umbrellas, wanting to
   get out of the rain and home to get warm.
'At least you have a home to go to,' I'd think,
Envious and angry at them for ignoring my existence.
Sat
Alone
Wet and hungry
Begging for change.

HOME IS WHERE THE HEART IS

ANNIE VINCENT

'For the love o' God don't be telling anyone – sure, they'll never believe it, they'll think it's us', my mum said, and I thought, why would nobody believe it? Why would anyone think that *we* were making Peg scream the house down? Whenever we were out my mum worried as we came back through the front door that Peg, her aunt, was in the house.

'Shh, is she in?' 'Shh, is she in the loo?' 'Shh, where is she?' 'SHHH! WILL YE?' She worried and shushed until nothing else existed, all focus up the stairs, the fear magnified by isolation and secrecy.

Peg lived at the top of the house in a bedsit. She had a sitting room/kitchen and a separate bedroom, but she shared our bathroom on the middle floor. Before we moved in she'd lived this way for many years, paying £1 a week as a sitting tenant.

Then Mr Clifford, the recently widowed owner, coerced by her I imagine, agreed to sell at a discount to us. He would've been unable to get a proper price on the open market with her in it. She, knowing that new owners would never put up with her nonsense and would harass her out, encouraged my parents to buy by offering to pay the £1,500 deposit. They never could've come up with this themselves, having four kids to feed, and so accepted this world of home ownership, not yet knowing the true cost.

My dad did say to my mum, 'Don't do it, you know what she's like.' But my mum said, 'Ah, it can't be that bad, and sure we'll never be able to buy a place of our own otherwise.' She put to the back of her mind the fact that Peg had abused her plenty not too many years before when, as a sixteen-year-old straight off the boat from County Mayo, she had arrived at the Archway in 1958 to work and send money home. She was to stay with Peg, the aunt everyone agreed was *a bit funny*. Maybe they didn't realise how hilarious she was, or maybe they just needed the money. Peg soon had her polishing the banisters thirty times in a clockwise direction, and if my mum didn't get it quite right, Peg would scream blue murder. The final straw came when, on one of these occasions, the banisters found wanting, Peg scraped her fingernails down both of my mum's cheeks, drawing blood. She ran downstairs and presented herself to the Cliffords, who let her sleep in one of their rooms. She left Peg's the next day. London was an easier place to find digs then, even with the 'No dogs, No Blacks, No Irish' signs. She later wondered why she had put up with it for five years.

But she then felt a similar pressing need to get away from the council estate we lived in near Finsbury Park as she didn't like the *problem families* being housed around us whose influence might rub off, like Bunhead and her kids, who moved in directly above. Bunhead was a platinum-haired, yappy-dog owner with a hoard of *trouble* kids. Bunhead had looks and a mouth like Bet Lynch. We loved the sweary rows she had with her men. We loved the instant gang of friends to play with outside the door. We hated the quiet terraced street we'd moved into, which was full of old people.

By the time I was fourteen, it had been going on for a few years. Us kids made jokes about the crazy woman in the attic; we called her the Bat in the Belfry. With all the screaming and rows, we had long ago stopped inviting her down for Sunday dinner, where she used to criticise endlessly with things like: *This chicken is so dry; oh, these potatoes, the salt! Really, I've never seen anything like it in my life, these children eat like pigs.* We didn't even have Christmases with her any more, as we had before we moved in. Not after she revealed a taste of what was to come on our first December in the house.

That first Christmas Eve, I was nine; the otherworldliness of being out in the middle of the night, feet crushing fresh snow on the short walk back from Midnight Mass, looking up through the swirling flakes at the cavernous sky, snowdrops melting on my chafed cheeks, getting back at 1.30 a.m. and before bed being allowed to rip open one red package that had been glittering under the tree for weeks... then the spell broken by my need for the loo as the gradual thaw set in after two freezing hours in the circular concrete church. I raced from the front room, intending to take the stairs up to the bathroom, but was stopped in my tracks by the unexpected sight of Peg, legs planted wide, standing halfway up the staircase.

'MERRY FUCKING CHRISTMAS!' she screeched as she grabbed the bottom of her tweedy skirt and held it up under her chin, revealing thick tan tights and cream underwear. Her eyes were looking right through me with what was, I recognised years later, the unseeing glaze of an alcoholic in blackout. Stuck to the spot, I tried yelling in an effort to alert my mum in the kitchen, where she'd gone to boil the kettle, but it came out wobbly.

'Mu-u-u-uumm? I think Peg's gone mad.'

Her screaming, once started, would go on for hours, ranting repetitive dialogues about things from the past with added expletives in unusual combinations like, '*YOU'RE ALL FUCKING SHIT-CUNTS.*' When she ran out of words she howled and yowled endlessly. My mum was her particular target. My mum, the only one who cared for her. Her other relatives, who lived in Ireland, never visited. I'd never met them.

Sometimes she would summon my mum up the stairs as if to have a rational conversation and would calmly twist the knife. One time, it went like this:

'Now Mary, do you remember the day your father died?' My mum had been eight years old.

'I do o' course,' my mum said.

'And do you remember the funeral?'

'Of course,' my mum said, starting to feel unsure.

'And do you remember going back to the house afterwards and it had been locked by the landlord because you hadn't paid the rent?'

'No...' my mum said.

'Well, I paid your rent so you'd have somewhere to live.' She was talking about forty years before.

Later downstairs, crying to my dad, my mum said, 'Why would she say such a thing? Nobody'd ever do that in Ireland on the day of a funeral, would they? The shame of it.'

My dad told her, 'Ah, she's only out to upset you – take no notice.'

Listening to all this, we pleaded with him to do something, but he skedaddled us up to bed and told us, 'Mum won't let me.' It was true my mum said stuff like: 'She's family...', 'She's helped us...', 'You can't throw an old woman out on the street, sure, what would people think?' Occasionally he performed a lose-the-temper dash, up the stairs two at a time with a hammer in his white-knuckled fist, roaring, 'I'LL FECKIN KILL HER.' But he never did. He only left dents in the banisters on the way up and quieter promises on the way down. 'One of these days, God help me, I *will* fecking kill her...' And then to the cellar to put his hammer away in his makeshift workshop, where he spent most of his time.

In the new house, my big brothers were hardly affected. They thought Peg funny and perhaps by the time we moved in, being teenagers made them possessed of more bravado. I remember Jack one time – maybe he was about fifteen – also running up the stairs like my dad, with a hurley in his hands, shouting and threatening. When he came down calmly some time later, he held a rubbish bag he'd found full of crushed-up glass.

'Here's your problem,' he said, 'whisky.' Showing us a sharp triangle of glass with a bit of Teacher's label on it. But it took us a long time to believe, much less understand, that perhaps drinking lay at the core of this tiny, vicious-tongued lady who poshed up her Irish accent. This little lady who had her clothes handmade in somewhere we'd never been called Chelsea, near where she had once worked as an apparently excellent State Enrolled Nurse in the *King's Hospital*. This tiny person who went to church daily, arranging the flowers for God around the marble altar.

I, however, no bravado at all, lay in my bed stiff and wide awake for hours, listening to the frequent out-of-control stompings as she stalked her linoed kitchen floor, which was my bedroom ceiling. It shook and I wondered when it would fall in, imagining her crashing through in a cloud of plaster and wood. I hoped when it happened it would be on the other side of the room so she would miss landing on me in my bed. If not that, I thought she would one night just come in and kill me in a mad frenzy, stabbing or strangling me. And I know my little brother Danny felt the same fear, holding his breath, his freckled cheeks puffed out every time he heard her coming, trapped in the back bedroom beyond the bathroom.

One Easter Sunday night began with the usual ranting. Peg started screaming and we all ended up on the landing in our pyjamas, my mum and dad and my big brothers shouting back at her, me and my little brother shaking in the shadows. My mum was telling us all to ignore her, to go back to bed. Just as we were dispersing, Peg pointed at me from the stairs and said in a witchy cackle, 'And you'll be a bigger streetwalker than your mother ever was!'

Taken aback, my fear turning to anger for the first time, I started shouting at her, 'How dare you call my mum a prostitute!' My mum seemed more concerned that I had been able to interpret what she meant by streetwalker than by the situation, and it made me realise that we would do this over and over again, just like we had been for years, and nothing would change. My mum was so upset and the whole thing, as usual, was chaotic and exhausting. I went back in my bedroom. The lights went out in the hall, which meant my mum and dad had gone to bed. I didn't lie down. I just sat on the edge of the bed without moving in a sort of trance. Peg eventually stopped pacing and screaming after a couple more hours. I knew by now that on these kinds of nights she would be quiet until tomorrow. In the dark I crept up the stairs, hand over hand on the banisters for guidance, the brass stair rods lit by the moonlight coming through the tall landing window. My breathing, my heart, sounded loud. Shivering outside her bedroom door, I nearly turned back. But I couldn't go back. I held the smooth Bakelite doorknob and twisted, pushed open the door a little and listened. Going in I was smothered by the familiar smell of mothballs. An orange glow from the street lights invaded the room around the curtain edges, made shadowy lumps of everything. I picked up one of her needlework cushions from the armchair. She moved a little, the golden webbing of her hairnet catching a bit of light, keeping her Maggie Thatcher coiffure in place. I froze. She was tiny. A tiny old lady. I put the cushion back and left the room, closing the door quietly. Back in my own room, tired and cold, I climbed into bed and fell asleep before I'd even got warm.

IT ISN'T SO BAD

EILEEN CARNELL

It isn't so bad
your eating disorder
so much support
so much research

It isn't so bad
Nigel Slater's ambivalent
Eating for England
or starving for what?

It isn't so bad
the literature shows
The Edible Woman
Cooking with Love

It isn't so bad
the subject of soaps
Helen Archer, so fragile
her power so alarming

It isn't so bad
it isn't alcohol
it isn't gambling
it's not harming

It isn't so bad
the mindfulness cure
or cognitive therapy
or psychoanalysis

It isn't so bad
that secret hunger
that gnawing pretence
that emptiness

It isn't so bad
recovery slow
lasting a lifetime
but slowly a cure.

SPIN THE BOTTLE

NICOLA JONES

I was twelve the first time I got drunk. My fourteen-year-old brother Jesse woke me one warm Saturday morning with a casual bottle of tequila to share. Like children – which we were – with apple-juice boxes as chasers. Sitting under a playground pirate ship in suburban Australia, we slurred about our history of sexual abuse. One bottle wasn't enough to ease that pain, so we paid a visit to the liquor store to steal more, shoving a school bully on the way and urinating in someone's garden while they watered the plants. Somehow it was quite apparent to the shopkeeper that we were neither of age nor sober. She grabbed my brother by the arm and a feisty little me punched her square in the face, breaking her glasses. We ran and hid in the school bushes, Jesse sniffing butane while I proceeded to lie on my back and choke on my own vomit. An ambulance arrived and for good measure I attacked the paramedics. Or so I've been told; I was well and truly in blackout by then. You know what? I lie. Jesse and I had actually shared a bottle of Rebel Yell bourbon several weeks before, but then we'd both also sniffed a whole lot of butane. 'Wow, look at that octopus!' I said, pointing to a poncho. Off I went to a sleepover in that state, freaking my fellow grade seveners out.

Like other thoroughly traumatised people, I had anything but a glamorous start to my drinking career. It continued in a similar fashion throughout my teenage years. By thirteen my peers and I were hanging with the older kids at parties, scraping coins together to buy Passion Pop and Mississippi Moonshine. My drinking did not seem abnormal because my mates drank just as hard as I did. Variously, we'd each be making out, passing out, falling down, throwing up. We flung ourselves about together, as trauma-bonded kids tend to do. In blackout, our bodies were not our own. Nor were they when sober, at times. You know what I mean? Smudged black eyeliner and band shirts formed a kind of uniform for us. Metal music mirrored our angst. Lacking funds, shoplifting was a casual pastime. Once we jumped a cab for a rush. Our teens were spent drinking in parks, wandering the streets gatecrashing parties, or waiting at petrol stations to hitch lifts to nowhere because we had nowhere to be. Vulnerable as we were, we felt invincible. 'You can't handle your booze,' they'd say. In fact we couldn't handle our lives and at that point the booze helped.

My first addiction was bingeing on food, a compulsion our family took to in earnest when Dad went to jail. I discovered the perfect solution: purging! Now I could happily numb out without consequence. If it was good enough for Princess Diana, it was certainly good enough for me. Turns out bulimia and binge drinking are a potent combination. Booze and bile. On a fairly regular basis I'd get obliterated, then cry about how fat I was while making myself sick. Life of the party! My group turned on me at one point for stealing cigarettes, alcohol and a guy my friend liked. I remembered none of it. Apparently, I'd also been engaging in dude-talk about how hot our friend Carmen was. None of the girls felt they could trust me after that.

Here I was, an exploding mess of a queer girl trying to figure it all out.

I couldn't reconcile my feelings for girls with the drunken sex I kept finding myself having with boys. At fourteen a counsellor stoked the fire of internalised homophobia by saying, 'The reason you feel attracted to girls is because of the abuse you experienced as a child. You want to save and protect those girls you like.' Well sure, I guess that made sense... Crushed in a Pantera moshpit one night, I was tossed up onto the pulsing crowd to gasp hot breaths of sweat before being ripped away by a bouncer. The first face I saw outside was Jesse's; he'd also been chucked out for crowdsurfing. 'Let me the fuck back in!' I shouted repeatedly at security before police dragged me screaming through the Valley mall. Dad collected me from lock-up later and I took this as the perfect opportunity to confront him about the past. Faced with his denial, I jumped out of the moving car to go sit in a dark schoolyard slicing my arms up. These are just the things I did. At fourteen, my violent, erratic behaviour had become too much for my mother to bear, so she kicked me out in a fight. Dad was back in my life but I couldn't live with him. A friend's family took me in, no doubt saving me from a far worse fate.

By sixteen my friends and I were living alone, underage clubbing on school nights and skipping class to watch *Oprah*. We actually enjoyed academia, so we'd read our textbooks cover to cover at home, then astound everybody by turning up at school to blitz our assessments. An angel of a teacher gave my friend and I a safe home in our last few months to ensure we graduated. Against all odds, we did in fact finish, and with decent grades, considering. Did I tell you I'd met a proud bisexual punk girl who I was completely awed by? Doc Martens, a tartan miniskirt, a Powerpuff Girls t-shirt and brightly coloured pigtails: her confidence was as vibrant as her attire. When wasted we'd all make out, but I was so shy I could hardly catch her eye sober. Once a bunch of us broke into the school pool to skinny-dip, admire each other's breasts and swap childhood abuse stories.

This was just how it was for us back then. Kissing in front of straight bouncers was how we gained entry to our city's biggest gay club, where we'd writhe around and nick half-empty drinks all night. It astonishes me that we ever managed to make it into clubs, as we were very clearly sixteen. Another time we snuck down into a seedy strip club, where we watched, aroused yet conflicted, as glaze-eyed dancers straddled sixty-year-old men. Another time still, we played pool in a bar on a school day, and there I acquired an abusive boyfriend twelve years my senior. That one sure did some damage. Jobless and scrounging off my after-school wage, he chipped away at my self-esteem by raving about big-breasted exes. He slammed cupboards in a rage, then me into cupboards. Jesse caught wind a year in and drove out to rescue me. The next one was worse. A long-haired, head-lice-riddled musician wrecked by hallucinogens, he hung roadkill on his wall and confessed to his paedophilic past. At the latter I ran and drank hard to forget.

By eighteen I could no longer deny I had a problem with booze, so there began a decade-long process of trying to quit. Knowing I had no off switch once that warm glow set in, I spent my eighteenth and twenty-first birthdays stone-cold sober. I even went a whole year without a drop. Before I go any further, I should probably mention that Jesse hanged himself around this time. One February night, while I was tucked up in bed a few metres away, my closest brother put a noose round his neck till the credits rolled. My soul splintered. Accident and emergency became a holiday destination for me; I stabbed and choked myself or tossed my body into the midnight ocean. Gentle boyfriends tried to love the cracked pieces of me back together. They held me, fed me, patted me, kept me alive. I repaid one of these beautiful saviours with a broken nose – sober, too. Life had brutalised me, so I lashed out, a wild thing. Some inner force propelled me onwards, frenzied but alive. My golden university days are coated in a drunken, bulimic haze.

One night I dragged my punk schoolmate to a pirate-themed party I'd been invited to by newly made queer friends. Of course I needed a few drinks to calm the nerves. A bottle of vodka downed, we rocked up in zebra-striped socks and skull bandanas just as a game of spin-the-bottle had begun. Here I was at twenty-three, finally kissing girls again. Enbies, bois and andros too. It was terrifying. In the early hours of the next morning I got arrested for drunk and disorderly – stumbling onto the road and tripping a woman over in stilettos. Oh lock-up, my old friend. From Pantera concerts to pirate parties, this time I sat in the cell still dressed as a wench.

My addictions gave me a kind of reckless bravery, so off I travelled solo to South East Asia. I had affirming adventures in Thailand and Malaysia, couch-surfing with locals, visiting Buddhist temples and snorkelling on paradise islands. I felt a growing sense of pride in my independence. My world crackled with possibility... then short-circuited. In Cambodia I was raped by a local man. Fleeing from him down an alleyway, like a river in monsoon season, I lost first one, then the other sandal as I squelched knee-deep in the mud, alone, terrified he would catch me. Cockroaches kept me company back at my guesthouse as I rocked and shook. Of course it was all my fault. I should never have asked that man for directions. I should have declined his offer to walk me to the station. I should have told him to fuck off when he followed me onto the bus. I should have... I shouldn't have... Please God...

The next night I hit the drink with renewed vigour, drowning the violation in liquor and a thick layer of denial. Paralytic, I set aside my complete lack of motorbiking experience to go buy binge food. This outing inevitably became a love affair with the bitumen; I cracked my cheekbone and wrecked the bike I'd borrowed. Back home at university, I finally had my first real girlfriend. I treated her appallingly. After eight hours of solid drinking on my twenty-fourth birthday, I went to drive my car to once again buy binge food. I sure did love a good kamikaze drunk-drive in those days. Naturally my girlfriend confiscated my keys so I attacked her violently. 'If I want to kill myself, that's MY PREROGATIVE!' I shouted into her bruised face. This was the power my addictions had over me. This was the black rage bubbling beneath my skin, behind that smiling facade. Next, I fell in love with an adorable queer kid and joined a poly relationship just before moving to London. London – where I could invent a whole new me and leave that old mess behind. Freezing in a tiny room on the Old Kent Road, with a bucket of sick under my bed, I discovered that addictions have a nasty habit of following you. By twenty-five, though, I'd finally made it: I was sharing bottles of Prosecco with queer folk in east London and doing lines of coke. Except that my whole month's pay was being blown on booze when I'd sworn I'd only have a couple of drinks. My promising charity-sector career had stagnated. I was working an extra weekend job to make ends meet, but still the ends were loose.

Birthday twenty-six went something like this. A full day's drinking and several lines of coke gave me just enough courage to make a move on my crush, Bobbie. There ensued a chaotic couple of years together. Neither of us would stop at a skinful: I'd met my match. One afternoon Bobbie and I sipped cocktails at First Out like proper grown-ups, then chugged cheap vodka at home, at a friend's house, at a warehouse party. It wasn't enough.

It never was. Then came the inevitable: 'Heyyyy, can you get us any coke? Look, we can't pay you now, but TRUST ME, we're good for it.' We really weren't. They knew it. Laughing, almost wobbling into the canal on the cycle back, Bobbie split her unhelmeted head open. Our night ended in my familiar home of A & E. I curled up in the hospital bed next to her, and when the nurses told us we could leave, I slurred, 'Nah, is cool, I'm good.' A holiday to Mozart's stunning city of Salzburg was a refined affair until the last night, when we decided to stay out drinking all night instead of paying for a hostel. 'Genius.' Again we attempted to score drugs on tick from total strangers without success. At 5 a.m., exhausted, we flopped down on a building site and awoke to a man staring at us in surprise. As mad as we were in active addiction, Bobbie and I were always a team. I'd never felt so secure in a relationship, so safe, so understood. My core connected to hers and there we were, tethered to each other in the swirl of a cyclone.

After a six-week trip around Europe on borrowed money that same year, my dear father skulled a bottle of whisky, then ran a hose from his exhaust into the open window of his van. Too intoxicated to succeed, he was found by my distraught stepmother, dangling out the car door. The whisky was to blame of course, so he'd just stop drinking whisky. I begged him to get help, on a crackling line across the ocean. He promised he would, and he did all he could. 'I love you so much, Dad.' A month shy of my twenty-seventh birthday, straight after a visit home, my father hanged himself from his four-poster bed. This time he was methodical. I was drinking shots of brandy within half an hour of receiving the news. By the evening I'd wrapped a cord round my neck to join him. My queer family wrapped me up in their arms instead.

That summer I married my darling Bobbie, who'd since been to an AA meeting. The day was spectacular, euphoric. Still, by 7 p.m. we were all snorting coke off a toilet lid and I ended the night at a goth club in my wedding dress. Lucky I got married in black! Losing Dad was the beginning of the end for me, and the consequences of my drinking were as scary as ever. I missed a flight to Barcelona, so in anger I downed a bottle of vodka neat, then shoplifted more booze from the airport. Deportation would've been on the cards if I were caught. Then what began as a nice sober picnic ended in seizures after I fell off my bicycle in blackout. 'But I hardly drank anything,' I lied to the nurses doing a CT scan.

My wife started going to AA regularly and actually getting well. *If Bobbie's sobering up... I'd better sort my shit out too*, I thought. Seven years ago my recovery began. Clearly, I could admit I was powerless over my addictions and that my life was utterly unmanageable. The way I saw it, my options were recover or die by this point. Slowly, my hard shell began to dissolve. I was raw, an infant, desperately clinging to these sober survivors. Love and support felt so abrasive at first. It was unfamiliar. I was not worthy. Over time, my fists have unclenched to release my death grip on life. The violence I've both experienced and inflicted can finally be exposed to the light. In meetings I am constantly amazed by what the human spirit can endure and overcome. Through the twelve-step programme I am taking all the subjects never offered over my fifteen years of education: self-care, boundary-setting, speaking up, and processing feelings. All this has given me a little pressure-release valve so I don't explode, break down or become overwhelmed as often, or in the same way. Recovery has largely removed the shackles of shame. In these rooms we have all lied, stolen, crossed boundaries and been violated. We've wet ourselves, fucked our bosses and set things alight. There is so much black humour in sharing our worst moments that we laugh from our depths. 'Recovery is the best fookin' after-party,' a fellow says.

I've had my share of relapses along the way. Like the time Bobbie and I thought it a fine idea to spend New Year in Amsterdam at five months sober. Obviously the trip was less about museums and more about marijuana and mushrooms. Candles flicker on kind faces in the church hall, a coven of women recovering together. We are atheists and Buddhists, queers and hets, sex workers and school teachers. Here is the community, the connections we sought in those empty bottles. It has been a gorgeous, painful old ride, this recovery business, spiralling in and out of hell, buoyed up to stars and down again. To be here, to have made it this far, I am one of the lucky ones.

HOW TRAUMA WORKS

KATIE WATSON

I've read a lot about trauma.
I've read a lot of theories, including
The theories about the theories of trauma
Spent years wading through expert opinion
And companion guides
Only to meet myself again at the same starting line
Of the first words I read about trauma.

See, I can't find myself in the pages, in the lists
In the articles, journals or reports
In the transcripts
From court proceedings showcasing how trauma survivors
Are cross-examined.
Can't find myself in TED Talks
Or in the monologues and biographies
Of women who courageously share their trauma
Can't map my personal geography
In the second-hand experiences of men that care
For a sister, a partner, a daughter.

What they don't tell you about trauma is this
These are the parts they missed, from documentaries
And government policies
That trauma has the ability to split
You into two halves that will go their separate ways

Or into multiple segments that disperse
Only to find
That when the pieces come back to you
There's not even a whole image to be made.
That you may have to reshuffle and renegotiate the salvaged
      parts of yourself
In an attempt to make it familiar and full
Force it to fit
But when you hold up that image to the sun,
Light still finds its way in through the cracks
Doesn't it?

What they don't tell you about trauma is this
That throughout your life
You will be punished for it.
That when a man instinctively grabs you by the wrist
To pull you away from a fire
It may feel like he is suddenly kissing you all over
That grasp becomes buttons undone
A ripping of a shirt
That hand on your wrist will feel like an intention of hurt.

Or when a doctor tells you, you have to have some tests
Down there
So you ask if a woman can do the checks
And your request is met with a confused silence
And that silence feels like an act of violence upon you too.

And what about the feeling of your heart breaking
When the woman you asked to take
The swabs, to perform your pelvic exam

The woman in whose hands you plan to place the residual debris
     of a trust system destroyed
Can't understand
The woman you're required to undress for
Questions with her eyes why you need her to lock the door
To turn the lights to dim
So she can't look too deeply in
For fear she'll see everything you're not able to yet
When even *she*
A woman
Doesn't even get it
Who thinks I'm still a girl with a habit for trembling
Thinks I was simply never shown how to stomach things
Never taught how to politely lie back, shut my eyes and think
     of England.

Sorry I can't do that.
Because all I see when I do is a country that is failing me
Erasing me
Day after day
A country that's trivialising
Downgrading
Reducing and subverting
Decontextualising me
Undermining
And othering my history.

To that nurse that saw me as a jumble sale
I want to say
I know you're working to a timer
To the clock

But so am I
I'm continually counting down
Until the hands stop
And I'm bursting at the seams I've been sewing over rotten for
    years
Until I'm literally on my knees
Because I can't stand up
That getting out of bed sometimes seems impossible
When your whole world has become horizontal.

To the man who once asked me
'Are you gay because you were sexually invaded?'
Do you stop to think that maybe
I can't just change into an un-raped body
There's no back-up life
No understudy
Do you stop to think that maybe
You could be the person
With your comments, that sets it all in motion
Causes all the commotion
That happens in the mouth of a natural disaster?

But even earthquakes, cyclones
Tsunamis and exploding volcanoes
Have an explanation.

What I wouldn't give to look into the earth's core
And see tectonic plates moving
So I could prepare a bomb shelter
For later.
What I wouldn't give to measure myself

On the Richter scale
And know exactly where I am in terms of devastation potential
What they don't tell you about trauma is that it will make you
    feel like you're not the expert of your own life any more.

About how at 3 a.m. you might wake up
To realise the coat hanging on the back of your door
The coat you hold round you in winter
Is actually a shapeshifter
And has morphed itself in the night into the outline of him
And your imagination is filling in the gaps

About how at 4 a.m. you might wake to check the latch
The bolts
Check the locks
Check all windows, all doors
Check the floor hasn't slipped away beneath you
Check your body is still here and intact
Check you still have a reflection in the mirror and that
It's moving to its own rhythm
Check your partner hasn't stopped breathing
Check you haven't rolled over during a nightmare
Only to suffocate your dog.
Check your car and door keys are out of sight
Just in case someone can fit their hand through the letterbox and
    steal entry to your whole life.
Check and check again

And how at 5 a.m.
You are awake and feel compelled to make sense of
Why you are the way you are

And you can't afford to wait until the morning to start doing that
How, at 5.30, you're assembling a mind map on the carpet in
    front of you
Creating personal timelines
Just so you feel you have some sort of framework to build from
To go back to
And your back is aching
And your knees are in pain
From leaning in too close to the story of your life
That now seems to belong to a stranger

How at 6 a.m., you accept the world is pregnant with danger
And how you may possibly have your head in the attic
Looking for a VCR player, gathering dust
Because you absolutely, 100 per cent *must*
Play childhood videos.
By 7 a.m.
You're watching them and nothing surfaces.

What they don't tell you about trauma is that it might increase
    your anxiety about the safety of others.
I often worry about women I don't know, but I know exist
    somewhere
And women I'm only guessing do. I worry about them too.
I worry about women not yet born
I worry about the baby girls who at this precise moment are
    entering this earth
And how the first things they'll see will be their mother's face
Or the sky
And I think about the moment when those same girls realise
There's this thing called trauma

And it will cut off your oxygen supply

I worry about the women who showcase a shame
A self-blame, that shouldn't belong to them, on their arms
And those who declare their complete brokenness by giving
    themselves
Temporary tattoos of their children's names.
But what about the women who want to remain neat and
    contained
In their deterioration?
What about the women where language has abandoned them so
    much
That you forget they have an accent, forget they have a location
    in the world
I worry about these the most.
I worry about the women who find no solace in drugs
I worry that if I look too close they will disappear
Blend, smudge, dry up
Become part of the atmosphere
I wonder about these frozen women
That seem to be melting, leaking
Becoming less definable to us
Losing measurement and dimension.

To understand them
Will be as hard as measuring water
And in an instant, they could be gone.

What they don't tell you about trauma is that the world will no
    longer look black and white, but grey
Because all you'll see is concrete

From staring down at the ground all day
What they don't tell you about trauma is that it will teach you
    some manners.
That you'll become a series of Can I? May I? Is that OK?
I hope you don't mind.
Please. Thank you.
Sorry I got in your way
Sorry I bumped into you when it wasn't even my fault
Sorry I've let you down today
Sorry I took the day off
Sorry I'm feeling ill
Sorry I'm still not quite there yet
Sorry about the way I perceive every offer of kindness as a threat
Or a joke
Sorry that my internal alarm system is broken
Sorry I couldn't give you what you wanted
Sorry my self-expression sometimes borders on assertive
Sorry that hope seems like a trick
Sorry about how I'll assume if you help me it's conditional
Sorry for this apology
And for the apology before that
Sorry that my vocabulary
Resembles the discourse of a doormat.
I'm sorry there are no other ways to be sorry
That I've run out of synonyms for contrition
I'm sorry there's no way round this
But through it
I'm sorry I didn't learn my lesson
When I went to see that film that had trigger warnings
Sorry I believe that being in a crowd of people is synonymous
    with suffocation

Sorry for my behaviour, and that sometimes it seems I'm
    becoming unhinged
Sorry I look at life, and death
And believe they're the same thing.

What they *do* tell you about trauma is to
Talk to someone
Wait for therapy, buy therapy
Take medication
Or take medication in combination with meditation
Drink chamomile tea
Research EMDR, neurofeedback, trauma-release exercises
Try reiki
Consider substituting CBT for psychotherapy
Take back words, cultures, entire spaces
And simply deem them as reclamatory.

All the advice is focused on fixing yourself
But fixing is not the same as healing
Repairs are not the same as growth
Putting on a plaster is not an act of love to the body
Avoidance does not equate to safety
Anger is not the same as acceptance
Numbing all of your senses is not progress.

Finally, what nobody is telling you about trauma is that it is
Constantly in a race with you.
But if it has the legs to race you
It has legs to walk away.

And no one has the guts, the stamina
To tell you about other ways to heal
That just maybe, you have to look trauma in the eyes, shake its
    hand
And tell it that you know it's real
Tell it that you see it, you really see it
And it doesn't have to plead for your attention any more
Tell it, You can no longer live here, just outside my door, alone
There will be a language barrier at first
But healing begins its biggest journey
When you allow trauma in, over the threshold of your home.

THE DISTURBANCES

MICHAEL LOVEDAY

I am climbing this hill track
not knowing   if it's the right one

the other side invisible
       as a moon's darker face

       pines in the fields
half-recognised

         as if known
      in an older life

a sea breeze arrives   it strokes my skin
      with tenderness

but look   it says   I am bringing
      the crows along with me
those scavengers

WEATHERPROOF

STEPHANIE HUTTON

She dressed for winter, whatever the weather. Protection from harm in thick woollen gloves and a hood drawn tightly around her face. The brutal winter when she turned eighteen had bruised her with bitterness. Her family split in two by a dagger of lightning. She'd learned her lesson. Be weatherproof.

The cold seeped through and mauled at her. She added more layers, exhaling with relief at her numbness. She became layers of cloth and wool and fur, her flesh a memory. Padded hands were too clumsy to grip food or a pen. Best to curl up and wait for winter to be over.

Heavy velvet curtains draped over the outside world. Winter continued.

Inside her chest, nested behind her ribcage, lay a tiny weathervane. It spun endlessly to match the cruel winds, clunking against her heart to quicken its beats. Its frantic movements matched the howling air that pounded against the walls.

She could not have said just when the thaw began. Fragments of her past, before the storms, before the freeze, fell like snowflakes behind her closed eyelids. She chose to pay attention. Her mother smiling at the smell of doughnuts. Her sister's twisted lips as she applied mascara to eyes that had not yet witnessed sights that could not be unseen. With no sharp sides, the fluttering moments of light changed from snowflakes to white blossom. Behind the bitter smell of loneliness, she caught a gentle honeysuckle fragrance of hope. Could it be spring?

Fearful of change, she pulled the hood over her eyes. In the darkness, she looked inside her chest. Under that cloth and wool and fur, the weathervane stilled. Her heart slowed to a steady thud-thudding.

She peeled off the gloves and wiggled her thin fingers, staring at them in wonder like an infant. Shaking her head, she released her face and cascades of curls from the prison of her hood. She shook as she unzipped her coat. A different kind of shake. Not from cold or fear but of first love or first kiss. Her legs found their strength once the heavy covering of tights and trousers was thrown off. She heaved open the curtains and let her skin sing in daylight.

Peering through the grimy window, she watched the world. Puddles gathered at the kerbside, remnants of recent rain. They seemed so small, one jump across to dry paving. Litter swirled next to bins lined up along the street. Enough breeze to make a mess but not mayhem. She tilted her face upwards and let the glow that had travelled 93 million miles to reach her warm her from the outside in.

LUCKY

J. L. HALL

A crackle under my skin. A feather on my nape. A short-circuit, a surge.

Fear.

These are the small bombs scattered under my feet and strewn unseen across my path. A weekly, sometimes daily, charge of fear that is triggered without warning. In daytime waking hours, I can rationalise this – I dig out my mental toolkit and rummage, calmly and with compassion, for the best aid to contain and neutralise how I feel.

To defuse.

At night, when it comes and I am in bed, deep in sleep, with my old, balding teddy bear tucked under my chin, it devastates. The fear surges then, untethered. My heart races long after I have woken and lie in damp shock with loose, broken limbs.

This is the best that I have been. I am 'lucky'. I have recovered; partly, mostly. There is no expected full recovery for complex PTSD from childhood trauma. Trauma meted out then can last a lifetime in these fits and starts. It is a life sentence casually, violently handed down without reason.

The brain protects us in childhood trauma. It is programmed to save our lives: to shut down, switch off, freeze, and escape when our bodies can't. Children's brains in the midst of trauma cannot process it or take it whole and file it in long-term memory storage, moving it to the past. The trauma lingers in the present. It remains unformed and blinded, butting into the walls of an

145

internal maze, back and forth, like the victim of a blindfolded prank. The brain may save us then, but we will pay later when we can at last stop and let go. Once it is finally over, the flashbacks and night terrors begin.

Just when we are safe from harm.

I have had treatment; it was mostly successful. Now there are small bombs where there were explosions. Now there are charges and surges where before there was near-annihilation. Now there are cracks, fissures, where before I was obliterated. I should be grateful.

But there is no romance to be found here. Trauma has not enriched my life, I am not a changed-for-the-better person who would never have followed such a Technicolor path without this. I struggle, and sometimes I struggle every fucking day. I burn with rage and grief and loss and injustice, and it is exhausting. The never sleeping through the night is exhausting. The constant anxiety, the fear of fantastical consequences if x or y should happen is exhausting. I am sickened to be so limited in my health, to never work the hours I need to have the life I am entitled to. I am heartbroken that I cannot have the future that I want to give myself. I am defeated by always being that one rung further down the ladder with the top just beyond my reach. This is not pity; this is anger. None of this is my fault: none of these crimes should ever, ever have been inflicted on me. There will never be any justice; it can never be undone.

Somehow, somewhere, in the midst of all this unending shit there is acceptance, there has to be; fury and regret are shackles to before. I can only live the life that I have now – there is no other. My life must be full and appreciated; I owe this to the child that fought every day to survive. Acceptance is where the healing begins: being thankful, appreciating the now, the moment as it is.

Without acceptance, without healing, there is no more recovery: there is only the terror of the past, again, again, again. So I try every day.

I try to remember that I am lucky. I am mostly well. I am healing and will heal more. Sometimes, sometimes I am happy.

In a twist of fate I lived when other children did not.

I am here; I am alive.

I am lucky.

DESPAIR

YOUNG GUN

ALEXANDER ALI

Twenty-three, busted again,
No idea. Numb. Didn't even see it coming,
Head in hands, asking again
For forgiveness, a chance, £5, anything.

FLASH FLOOD

PETER JORDAN

My head is clear but I can't move. I try to sit up but nothing happens. My right eye doesn't open fully. It takes a second or two to focus. I'm in my bedroom.

I remember falling at the front door, crawling up three flights of stairs trailing a bag of broken glass behind me. Then nothing.

My landline rings. I wonder if it's Simon. Simon has been my sponsor for the past two years. I met him in rehab. Like me he's an alcoholic, but Simon is in recovery. He has a god in his life. He's living the programme.

He gave me his two goldfish to look after while he's on holiday. He thinks this little act will keep me sober. He's wrong. Before Simon gave me his goldfish I knew I was going to drink. The compulsion for alcohol had returned.

Here lies the paradox: I don't want to drink; I know from bitter experience what happens, but a part of me does want to drink, a part of me that is small but immensely powerful, a part of me that says, This time I'll be fine.

Sometimes I think I'd like to get a little bit drunk, but Simon tells me getting a little bit drunk is like getting a little bit pregnant. I'm a binge drinker and each binge begins with a mental obsession that compels me to lift the first drink. This compulsion to drink is the first part of the sickness that defines me. Once I lift the first drink, I'm beaten. Lifting the first drink starts a physiological craving. This is the second part of my sickness. The craving changes me completely, and

152

the more I drink, the more I want, until I black out, then eventually pass out.

I hear music. Shauna is home; she lives in the flat below. She looks different every time I see her. Sometimes I walk by her on the stairs, say hello and don't immediately realise it's her. She has that chameleon-like quality that great method actors have. She should have gone to Hollywood. Instead, she's trapped in a flat mixing antipsychotics with class As. She'll put on a track and play it over and over again. Today it's Nena's '99 Red Balloons' – the German version. Shauna is stuck somewhere in the mid-eighties, when she was a child and life held no fears.

I shout, but no one can hear me. I need to sit up to shout properly, but I can't move. So I lie looking at the ceiling, listening to eighties Europop. Please don't let me die to this song. If I'm going to die then let her play 'Snowblind' by Black Sabbath. When I was a kid I loved that song. I thought it was about someone who got stuck in a blizzard, until I realised it was about coke addiction.

I remember my first drink. I was fourteen years old. If I saw the world in black and white before I took that first drink, then taking it turned the world to Technicolor. It seemed I'd found the answer to my prayers. Drinking took away the fear, that feeling of being less than. All of a sudden, I measured up. I felt part of the universe, no longer an outsider. The problem was, it never lasted. Within a few years I was a full-blown alcoholic. Something happened after I crossed the line from social drinking to alcoholism. People talk as if the line is something defined, something you step over: one minute normal, the next, alky. In truth, the line is blurred.

It seems things can't get any worse, but I've had rock bottoms before. Rock bottoms alone are not enough to make me quit. I need to change inside. Simon talks about the jumping-off point, the time when he decided he'd had enough. It was a rock bottom connected to a psychic change.

Simon says I should 'move a muscle' when I'm in mental pain: *Move a muscle, change a thought.* But I can't move. I'm truly paralysed.

I'll play I Spy.

I Spy with my little eye something beginning with A...

This is an easy one. *A is for alcohol.* There are four empty vodka bottles on the dressing table. Three are Smirnoff and one is Vladivar. I don't remember buying the Vladivar. I can't see the floor but I know they're there as well, all empty.

I read recently that more people drown in the desert than die of thirst. Flash floods are the killer. It doesn't rain for a long time. When it does, people aren't expecting it, and it really rains, for days on end, and people just drown.

I wake in the early morning of my second day. I know it's morning from the angle of the light shining through my window and on to the bedroom wall, and the sound of the traffic: of commuters going to work. The need to drink alcohol has left me entirely, but I desperately need to rehydrate. It isn't simply the thirst. My body is full of toxins that need to be flushed. The problem is I still can't move.

For a long time I stare at the bedroom wall. The length of the shadow cast from a clock sitting on my bedroom windowsill marks time. As the sun dips, the shadow rises up the wall.

I return to I Spy. I can't see anything beginning with B, but I think I might die of boredom. Sherlock Holmes took morphine to stave off boredom. Maybe the police will investigate after my body is found, maybe a modern-day Sherlock Holmes will look around my room, and as '99 Red Balloons' ascends up from below, he'll deduce: All is not as it appears, Watson. Something hastened his demise.

What *do* you mean, Holmes?

'99 Red Balloons', my dear Dr Watson!

You weren't bored again this morning, were you, Holmes?

I spy with my little eye something beginning with C.

I look at the ceiling. *C is for crack.* No, not the drug; I'm talking about the cracks in the ceiling. I'm sure I've noticed the big cracks but I didn't notice the little ones. They look like they've been there for a long time, but I don't think the ceiling is going to collapse. They're just a part of it. I suppose if you look closely at anything for long enough you'll see little cracks.

I used to think I was a born survivor, one of those people you read about in *Reader's Digest* who gnaw their own legs off in a snowstorm, then slide a hundred miles on their arse to the nearest hospital and now they have a new career as a skiing instructor. And maybe I was a survivor at one time, but not any more.

D is for dehydration.

That would be a good one for my mother – died of thirst. When her friends ask over the garden fence with clasped hands what I died of, she'll be able to say: He died of thirst.

Oh, was he an adventurer?

Sort of.

The phone rings again; I'll bet it's Simon.

I fall asleep, worrying about his goldfish.

When I wake it's the late afternoon of my third day. I have a harsh taste of copper in my mouth. The bedroom window is closed but I can still hear the traffic: people living their lives, coming home from work, collecting their children from school, doing what I can't do.

The thirst reminds me of the time when I was a kid in hospital. For two weeks they kept me on a drip. I wasn't allowed anything to eat or drink. When they took me off the drip, my mother asked what I'd like to drink. I'd been dreaming of cold lemonade for weeks, but I said tea. I'd like a cup of tea. Trying to impress, always trying to appear something other than what I am. I would do anything to go back to that time and tell my mother that I'd like a glass of lemonade.

The peculiar thing about my present situation is that, although my thinking is abnormal, I'm perfectly rational. Instead of worrying about myself I'm worried about Simon's goldfish. I can't remember when I last fed them. I'm quite sure I fed them for the first day or two but I think I may have added the whole container of fish food some time in the middle of the binge. Again, I fall asleep worrying about them.

When I wake, my jaw and tongue are sore.

E is for electric shock.

My muscles are in spasm, my buttocks, thighs, calves, biceps and stomach all cramp up and release. When the spasms are over, and they last maybe five, ten minutes, I'm exhausted, but I find I can move. I turn onto my side and manage to get myself semi-upright at the side of the bed. I'm still wearing my clothes, even my shoes. On the floor is the bag containing the broken glass from a vodka bottle I dragged up the stairs three days earlier.

Although my muscles are no longer in spasm, I'm shaking badly. In this fashion, I make it towards the kitchen. There's a long mirror on the landing framed in gold. I see myself. But it's not me; it's an intruder, a bearded skeleton who has ransacked my flat.

I make it to the kitchen water tap, and quench my thirst. For a long time I stand, hunched over the sink, slurping cold water from the cupped palm of one hand. Then I reach to the cupboard for a chill pill. Diazepam will give me a soft landing, but it's also a muscle relaxant. The tablets are in one of those little bottles that have a safety cap to stop kids opening them. My brain tells my hand to squeeze the lid while turning, but somewhere along the line my hand doesn't receive the signal. A task that would take me ten seconds now takes minutes. This is how it will be for the next few days. On the bottle it says, *Take one as required*. I take four and, in a couple of hours, I will take another four.

I return to the kitchen sink, sipping water, but my head is still in the bedroom. I know I've forgotten something.

And then I remember… *F is for fish*.

END OF AN EPISODE

ROB TRUE

Drill, Rawlplug, 500 millimetres, drill, Rawlplug. Darren holding the other end of the trunking, supporting the weight, as Theron puts a screw and washer in place. Trying to ignore the vision repeatedly flashing in his mind. Hanged brother. Sweet, death-face distorted, purple. Lolled to one side on stretched neck, slowly swinging from rope. The horror breaking through bricks and metal and screws.

In goes another, drill gun-rattle, hanged brother, level up. Down the ladder, hanged brother, move along and up the steps again, hanged brother, concentrating on the screw, rattle of gun through sight of Paul hanging. Darren drilling a wall across the corridor, sound-shattering echo through Paul swinging, peacefully.

Theron climbs down to get more trunking and as he bends over he sees boots in front of him. He straightens to see Paul there like an apparition; solid, but ghost-like vision. Paul is telling him something, but there are no words, just a strange, alien noise as Theron tries to comprehend, slowly aware of Darren talking to the client nearby.

This is not real, this is not real, he repeats like a mantra in his mind as he raps knuckles on his forehead, trying to dislodge the reality before him.

That evening, he lies in a bath, trying to wash away the pain. He's meeting a friend at the Ten Bells and has to catch a train. Theron dresses himself while in a trance. He looks at his hands like they don't belong to him and he's surprised to see them, as they change from transparent, luminous, to rotting colour of old flesh wound.

On the train, Theron is struck by a ridiculous excitement that everything's amusing and absurd. Everyone like hideous puppets. He watches out the window. Dream journey, back through ancestral past, as the track takes him through ancient towns of dead relatives. He sees the backs of houses in place of the slums where they'd once lived. There are gaps too, where more recent blocks of flats that he once knew have been demolished. He remembers dramas of life and death, delusion and disaster, beatings and delirium, and Theron feels like he's in an alien world, different from what he had known and understood.

As the train passes through a tunnel, the window becomes a dark mirror. Theron looks into his own empty eyes and sees the abyss, infinite and terrifying. He notices a young couple laughing together behind him. They are laughing at him. Anger wells up, fierce as fire in his blood. He turns to look at them, but they won't look back. He stares madly at the man, trying to catch his eye, provoking conflict.

Are you fucking sure? I'll smash your face through the back of your head, cunt.

He sends this violence telepathically on laser beams through his eyes. The man looks away laughing and, as Theron goes to get out of his seat to attack the fella, he's stopped dead by a terrible scene. The whole carriage is looking at him. Every couple, every group are all talking about him, laughing at him. He is at one end and can see the whole length of the car. All those faces, mocking, judging, sneering. Dream vision of smirking masks. Theron is both livid and afraid. Violence in a nightmare show. It seems like he is in a film.

An old couple right opposite him are laughing too. Frail and decrepit as they are, he wonders how they would dare to deride him so obviously.

The train stops and the lad who first laughed gets up and makes his way off the carriage.

'Sorry, excuse me – thank you.'

Polite as you like. It don't make sense. His behaviour doesn't match Theron's understanding of an enemy belittling him. He looks back at the rest of the carriage. Everyone minding their business, chatting and laughing, but not at him. Confused, he can't escape his anger.

The train pulls into its final stop, where Theron gets off. A wave of hurrying humans, ugly and vivid in electric-light glare of rude, abrasive station atmosphere swarm at the train he's leaving. Echoes of movement and voices. As they come at him, Theron wants to lash out and smash their heads.

Just one of you get in my path and I'll beat you to the fucking floor.

But none of them do. They part before him, like magnets repelled. One look at his face is enough.

In the pub, as the first pint goes down, Theron levels out and begins to relax. The rest of the night is spent pouring lager all over his adrenaline, to put out the flames rushing up.

Saturday, at home, Theron sat in dream room, staring at nothing. The colours are strange with the odd air, moving in slow currents and eddies around him. His wife and son, unreal somehow, seem distant and out of reach. It's like he is seeing it all from another dimension. He wonders if he is even really there, as he looks at Jake playing and Jane clearing up. With their sounds slightly muted, distorted scene, beyond communication, it's as though he's watching through a thick glass wall. He thinks if he knocks on that wall, they might not notice.

'Why are you staring at me like that?' Jane says, annoyed by his intense atmosphere. Theron knows now that Jane and Jake don't like him. They don't want him around any more. He feels his isolation and loneliness among the two people he loves most, and is lost. His eyes float off into desolate depth of dream-blue walls and Jake looks at him with curious fear. He knows his dad behaves oddly sometimes and isn't like the other dads, but moments like these make him uneasy.

Theron laughs at nothing. It's a crazed laughter and he has no idea where it is from, or what it's for. Maybe it's just laughter at life, absurd and meaningless. What a joke. Nonsense. His laughter trails off and tears spring up in his faraway eyes, nowhere gaze in oblivion face, then roll down his cheeks. Jane sees his despair and comes over to put her arms around him. She holds Theron tight and he cries quietly into her dress.

'It's OK, sweetheart. It's all right now,' she says, and like the words are magic, they sweep the darkness away.

PRESTIDIGITATION

GARRY VASS

At night the houses vanish
behind a magician's curtain.
I walk on softened sand
among dogs and broken bottles.
My health improves. In the distance,
there's a bandstand posing with its ghosts.

Not much left here: the hotel
boarded up, the parks abandoned.
A golf ball bounces along the road
and the gorse bushes smell of blackened rivers.
Eggs hatch while crows make holes
in the sky behind the spruces.

I'm here all year, at once
smothered by dead leaves and
sprouting green tumours that flower
and shed their petals. I must eat only
from the bowl left steaming on a sill,
with my hands like spoons, then run away.

The sea is dark blue, a mutiny of water
held in a pincer by the pier and the beach.
Children's hats float there, pecked at
by gulls. Far off there's gunfire and the sound of

electricity substations exploding
in showers of Hogmanay and Your Round.

Waking up, I grope for my pulse
and shoot it as it attempts to escape
out of the barred window. It's bouncing
its ball against my sides, catching itself
in a mitt, throwing again,
waiting to be let out.

THE MOUNTAIN HEARS ME

ADAM KELLY MORTON

I meet Siobhan on 26 January 2008, at the Dieu du Ciel brewpub at 3 p.m.: opening time. Just off the Main at Laurier, it's a dark, warm place with exceptional beer, and tables that make your hands stink of copper. Apart from the staff, we're the only two people in there.

Siobhan is a talent agent in her mid-forties: a Betty Page type with pale skin, bright-red lipstick, and bags under her black eyes. She's seen things – including me up on stage.

'You could be the next Hoffman,' she says to me, and sips her beer, leaving a red kiss on the rim.

I take a pull of my Gaelique cream ale before asking, 'Dustin or Philip Seymour?'

'Philip Seymour.'

I get it: I have his chubby, mama's-boy face. I tell Siobhan that I graduated from one of the best acting schools in Canada but that, ten years later, I still haven't caught a break.

'There was an actor I repped,' she says. 'One of the best I've ever seen, but you couldn't work with the guy. You remind me of him. In a good way.'

Danielle, the tiny Québécoise waitress, brings over two more pints of Gaelique. I look at her little ass, and Siobhan catches me looking.

'Your round,' she says.

'Sure,' I say. We drink for a while, watching the place fill in, mainly with French-speaking students. AC/DC is on the sound

164

system. I gulp down my beer and order another round. I'm starting to feel good.

'I'm surprised they're playing "Down Payment Blues" in here,' Siobhan says.

'I'm impressed that you know it,' I say. We talk a bit about music, and the next round comes. I start in on it.

'You're lapping me here,' Siobhan says, taking another pull of her beer. 'What are you doing tonight?'

'I'm meeting a friend,' I say. 'We had a falling-out.'

'Yeah? What's her name?'

'Wyatt.'

She doesn't believe me.

'He's an actor too,' I say. 'I wanted to do *Godot* with him, but got tired of waiting.'

Siobhan smiles. 'Har har,' she says.

'Yeah,' I say, and gulp some beer. 'I hate it when people can't confront their fears. Anyhow, I told him at the time that he was being a coward. Now I want to make up with him.' I finish my beer and signal to Danielle for two more.

'Where are you meeting?' she asks.

'Cock n' Bull.'

'Jesus, I haven't been there in ages.'

'It's a nice place,' I say. By nice, I mean that it's nice to get drunk there, and possibly pick someone up.

'I don't go downtown any more,' Siobhan says.

'I don't blame you,' I say.

Another round appears as more people pour into Dieu – mostly hipsters wearing anoraks and Canada Goose parkas. Siobhan is starting to look pretty gassed.

'One more and I'm out,' I say.

'What time are you meeting your friend?'

'Eleven.'

'It's only eight-thirty.'

'I'm going to stroll a bit.'

She leans in close to me. 'Do you want to come over to my place?' she says. 'I'm right around the corner.'

'No, thanks, Siobhan.'

She sits back, as far away from me as she can get. We drink the last round in silence. The bar is too noisy to chat.

I drain my pint, get up, and pull on my Canada Post parka – a gift from my stepfather, who worked there. It doesn't look good, but it's really warm.

I hold open my arms for a hug. 'See you later, Siobhan.'

'Fuck you,' she says. She stands up and wobbles out, dragging her coat over her as she goes. Oh well. So much for her repping me. I finish her beer and make my way to the door.

Outside, I don't feel the cold. I walk past the little bistros and ladies' boutiques on Laurier. There's plenty of time before my meet-up with Wyatt, so I step into the Dépanneur Paradis de la Bière. Suj, the mustachioed Indian owner, adjusts his spectacles as I hold out a six-pack of Labatt 50 for him to scan. He is surrounded by hundreds of bottles of microbrews.

'You sure you want to drink that piss?' he says.

'Can't taste it at this point,' I say. 'Makes no difference.'

'Twelve-twenty-five,' he says.

'Pack of Gauloises red, too.'

'Twenty-fifty.'

I pay and unwrap my smokes, take one, then open the case of beer on my way out.

Walking west on Laurier, I zip up my Canada Post parka, open a beer, and light my smoke. After a block or so, I stop and stand against a street light. I drink and watch people go by. Across the street, there's a ground-level apartment with green lights pulsing inside. A few hipsters are standing in front of the place, smoking. I walk over and take a look through the window.

It's a typical Mile End party, with fashionistas toting cans of Pabst Blue Ribbon, milling around a loft space with high ceilings and loads of plants. There's a redhead girl in there who looks like a doll, with pink cheeks and long eyelashes, wearing a sunflower dress and red ballet shoes. She's standing alone, so I go in.

No one seems to notice that I don't belong there, so I cruise on up to her.

'Hi,' I say.

'Hi,' she says, pulling at the strap of her sunflower dress and looking away from me.

'I'm Alan,' I say.

A bearded young man wearing gold chains and a teal tank top walks up. He puts his arm around the doll girl and glares at me.

'This is my boyfriend, Marcello,' says the girl.

I stumble back a bit, then offer him a 50 from my case. He already has Pabst in his hand, but he takes two bottles from me anyway, and hands one to the doll.

'Thanks, pal,' Marcello says. I nod at him then turn around to look for someone else to talk to.

A girl who looks like Audrey Hepburn in a sixties stewardess uniform with a hat walks up to me. 'There's no smoking in here,' she says.

I look at my lit cigarette, then for a place to put it out, finally deciding on a potted snake plant. She scowls at me. 'Are you here with someone?' she asks. I shake my head. 'Then you had better go.' I nod and make my way to the door.

Outside, I do up my parka and open another beer. I'm feeling the cold now. My cell phone reads ten past ten, so I text Wyatt: 'Heading to Bull.' There's a taxi stand by Esplanade, so I make my way over. A gold Pontiac Bonneville cab with mag wheels is waiting there. I open the door and get in.

'Cock n' Bull, Sainte-Catherine, please,' I say. There is reggae music playing inside the cab, and it smells like hair gel.

The cab driver looks at me in the rear-view. '*Tu bois ce soir, mon ami?*'

I lift my bottle to him. '*T'en veux, toi?*' I say.

'*Non, merci.* No drink in my taxi,' he says.

I finish my beer, put the bottle back in the case, and close the flaps.

'*Bon,*' he says, and starts out. 'Let's go: Cock and Bulle.'

He turns up the music; it sounds like a Haitian party. Everyone's joyful. It's loud enough that I can crack open another 50 without being heard. The driver is having a good time, bobbing his head to the beat, minding all the brake and traffic lights on Parc Avenue.

As we start climbing the hill through Jeanne-Mance Park, I look up at the mountain. Several lights are burned out on the cross. I take a big pull of my beer and mouth the words 'Fuck you.' I hope the mountain hears me.

The fare is $12 as we arrive at the pub. I flick a twenty at the driver. He shouts something at me as I finish my beer. I descend the stone steps and pull open the big red door.

The Cock n' Bull is packed with its usual mix of students and codgers, suits and sluts. The Old Man Band is on the floor, playing Rafferty's 'Baker Street'. Wyatt isn't here yet.

I walk up to the bar. 'Four pitchers of 50,' I shout to Grace, the Irish mother who owns the place.

'You want to start with one this time?' she says.

'Sure. Here's money for four.'

'Pay as you go.' She gives me change for one pitcher.

Good old Grace. Reminds me of my mom, only my mom would be drinking with me. One St Patrick's Day we got drunk here together. My stepfather had to carry me out over his shoulder. That was ten years ago. Not much has changed.

I look around and find a table to sit at. I'm listening to the music and checking out the scene for potential women. There aren't any yet, but it's early.

Half a pitcher later, Wyatt comes in, shaking off the cold. He stands there, looking at me. I pour him a beer.

'Come on,' I say. 'Let's start with this.'

'Thanks, Al,' he says and sits down.

'Cheers,' I say. 'I'm sorry about all the *Godot* shit.'

'Don't worry about it,' Wyatt says. 'Cheers.'

We drink. 'How many have you had?' Wyatt says.

'A couple,' I say.

We drink for a while. Wyatt's a lightweight, nursing his beer. 'Come on, man,' I say. Wyatt takes another sip. It doesn't matter. We're having a good time, singing along to a few songs: Lightfoot's 'Steel Rail Blues' and Dylan's 'It Takes a Lot to Laugh, It Takes a Train to Cry'.

A while later, there's an emaciated woman sitting beside me. She's middle-aged with grey, rotting teeth. I grab someone's empty glass and pour her a beer.

Wyatt leans over to me. 'What are you doing?' he says.

'I bet she's got wisdom,' I say to him.

Wyatt starts putting on his coat.

The woman takes the beer. 'I'll take some money for the Metro too,' she says.

I'm pulling out my wallet when Wyatt lifts me out of my seat. 'C'mon. Let's get out of here,' he says. Before I can say anything else, he has pulled me outside, my Canada Post parka in his hand.

It's gotten really cold out. 'What the fuck,' I say, swaying.

'Put on your jacket,' Wyatt says. So, I do. 'I wasn't going to let you get too close to that woman. Come on, I'll drive you home.'

'Fuck you,' I say to him.

'Come on, take it easy, Al.'

I try to punch him: a wild haymaker that Wyatt dodges as I fall down beside the stairs.

'What the fuck are you doing, Al?' I pull myself up, crawling a bit, then stand in front of Wyatt. 'Let me take you home,' he says.

I spit in his face.

Wyatt stands there for a bit, with my gob trailing down his cheek. He wipes it off with his sleeve. 'All right,' he says. 'Fuck this. I'm done. Hope you get home safe.' He walks off. I watch him go.

I can't stand still without losing my balance any more, so I start walking east on Sainte-Catherine toward Guy Metro station.

The next thing I know, I'm lying on the ground. An ambulance comes. Paramedics pick me up, put me on a gurney, and load me in.

My eyes open: fluorescent lights in a light green hallway. I'm on a gurney, wearing a blue gown. A butterfly IV is attached to my arm. I touch myself all over, to see if all my parts are there. My chest hair has been shaved off in three circular patches. I sit up and look beneath the gurney. My clothes are there, in a white plastic bag with blue lettering on it: *Hôpital Royal Victoria*.

A middle-aged, black nurse walks by on her rounds.

'Excuse me, Miss,' I say. 'Do I have to stay here?'

She lifts an eyebrow. 'It's not a good idea for you to go anywhere.'

'But, do I *have* to stay here?'

She crosses her arms. 'No, you don't,' she says.

'Thanks so much,' I say. I wait for her to go, then pluck out the IV needle, press the bandage back on and step down from the gurney. I quickly undo the string of the plastic bag, yank out my clothes. They're scrunched up and wet. They smell of piss.

I pull on my clothes, boots, and parka in the hallway and make for the exit. A resident is stationed on the way, looking at someone's chart. 'Thanks, Doc,' I say to him. I walk down the hall, down the stairs, and out into the night.

The cold whacks me, wind whipping down the mountain. I find my cell phone. The screen is shattered, but the phone is still working, somehow. Battery at 5 per cent. I have a text from Wyatt that says: 'Get home OK?' and another from my mom: 'Are you coming for roast tomorrow night?' It's 5.15 Sunday morning. I shiver my way down the hill. There aren't any cars on Pine Avenue. Only wind.

I reach Pine and Parc and look around. No people. No cabs. My teeth start chattering.

'Uhhhh,' I say, trying to warm myself, but my clothes are drenched beneath my Canada Post parka.

'Uhhhh,' I say again. It's a moaning sound, coming from somewhere deep inside me.

I just want to get home. Home to my apartment. Home to my mom and stepfather's house in the suburbs. Home to roast.

'Uhhhhhhh!'

I remember when I was a teenager, coming home and finding my mom asleep in the kitchen, drunk on box wine, the-black and-white television set on the kitchen counter showing some infomercial or white static noise.

'Uhhhhhhh!'

There are still no cabs.

'UHHHHHHH!'

It's a guttural moan, from my core. Turning to a wail.

'UHHHHHHHHHHHHHHHHH!'

A wail for life.

A wail to the world that I don't know what the fuck I'm doing any more.

Wind is coming down the mountain.

A cab, light on top like a beacon, comes down Pine. It slows down and lets me in.

Somehow I make it back to my apartment. It's dark inside, but I make my way to the bathroom, strip off my piss-soaked clothes, and flick on the bathroom light.

I look at myself in the mirror: there are bruises up the left side of my face, and part of my left eyebrow is hanging, swollen and blue over the socket.

Naked, I stare at myself.

I made it. I'll grab a sleep, then get a lift home. Have some roast. Some wine. Nothing will stop me.

Nothing but me.

HOLDING JOE

JAMES O'LEARY

In a locked ward with safe surfaces,
we are sitting still in the visiting room
when you tell me you tried it again –
this morning – between room checks.

We are sitting, still in the visiting room.
I look at the soft-rubber coat hooks.
This morning, between room checks,
you nearly succeeded.

I look at the soft-rubber coat hooks
and quietly ask how you did it.
You nearly succeeded.
I don't know what to do for you

and quietly ask how you did it
when you tell me you tried it again.
I don't know what to do for you
in a locked ward with safe surfaces.

THE HOLDING PLACE

SUSANNAH VERNON-HUNT

Patrice and his friends came with their scythes and sheared down the waist-high grasses. A roughly hewn field now, tamed and sloping to the fence that tracks around the old French farmhouse. 'Patrice has grown so tall,' Mum said. She is detaching and wishing. Frankie in amber. 'Mum?' She holds for a second. And comes back.

Just under a year before, Frankie, my younger brother, myself, Mum and Dad had ferried and driven down to an isolated rural south-western spot. Just a day's drive away from the foothills of the Pyrenees. Near only to a bustling market town, with a crumbling turreted castle, scooter garages, bars and some scattered working farms. We were there to look at a non-working farm, up for sale by an elderly couple and set in a decent expanse of land. It was October. But the aim was to spend the summer months there, with my large family coming, going and overlapping when their time was freed up. It had been a long business, but Mum had seen the photos and was pretty sure that this was the one.

Dad was getting ill now. Tetchy and restless. Probably not the most sensible time to buy an old farmhouse, but Mum had sensed his fight for time; and perhaps there was a need in him to make something happen. And so like old Baudelaire said, we leave for leaving's sake. Although Dad was too frail to drive the car, he cannot bear my mother driving. Mum leaning forwards, hands clamped on the wheel at ten to two, would become vociferous, 'Indicate, you damn bastard!' to sudden timidity, 'Sorry, God, so sorry,' then, 'And it's a left here,' as she ferociously swings right.

'Jesus Christ, Liz! You're going to kill us all.'

Frankie and I, giggling, falling in together on the back seat. Your soft chestnut hair brushes my cheek. And that wide, open smile.

You were happy. I know it.

My parents decide, almost immediately, to buy. It isn't beautiful, but it has an open face. Through the kitchen windows, the view is bare now in these cold months, but for an occasional spire and line of cypress tree. But we know it will kick afresh come spring, and later break open, a hot yellow sun shining on vast fieldland, horizoning vast skies.

The local French builders, plumbers and electricians will start immediately, as soon as we leave for home. The barn tended to first. Inside, its two huge doors, unhinged now, but, come summer, will swing wide, letting into the shadows a shock of light and heat. Half-hanging shutters in the kitchen will open soon as well, letting in the thrum and swell of birdsong. The glory of an isolated morning, moving the day long and slow, through to lazy afternoons, purple darkening skies, fox cries, and the country secrets of night-time. Fencing, running up, down and all around will be mended and made stronger too, like a wide embrace. As if holding us in, with all the having and the losing. Not that Mum could ever have known that then. How clever of her, to be one step ahead of the trend, the farm bought for sixpence. But she knew none of that stuff. This was no acquisition.

*

Before the final signature on the document is made, Monsieur Lesant offers us the place for a few nights. Maybe it's planned, maybe it happens by chance, but later that evening, Patrice, who lived with his family at the neighbouring farm, and the same age as you, Frankie, comes knocking and stands in the doorway. He is grinning, with two rifles slung over his shoulder. 'We go together? Hunting the rabbits. Very nice to eat!' I see you look at him. You hesitate. I am confident in what you are going to say, and am shocked when you say, 'OK, yeah.'

Patrice is a brawny, country lad, and you are London lean and can run like an arrow. It's boy stuff, eye-challenged and gauntlet thrown. Dad goes outside with a glass of red wine, coughing up his guts. I watch Mum as she does that funny thing with her lips. They are hardly moving, just tight little quivers, forming words that only she can hear. It is so strong and instinctual, something she has done for as long as I can remember, connected to her almost naked anxiety. She knows, I know, that you don't want to shoot rabbits. Unease lies all around.

That April half-term holiday, so many years before, with the Welsh farmer, you chose the runt from the litter of Jack Russell pups. 'This one, please Mum,' as you tucked him into your Levi's corduroy jacket. And days later, you came to the kitchen table and started to tug me away. 'Come on, come, now. I've got something. Something I want you to see.' You took me behind our gnarly old mulberry tree. There was a bundle of leaves, heaped up, with a little opening. We were down on our knees, and you told me to look inside. I saw two beady eyes. 'It's a pigeon,' you said, 'he's been here for two days, and he hasn't moved. I've made him a safe place. He's dying.' I asked how you knew. 'You can just tell,' you said, 'His wings are all flyed out.'

*

These memories, embedded from so long ago, jab, hot and fresh, as you yank the rifle onto your back. The two of you walk up the track. Patrice is holding a torch; it dots its way, moving you further away into the black country night. Unease calls again. It creeps through this lovely farmhouse. Mum makes soup. I smoke a cig. Dad coughs.

Some hours later there is a noise at the door. Frankie walks quietly past the kitchen and towards the back bedroom. Mum looks at me. She says nothing, but I know. 'You go and talk with him,' her eyes implore.

I find you as I often do, sitting, knees apart, arms resting on them and face looking down. 'Hi,' I say. A long pause as I sit down and hear your breath, hot and quick. Waiting for your ribcage to stop its heaving.

'Why did I even go?' I have to bend in to hear you. 'Why did I— Why?...' Your hands are raking your jeans, up then back. I rest my hands on them, but you push them off. 'Fuck, why?... That field, jumping with rabbits, big ones, and big... Jesus, pregnant ones, and little... I just thought he wanted to – I don't know – show off, or show... he shot three of them, you couldn't fucking... you couldn't miss.' Your voice is stuttering, breaking. 'He shot... The last one, it didn't die, it was twitching, blood coming, like everywhere, blood. He wanted me to kill it, I turned my gun, it... I shot the earth, but it... it must... It hit something hard and he's fucking shouting at me in French. Why do I... all the time, I just can't... it didn't die and he kills it, up close, so close, and blood is spurting up and he's laughing... he's laughing. Just, oh... just—'

I remember your tears splashing like explosive stars onto the stone tiles. I want to pull you into the whole of my body. But you don't like that stuff. Fuss. I stroke your back, slowly you relent. I pull out a scuzzed-up tissue from my pocket. You smudge it to your eyes. We sit side by side. An occasional hiccup. It was wretched. My brother, distressed. I am your sister. Always your big sister. It is my need that wants to pull you in. You are not cut loose and adrift, your crying unheard. But you didn't need me. I am useless.

Then, startled, I watch you jump quick to your feet. 'I'm all right, I'm all right. Tell them goodnight, yeah? I need to be... I need to sleep. Thanks, yeah, thanks. I'll see you in the morning, OK?' A quick kiss, awkward, on my cheek. I kiss your cheek back. Your hair is long, to your shoulders, it's gone into little tendrils of dirt, sweat and possibly blood. I kiss you quickly, just one more. You pull away with a half-hearted grin. My love for you rises in me like a heat.

As I close the door behind me, I have the strange feeling of falling away from the lamplight in your room and into black. The world is bright. Sometimes a wondrous, and sometimes a brutal bright. Tell me, is it too bright for you? I fear you are in deep waters. And you will simply let the pull-tide take you. I cannot make you resist, I cannot pull you up, out and away, but don't go too far out or too far down. Let me always be able to reach you. Promise?

The next morning, Dad's coughing wakes me. In the kitchen Mum is drinking strong black coffee. I go to pour myself a cup, and suddenly Frankie is in the room. He has his wide-open smile and holds out to Mum a winter bouquet he has just picked. Tall yellow grasses, twigs with shiny, lime-green leaves, and spirals of flopping ferns. 'What a beautiful bundle this is.' She is smiling and takes them and puts them into an old glass jug. There, on the table, a jug of sweetness and love. You hug your mother. Her eyes are closed, and her face is at peace. She holds on to you tight, and a beat too long. You let out a little bashful laugh. I laugh too, and then Mum. All dark troubles and tension set loose, made free by our laughter. Dad comes in, trying to hold back a few nasty throat splutters. 'Hey, this looks nice. Get your old man a cup of coffee before he kicks the bucket!' We were happy. You were. I know.

Mum could never have known. Dad neither. Not anyone. That this was the last time Frankie was ever to be in the farmhouse with us. Later, in the tremendous heat of the coming July, you were to leave us all. No goodbye. No letter. This was not a paper trail. This was an absolute.

You found a virtually unfindable place, in the magnificence of Richmond Park, the garden of your childhood. You took many pills, swallowed with whisky, and lay yourself down and died. 'I know every inch of this park,' you told me. This vast park. And you did. Your body found, completely by chance, three weeks later. Three unendurable endured weeks.

Sometimes a spark of shameful anger gives way. You never saw Mum come to me in the middle of the night, in that pale pink sleeveless nightie, arms of bone, a wraith. She lay down beside me on my bed. Her face so close to mine. With the dirty breath of sorrow. She no longer brushes her teeth. She no longer does anything except breathe in and out, the one act given up in exchange for the barest bone of life. Her little one has disappeared for seventeen days, and she knows – she is his mother and therefore she knows – that he has gone. And she says, 'He was just sixteen, but that is sixteen years of a life. Lived. And then and then...'

'Maybe enough for him,' I say in return. We hold each other until we may break each other's bones.

*

The months preceding your death, from March to July, had been chaotic and desolate. You were, without warning, expelled from your boarding school. The new and ambitious headmaster, brought in by the school board to tighten the reins, sent a curt letter of dismissal. You a junior, and along with four seniors, were seemingly bad influences. You had been writing, with the help of Mr Rappaport, the English teacher you loved, a short play about the Greek Gods. You were building a 'medieval hut' with your friends behind the playing fields. 'Am I bad?' you later asked Mum. The headmaster continued his slaughter of the innocents for about a year, until the parents rose up, and he was sacked. A fine new man, I heard later, was brought in. But for you, sadness, like a sheet of tracing paper held over your life, was now emboldened. It was all too late. 'I never get the good luck,' you said. My voice began to rise up to tell you off for such silly talk. But it never came.

That first evening you came back was terrible. As the muffled sobs from your bedroom crept down the stairs, my father, inflamed with the injustice of it all, and hotly protective, spoke with a quiet, bitter anger. 'It's wrong. That fucking bastard of a man.' And in that big, messy kitchen, unease came calling, yet again. You moving further out of touch, dark waters lapping around your ankles, the tide lulling you in. As I stood outside your bedroom door, I held back from knocking. I wish now that I had not. I wish that.

And you were too young to be suddenly so solemn, aloof, disengaged with the very wanting of living. And I did not look long enough to see you. I was not really looking at all. Maybe my new-found freedom after leaving boarding school was fizzing me up too much. Soho gigs with boys and joints. My 'Activist!' youth theatre, Dylan and Bowie. London, enticing me. And you, just disappearing for days at a time. Defiantly solo. Throwing off my gentle questions with your eyes. Your bedroom door closed. My brother, inscrutable, unreachable. Sad.

You made fires in the big old drawing room with its delicate wooden fireplace. I would come and kneel by you, just watching the flames. One time I began to feed it with snaps of dry wood. You stopped me: 'No, don't. Just let it die out.' I began to cry. 'Oh don't,' you said. I sniffed and stiffened my face.

'Fires need to burn, that's what fires do.'

'Yeah,' you said, 'and then they return to ash.'

I let out a little hapless laugh, 'Christ, Frankie, "ashes to ashes" – you don't have to be so bloody heavy.'

You stood abruptly. 'Oh, just fuck off, then,' as you went to the door. 'What's wrong in watching a fire just die out?'

'Nothing...' I began to say. 'Nothing, but—' The door shut out my words.

There is nothing wrong in watching a fire die to streams of flaked ash, embers glowing, going. But only that you do. I was confused. A fire of flames, but flames all flew out.

And then, quite inexplicably and suddenly, your mood changed. You still went out for hours and hours, without ever saying much. You still read, with your beloved dog resting protectively and coiled up on your tummy. But you smiled more. You laughed a bit at my silly impressions; you roughhoused with your brothers, and would give Mum quick spontaneous hugs. I had been accepted on a theatre arts course, to start in September, and was ecstatic. You were happy for me, too.

You played 'Let It Grow' by Clapton in your bedroom. I felt light-hearted when you told me that when you met up with Lorraine, your dear friend, she played it on guitar, and you sang with her. You, singing! And, of course, Mum was almost delirious at this sudden change. 'I think he really is happier now. He is. And I don't care why. It's just so good to have him back.'

The casual cruelties of this world stun me. We had him back because he knew he was going to go. I'm told it is often like that. You were calm, at peace, everything falling into place. You had taken your one true vote. And now it all made sense. It was so simple. You just hadn't seen it. But now, there in the palm of your hand. Death. Take it. It's yours.

That August after you died, all four of my elder brothers and my sister visited La Ferlot for the first time. My brother with his wife and the first of many grandchildren. Little baby Lowri, passed from hand to hand, plump rose cheek, finger stroked and kissed. The holiday had been planned for months with no idea of what was to precede it. And finally, with all the relatives and friends, the police, the autopsy, the coroner's report, all dealt with; it was just your funeral. It was the saddest day of my life. And then the whole family left for France.

I think my parents had bought La Ferlot as a home for an ever-growing family to have always, as a place to nurture and pass on. But really it was a dream. Families shift, grow and change. Imperceptibly and hugely. And for all of us to spend holidays together was unrealistic. And yet at that precise moment in time, the house came into itself in a way no one could have foreseen. Not a home exactly, but a place of holding. A sanctuary for a shell-shocked family, but a family that was in the very moment of living, of things happening. Life, now.

Too much red wine, outdoor fires, a beautiful table, made by my brother from a huge wheel found at the back of the farm. Staying up to the early hours in the barn, music playing softly. Late one night, I heard Mum crying deep, quietly hidden sobs in the bathroom. I stood outside. I wanted to hold her. But she needed to be let be.

Dad was really quite ill now, and of course he struggled with the body blow, punched straight into his heart. He could lie in the heat, letting the sun warm his bones. Sometimes on very hot nights he slept outside. 'The stars, God, the stars,' he would say.

Despite everything, here, my mother was able to relinquish some of her pain. Able to take in great gulps of air, rather than tight quick bites. She could walk freely among those who loved her and let her be. Fading fast were the needle-thin cocktail ladies from our home town, stalking her with their supermarket whispers, 'Her, that's her.' Their tight, bright lipsticked smiles and stuttered, embarrassing condolences. My shy, gauche mother who detested gossip and got on better with Gladys, the cleaning lady, than this 'set'. Those ladies, who we imitated, with their 'la-di-dah' voices and stringent laughs. And the one you once pushed, Frankie, because you thought she was being nasty to Mum. Mum didn't even mind. I tried to keep her safe and away, free from those women, just like you did.

Here too, she was safe from the hellish visits of Father David, the Catholic priest who had baptised all seven of us. His questioning and judgement when he had to bury one. Suicide, once a sin, and still one for him. Fumbling through the funeral service, offering a pittance of compassion. The old-school Vatican crow. Useless cunt.

My mother took off her shoes at La Ferlot and left them in the wide, stone-tiled corridor. She went barefoot. She unwound the belt of her summer frock and left it hanging over a chair. Let her black hair go unbrushed and unkempt. You went a little bit Woodstock on us, Mum. Your stunned pain cupped here with some decency.

And you were gone, but sometimes I felt you, Frankie. My head throbbing with a summer longing. You, hazy in my thoughts by the lake; the lack of you easing, shifting in and out of the sun and shadows. Sometimes baby Lowri, gurgling contentedly in her Moses basket and sometimes crying out into the night.

Late one evening, just outside the barn door, I stood very still as I watched my mother. She wandered down the sloping field, right up to the fence. Her face held up to the darkness. My mother's heart, unclenching. My eyes blinked. My hand moved forward slightly. She was as still as a drop of rain suspended on a wire, about to fall.

FOX FIELD AND COCONUT SHELL

ANTHONY JAMES

The Fox Field was a seductively idyllic place to die. Late April, and the sun's warmth rich and strong as summer. I used to walk to the village shop in less than ten minutes, but now it took me about three quarters of an hour, with three long, breathless, head-spinning rests along the way – three quarters of an hour to walk back, carrying my bag of six bottles of cheap wine or sherry; at least three more rests. That evening, I turned off the river path, went through the bluebell wood and lay down in the long grass of the field. The sunlight flooded down on my face. I looked up into a light blue sky of infinite depth – blue and blue and blue; enveloping, slightly maternal, serene and erotic. As always, these days, I was drifting off into exhaustion, into sleep, into that still zone between waking and sleep; and into that zone between life and death.

I did not want to get up and move – ever.

Time shifted and overlapped. There was no division any longer between past and present. My daughter and I had called this place the Fox Field because we saw foxes here – before adulthood and an academic career had taken her far away. When my wife still lived with me, she had also called it the Fox Field. That was before the contempt and vindictiveness on both our parts had set in. And this village in a valley by a river? Four decades before, aged seventeen, and reaching the last stages of the violent abuse by a brother nine years older than me that he had begun when I was three, I had travelled to

London with some overtime pay from the forestry labourer's job I had drifted into. I was gripped by a passion for books and for history – most of all the history of revolutions and rebels – and my first destination was the tomb of Karl Marx at Highgate Cemetery. The massive monumental head in the cream-hazed spring sunshine; the quietness with the background London roar, and carved into the plinth: *The philosophers have only interpreted the world in various ways; the point however is to change it.* Karl Marx was all very well, and books had saved my sanity. Books were my real family – not the brother whose presence was a smear of dirt and grime across my childhood and teenage years, or the mother who connived in his abuse of me, or the weak, depressive father who died when I was eleven. And yet, as the victim of male power at home and in the boys' grammar school I attended, where several of the male teachers were more violent bullies than the worst of the kids, I was looking for some other figure of inspiration. A heroine, perhaps. So, I wandered through London all that weekend, an intense, wide-eyed, long-haired youth, far too shy even to speak to a girl. Finally, in the Camden Bookshop, I picked up a book by Emma Goldman, the Jewish-Russian-American anarchist and feminist. Her face looked at me from the book's cover. A famous song described how the painter Van Gogh had eyes that knew the darkness in the singer's soul. I felt the same about Emma Goldman. Decades later, after a strange set of circumstances had brought me to this village in a valley by a river, I discovered that Emma Goldman had also lived here back in the 1920s. Hounded from one country to another, she had married an anarchist Welsh miner in order to be allowed to stay in Britain. She had lived in the station house about a quarter of a mile from my Fox Field.

Oh my cursed (or blessed) legs! I think I came very close to dying in that field. I once read about a soldier in the Spanish Civil War who said with the wonderful humour of his country: 'I conducted myself with great bravery in the battle, but my legs showed a great tendency to run away.' It seemed that my legs also had a will of their own. Of their own accord they stirred and carried me with small, liquid-muscled steps out of the field.

I did self-employed work as a salesman, and I had not yet given it up. The previous winter, already very ill, I had set up for a day in a large store in an isolated little town. The snow had come down and the buses had stopped running. I walked three miles in a blizzard along a country road empty of all vehicles, reaching the state of mind in which I sincerely wanted to lie down in the roadside ditch and fall asleep, letting the snow cover me. My legs – my stubborn, wilful, undefeatable legs, or so it seemed – refused to stop walking. I reached the next town and the railway station. The train to the nearest city... the spare room in a friend's house... next morning back to my (and Emma Goldman's) village.

A few days after my evening in the Fox Field, I was still working. Another town, another store. Another day selling items to people that they did not really want. I hired my skills to a company that acted for small businesses wanting to break into the market with their products and for charities wanting to sell fund-raising items. I knew the managers on my circuit of stores. *I no longer knew myself.* The manager stared without comment at the yellow-skinned, exhausted and bloated invalid I had become; a remnant of the smart, if unscrupulous, salesman he had known for years. But he let me set up in the foyer of the store.

Long ago I had learned simply to switch on my professional self, even in the most horrendous circumstances – and sell and sell. I never slurred, never swayed, never lost my focus, even after the second and third bottle of wine on an empty stomach. Now, after ten minutes I took what seemed to be a bottle of mineral water from my bag and took a swig. It was half water and half vodka. I drank while working like this for years, from an innocent-looking bottle, concealing the smell of my breath with a few dabs of clove and eucalyptus oil around my mouth. For years, I drank everywhere, whatever I was doing. On buses. On trains. On planes. At my daughter's graduation ceremony. In the doctor's waiting room. In court, right in front of the judge, when I assisted my stepdaughter in a case brought over access to her children. This time, my body rebelled. I vomited. The store manager must have been watching me on the CCTV, and he dialled 999. The ambulance arrived astonishingly quickly. I refused to be taken to hospital that day. But eight days later, less than two weeks after the evening I lay in the Fox Field, I *was* at last in hospital. I learned later – not much later – that everyone expected me to die in hospital, although no one quite said so, not even the consultant. I had certainly been dying for several weeks. I had advanced liver disease and liver failure.

In that spring of 1974, the time of my weekend in London and my discovery of Emma Goldman at the age of seventeen, I had already been drinking heavily for over a year. In my late teens, when I began to suffer from serious depression, I drank even more heavily. Prolonged violent abuse from an early age had left me with a wretched sense of worthlessness, which is what so many victims feel. Perhaps there is an element that is more common in boys and adolescents: as a male, you feel cowardly, dishonourable because you did not fight back enough. This was the psychological splinter of glass that was lodged deep in my self-esteem. Whatever I did in later life, the poisoned splinter could never be quite plucked out. In the 1980s, when the war on the streets was at its worst, I went to Belfast to see things for myself. No one made me go, I just went. I sought out other dangerous situations and dealt with them fairly well. In my teens and early twenties I was too cripplingly shy and socially isolated to reach out for a relationship with a woman, which I longed for. Yet later, I was married twice and as the years went by I had surprisingly numerous relationships with women, some of them very intense, romantic and tender. I went to university as a mature student and graduated with honours. Never enough. Never quite enough! The splinter was embedded too deeply. I drank to numb the pain of awareness. And in my teens, I also drank because I was *good at it*, I could hold it, so I felt tough, heroic, fulfilling a man's role. The feminists and revolutionaries I admired hadn't quite convinced me; I still thought all too often in a conventional way. As the years passed, I drank more and more: finally, four or five or six bottles of cheap wine or sherry every twenty-four hours.

In that last spring I lived to drink and to buy the next six bottles, just as a heroin addict lives only to buy heroin and inject. I slept or lay half-awake in a fog bank of exhaustion, losing track of the days, losing insight and perspective. I did not know or care how ill I looked. I did not know how close to death I was, or if I did, it was only a vague and apathetic sort of awareness. I had no idea how to get out of the situation. I lived alone. I spoke to my daughter on the phone most days, but I concealed the seriousness of my condition. Having a washing machine and a tumble dryer, I was able to keep myself supplied with clean clothes and clean underwear. One day a week I still worked, earning my commission, banking money, making phone calls.

I moved about the house with weak, small steps and leaden reluctance in my limbs, sitting down to rest in each room, taking hours to bath and dress myself.

There remained Kathy, my GP. Recently, as my liver could no longer process alcohol, I began to appear drunk or at least affected when I saw her. I was still able to register her mixture of sadness at my ongoing destruction, together with her never-suffer-fools-gladly toughness. 'So, what's the overall picture you are seeing?' I once asked her with alcohol-fuelled heartiness and expansiveness.

'I see an alcoholic drinking himself to death,' Kathy said tersely. But a few minutes later she spoke softly, rather sorrowfully: 'It's time for you to go now. I'll see you next time.'

In my teenage years, when I needed them most, I had only encountered doctors – and the occasional psychiatrist, because of the depression – who were indifferent, bored, untalented and fundamentally callous. At that time, I never found a doctor who had Kathy's efficiency and compassion. It was Kathy who got me an early appointment with the consultant at the nearest large hospital. My daughter arranged transport by phone. I packed a small bag of books and clean clothes. I had always hated the idea of being in hospital. But I hated this present existence anyway. Grey, lingering exhaustion. Unconsciousness. Walking to the local shop to buy more wine and sherry, although I could barely stand. A clawing ache that never went away in my distended stomach. Endless booze that tasted foul in my mouth. Nothing else.

Early May, and I arrived at the hospital on an afternoon full of the still gloom of a low, grey sky. The consultant was a man with heavy, dark-haired, Welsh good looks. He was calm – but of course he had done this many times. And cheerful – but he was not the one who was severely ill, and gloom would not help his patients. Wouldn't you be better off in hospital? I agreed that I would be. He spoke weightily.

'There is, of course, a thirty per cent mortality rate in cases as advanced as yours.' Was this an argument for staying in hospital, or a warning not to expect too much? Was he this candid with all his patients? But then, I must have seemed like a person who did not lack intelligence, and I spoke objectively and unsentimentally about the state I was in.

'You mean I have a seventy per cent chance of survival?' I was surprised by how brightly I had spoken. He nodded.

Actually, it later emerged that he had thought that I would probably die within a fortnight. And so had Kathy my GP. There is an excellent story by a Russian writer based on his experiences as a cancer patient in the 1950s, which I first read when I was about sixteen. He begins the story: 'When I arrived in Tashkent that winter I was practically a corpse. I came there expecting to die.' But I did not feel like this at all. Despite my massively swollen belly, the dramatic amount of weight I had lost and my discoloured skin, I never believed that I would die, not even that there was a 30 per cent chance of my dying.

Yet the first thirty-six hours were far from easy. I was able to eat – I even had more appetite than I had possessed for many weeks. On my own in a small room, I was brought beans on toast by an auxiliary nurse, a slim woman with short fair hair and small, sparkling ear studs that kept catching my eye. The young man who was the consultant's chief assistant arrived, pleasant and mild-mannered. The procedure by which he drained off a sample of the fluid from my massively swollen stomach was not pleasant or mild at all – the needle went into the stomach wall. The pain was hideous. The auxiliary nurse let me grip her hand

and kept eye contact with me, kept talking to me, kept asking me questions. Strange. I had never seen her before and never saw her again, yet how great a difference she made. I also sensed that her kindness was genuine. Glimpsing the sky beyond the windows, I saw that a mist-laden night was falling, mild and obscure.

Then things got difficult. An aching wedge of pain pressed and pressed just below my ribs. My hugely distended abdomen must have dragged on and expanded the normal stomach cavity; because my liver and kidneys were barely functioning, my body was retaining a huge amount of fluid. Ironically, this was one of the reasons why I had kept on drinking continuously – the alcohol numbed the pain. Now the supply of alcohol was gone. I asked repeatedly for something to relieve the pain as I lay in a bed that had been wheeled into a room just adjoining the nurses' station. I tried not to ask too often; I tried to speak with courtesy through the red blur of pain; I tried not to slide into the self-centred, shrill hysteria that is so common in those of us addicted to alcohol. And there was a tiny answering vibration in the blue-uniformed women around me. Ill and in pain and in a strange place, I was still sharply sensitive to such reactions in others. Also, due to my appearance alone and from what they were already reading in my notes, they believed I would soon die. Still, a pattern was set. Respect for respect. The nurses explained that they could not give me painkillers until the results of the blood tests were available, so that they knew what they should or should not give me. Finally, they gave me an injection of something that greatly distanced me from the pain. My bed was wheeled into a ward.

I am lying on the bed in the ward. My old suede jacket that has accompanied me on so many adventures is pulled over me and I am dressed. I vaguely remember that I got up to go to the toilet, with one of the nurses holding my arm part of the way. I refused to use bedpans – ever. When I return, I have no energy to undress and get into bed. The great fog of apathy, diseased fatigue and alcohol in which I have lived for months has merged with a weightless and multicoloured state of euphoria created by the powerful injected painkillers. My wife appears at my bedside. I dimly apprehend that she too thinks that I will die. Sad, she is so sad. There is to be no reconciliation, no romantic happy ending. She will go on visiting me – if only for a few minutes each day, bringing me clean clothes. The calm, undeviating integrity and decency of the woman who once loved me: more than I deserve. My daughter will visit, coming hundreds of miles to stay for four days. She is in the middle of working on her Ph.D. at the age of twenty-four. There is an uneasiness, an awkwardness; the old, unbreakable alliance is like an oak branch rotted from the inside, seemingly still in place, but soon to fall away. But the axe blow will be postponed in my daughter's case. A German philosopher once said: 'Die at the right time!' If I had died that week in May in Ward 4, Princess Royal Hospital, at a time when sympathy for me was at its highest level, then those who knew me could have said: 'Well, he was a bastard, he caused a lot of unhappiness. But he was his own worst enemy, and he also did some good things.'

Die and be pitied – and even occasionally praised. Live on and be resented.

Clear. Yes, clear. CLEAR. The fog has lifted; it has dissolved away in the morning light. The half-life, semi-consciousness, the putrefying cloud in which I have lived for months has gone. I am also surer than ever that I will live. It is my second morning in hospital. I decide I will go to the hospital shop, although I am still desperately weak and unsteady, stomach swollen, skin yellow.

The 'domestic' staff are cleaning the ward. I ask one of them directions to the shop, but she can see I am not taking them in. Ellen leaves her work and walks with me down the stairs and along the corridor to show me the way. She is a petite, tough woman with short dark hair. In a sense I have known her all my life; or rather I have known women like her all my life. They battle on, they expect nothing, they know the world is stacked against them; they face the next blow and the next; they have no illusions about the rich, the powerful and the pompous who infest the world – they do not admire them and they are not impressed by them; they deal with them as best they can and laugh at them privately. Some, like Ellen, never become choked by bitterness and they keep a certain generosity of heart... amazingly. My only cause for resentment is the way in which the cleaning and catering staff are treated – the people who clean the ward, the bathrooms and the toilets, as well as bringing and serving the meals. They are put upon by their own supervisors and treated as if they are invisible – or with contempt – by most of the doctors and some of the nurses. I stand up for them whenever I can and declare loudly, as often as I can, in front of doctors and nurses, that the whole place would cease to function without their efforts.

On my second morning I also go walking outside, managing to walk around the car park. And each day, without fail, in sunshine or in rain or in the white-grey chill that the British May can bring, I walk, further and a little further. I know, I feel that these walks are helping me to recover, healing me. Since childhood I have been used to making my own decisions in solitary, secretive fashion. I ask my wife to bring me loperamide for diarrhoea and milk thistle, the herbal remedy that helps liver function. She does not like this, but she brings them; for her, complete openness with the doctors and faith in their solutions is a given, almost sacred. The husband she remembers is twitching, stirring, rearing up before her eyes again. When we still lived together, she had said to me: 'You are a victim of your own arrogance.' When the breach with my daughter comes later on, she too tells me: 'You pretend you have changed, but you haven't.' The alcoholic old bastard always thinks he's right. And yet... The beautiful and glamorous and very ambitious Sri Lankan doctor on the consultant's team is always out to make her mark; she hopes to take the consultant's job when he moves on, and perhaps she well deserves it. If she knows I have diarrhoea I will be sent for tedious blood tests and X-rays. I take loperamide and the problem is gone in twenty-four hours. And in fact, some weeks later, two male patients complain of diarrhoea and there is a scare about C. difficile infection on the ward, and all but one toilet is closed. But the doctor had over-reacted: the scare is unfounded. Perhaps the alcoholic old bastard knows a thing or two after all.

My stay in hospital – like most stays in hospital – is like a parabola, the arc made by a ball thrown into the air. The beginning is simply being glad to be alive. Appreciation and gratitude for any kindness or help or skill grows and grows, and strength and health increases too. Then the point is reached at which restlessness and impatience set in, and the desire to get out grows stronger. I have more books now. I write down a record of what happens. My wife is a university mentor for degree students with disabilities. One day she tells me that one of her students is having endless trouble getting to grips with the influence of Karl Marx – could I write some notes to help her? How much I enjoy sitting up half the night writing these notes, my handwriting jagged because my hands still shake! I go on walking further and further.

There are two poisons for the lifelong excessive drinker as well as alcohol itself: one is the comforting delusion that we are not free to make choices, and the other is selfish self-absorption. I walk and I write and I read. I observe other patients and also the doctors. I secretly self-medicate when I think it is appropriate. Mainly, I think, I manage to avoid both these poisons. I read or write until about four in the morning when the early summer dawn is turning the sky milk coloured and faintly luminous. I sleep. I wake at eight. Breakfast. Shower. My walk. Lunch. Doze. Read. Evening meal – my appetite is good, the food is good. My wife visits, sometimes we are amicable, sometimes we are not. I walk again. A nightly anti-coagulant injection, which I refuse to have in the stomach, always in the thigh. Night, people settling. Malcolm dies. At least, it is fairly certain that he dies. Malcolm was a man in his thirties – at least twenty years younger than me – showing the same symptoms of liver disease as mine, and over about three weeks there is no improvement in his condition. There was the same massively swollen belly and yellow pallor on his skin. He ceased getting out of his bed in a side room off the corridor leading to the ward, and more and more often there were alarmed, whispered conversations among the nurses after going into his room; several times they called the doctor in to examine him. One morning he had disappeared from his room and his bed was empty.

Tracy, an auxiliary nurse, looks at the books on my bed – a biography of Jane Fonda, a collection of writings by Emma Goldman (well, naturally!) called *Red Emma Speaks*, and *The Sea-Wolf* by Jack London, a massively underrated and misunderstood novel that I was reading for perhaps the twelfth time. Tracy tells me that she has an academic degree, being thus overqualified for many jobs in the National Health Service, but fortunately she likes the job she is now doing. They are giving me large doses of steroids. The fluids retained in my body are getting less every day – when I arrived and looked down at myself, my body was like a heavily pregnant woman's. But the steroids sometimes make my emotions seethe like a pan of pasta sauce with the heat turned up under it. Tracy, with her stylish spiky hair, humour and easy gracefulness is one of those women who warm and improve the atmosphere of any room they enter.

It is just before dawn following a sleepless night. I sit on my bed in tears and Tracy sits beside me and hugs me. Two nurses pass quietly. One of them speaks to me, amused.

'You've got your pyjama bottoms on inside out.'

'So I have,' I say, looking down, my mind still full of my own pain.

'It's unlucky to take them off and change them.' The nurses are trying to distract me and lift my mood.

'I thought that only applied to a woman's knickers.' I am remembering something I had read in a book years ago, and my thoughts are still far away.

'I know I put my knickers on the right way today,' Tracy says to the nurses. 'But you two had better go and check.'

Suddenly we all slide off into shivering laughter, laughing into our hands, trying not to make enough noise to wake the uneasily sleeping and grunting men in the low-lit, faintly humming ward.

Beyond the hospital car park is the access road into the hospital grounds, and after some distance there is a playing field alongside the road. A gate in the fence opens onto the playing field, and crossing one corner of it, you can go through a gap in the fence and into a little wood of old, ivy-grown trees. Here I find the coconut shell on the grass – a perfect half. I pick it up and turn it over, looking and looking, wondering how it ever came to be here. Hardly anyone comes this way. The little patch of forest is overlooked and isolated. There is no rubbish. I am going to keep the coconut shell. It is for some reason incredibly precious and incredibly significant.

The day is full of burning, intense June heat, even the green leaves on the trees are softly flashing, reflecting the brilliant light. I am going home on Monday, in three days. I will fix the coconut shell up on the wall in my house, and inside it I shall put the waterproof plastic bracelet that has been on my wrist since my admission, which bears my name and hospital number.

The philosophers have only interpreted the world in various ways; the point however is to change it.

DOWN AND DOWN

ANDY MOORE

Down and down brother,
Down and down.

Down in cold bone delirium
Down in memory brother
Down with the bloodied tides
and hopeless symmetry.
Down with the alleyways, housing estates and cold buttered
    mornings,
Down in the primary school's dull claw, the playground's
Concrete and sorcery
Down, born and woven anew
in the bonfire's breathing shadow,
Down in music brother,
cut up in melody, word and bone,
Down with cat eyes and dog heart,
good women and the keen lash,
Down where the skies arc cracks in memory
Down in Belfast city brother,
Down where the codes are written.

Down and down brother,
Down and down.

Down where the clacking tongues rust up,
where the rutting glare and fuck in idle finery,
Down in London city,
Down in bliss brother,
Down in bars with mongrel blood on broken glass,
Down with the tilting roar,
the hammer and the glee,
Down in toad oblivion,
Down with the holy worm brother,
all eyes and snare,
Down in the glooping static,
where the fleshy promise burns up on re-entry
Down with cunt eyes and banshee heart,
Down with the powder and Crow,
Down and only,
Down and sold brother,

Down and down brother,
Down and down.

Down where the narrative's torn and flawed,
where the thread's fractured,
Down where the metaphor won't stick
Down in the source,
Where the Id sleeps heaven and wakes to destroy,
Down in the birthing serum, the scared hate,
Down on the cold road,
Down and sorry brother, sorry I wasn't
for, of you and more,
Down and tired brother, down and tired
Down and I'll leave now brother,

peel skin from the grave of bed sheets brother,
Down and I'll gather up screaming molecules, spinning hell
    brother
Down and I'll walk brother, I'll walk,
begin again.

HEALING

THREE BISCUITS

NADA HOLLAND

At the twelve-step meeting, the Saturday before, Kat had listened as Arthur, the man in the City-type outfit, told his New Year's Eve plans. Or rather, his wishes. A cell, Radio 4, the papers. *So fuck you again*, he ended, *which of course really means fuck Arfa. I need to be around sods like you to have any chance of surviving.*

The topic had been 'action and prayer, not magic'. The next sharer was Stellar, a red-bearded raver type in a petrol-blue Aran jumper.

Yeah, I always just want things to go away, like magic. Quick fixes. I'm clean now for sixty days.

An encouraging murmur went through the room.

But I want my recovery to be like magic too. I really don't want to do the work. Action, prayer, that type of thing – I just don't have the patience. His handsome, ginger face was gold skinned, not pale; deeply grooved, shadows under his eyes, a sexy, smoky, petrol-blue-flame kind of look.

He looked familiar, a phenotype, thought Kat. The bloke with the girls at the party, the smiley busker under the bridge, the rock star if things had turned out a little different. *If only.* She looked about the room. About half of the thirty-odd of them fitted that bill. Had that manqué-star quality, charisma, small-time divas, failed leaders, benevolent despots gone rogue.

The other half were enablers, the mousy, retreating manipulators, much put-upon, silently seething with rage. Withdrawn, shrunk back to mere spectres, even here, with their beige colouring, their shapeless dad jeans and shoes – or, conversely, blown out of shape, helplessly bloated to the size of whales. Serial killers, Kat thought to herself. Bruisers, mad as hell, the lot of them.

I've used for twenty years, Stellar went on. *I don't know anything else, don't have a single life skill. I've always just gone for the easiest way. When you're down, do some weed, when you're tired, some coke, when you can't sleep... Well, you know what I mean. I've always been the one who kept going, last man standing, light of the party, the one who will climb on the roof, swing from the ceiling, that's Stellar, you know, that's me. Even if I did most of it in blackouts, never was there to even enjoy it.*

Hint of self-pity, Kat noted. Defining quality of the active addict.

But without all that, Stellar went on, *I don't really know who I am. I'm finding that out now. I've lost my identity. I'm trying to get back with my friends, but twenty years is a long time, that's also just dawning on me. They have lived lives, time has moved on and it's really hard to reconnect now. I don't know if I can ever be the man I was before.* Pause. *I'm sure I still have a lot to learn in recovery.*

A hushed chuckle in the circle.

Anyway, I'm glad to be here, Stellar ended. *Thanks for listening.*

Thank you, Stellar. Silence.

A dark, big man with glasses and a silver glint to his short black frizz spoke up. Solidly built, in a cashmere sweater. Handsome.

Kat sat up.

I have a sixteen-year-old, and he's taken up smoking, he began. *It's very hard to watch as a dad. Weed certainly was a gateway for me. I try to talk to him, but it's really no use. His mum is like, 'At least he smokes in the house, not in the street.' I'm a bit more boundaried. Let him freeze in the park, like everyone else... In truth, I feel pretty helpless. He has his own journey to make, his own mistakes. But it still kills me.*

Kat listened, half pitying the man, half judging him with his wayward kid, some part still sort of fancying him; he was one of the charismatics. A failed tyrant, forced to take this demotion at last, grow this softened, wiser aura.

The mousy types were silent. A pale woman Kat had seen here for years sat fidgeting in her seat, her lips moving occasionally, forming inaudible phrases. She had never spoken, not once raised her voice to share, though she'd never missed a meeting. Had never been clean, Kat knew. You could see it. The neat plastic shoes, orange or black, the thin, strawberry-blonde hair. The tangerine-plastic earrings, the careful Petticoat Lane leggings-and-sweater ensembles. An orange Sainsbury's carrier bag, like a purse, always parked at her feet.

Never staying to chat. Topping up her paper cup once more from the coffee pot, after the meeting. Taking three biscuits. Before disappearing. Poor thing.

The room was silent. Kat scraped her throat.

I'm Kat, and I'm an addict.

LOWELL IN ST ANDREW'S, NORTHAMPTON

JOHN O'DONOGHUE

Robert Lowell spent two weeks at St Andrew's Hospital in early 1976.
John Clare had been a patient in the same hospital over one
*hundred years earlier.**

Here, where Winter works its old arthritic way
to Spring and looks like it just might not make it –
there's death in the air, a chill around my heart
after so much fire in my sad, ashen head.
The corridors are cabbagey and I am
missing all I've left behind. It's come to this:
landlocked in this foreign place, far from home, with
only the daily round of meals and pills and walks
to remind us that though all lands are strange to
the mad, there's one we have to get back to as
soon as the blood needle and the little white
stepping stones of lithium allow. At night
I try to recall those lines of his – *I am...*
He's beside me – my only company here.

---

* Robert Lowell was an American poet who lived in England between 1970 and
  1976. He had recurring manic episodes and was admitted to St Andrew's in
  early 1976. John Clare was a nineteenth-century English poet who lived in the
  hospital for the last twenty-three years of his life.

I think of what he called this place: *a foul
Bastille*, and imagine what he must have
daily long endured. There's a soft echo
down the decades of his life here, routines
we have in common, but I know for both
of us it's not just time that colours how
we see St Andrew's. A long century
and more apart, the walls may look the same
but the windows now let in a light that's
different. And I think John Clare escaped
each time he wrote a line, with each poem
dreamed himself again at liberty. This
Bastille is overthrown not by force
but by remaking the broken self anew.

John Clare's beside me in Group Therapy
and he's not quite right. Like me he is
for ever foreign here, at once inside
and outside the room, his dialect too
awkward, impure, odd. The young doctor asks
us to say one word that sums up how we
feel but both of us are dumb. We've made our
lives of words but now they will not come, so
we sit, while everyone manages
to pass the parcel of themselves without
dropping their precious package. Just me and
him now, all eyes turned towards us. He leans
across to me, his soft breath in my ear,
and whispers so only I can hear: *Damned*.

As Clare stumbles on Byron's long cortège
it's as if an England he once was part
of has died. The crowd might mourn the noble
Lord but he is struck by something deeper.
Some might say this ends the Regency but
he sees in the hearse, plumed horses, lines of
carriages, and weeping multitudes
the death of his career, will live to see him-
self snuffed out by a decree, put away
where no one will remember him. As long
as Byron lived he was part of something,
of Poetry, the Fancy, the Times. He
walks away, melts back into the city,
a fugitive now from Fame and Fortune
and tramps the streets alone till darkness falls.

After days of grey skies at last a hint
of sun. The grounds this morning are the green
of billiard tables, and though behind
me stands the hospital, for now I'm well.
Out here there's freedom in the air, as Spring
whispers a promise. I wonder if this
walk was one he took, if year after year
he too felt these stirrings I now feel? I
turn and take the path back to the ward, lost
in my daydream of him, wondering if,
over time, you could ever feel anguish
at Spring's return, your life trapped in a kind
of eternal winter, one day the same
as the rest until there are no days left.

In the portico of All Saints' Church,
Northampton, I sit and wait for John Clare
to materialise. The church is as English
in its way as he is: magnificent
and out of place, its grandeur rising skywards
from the Fenland town I've come to. He'll turn
up I'm sure if only I'm patient enough,
for poets find each other in the oddest
places. And so I haunt the portico,
looking for him in the visitors who
come and go, broad now and balding, the youth
turned squire of no manor or estate. But
he won't be spotted, goes incognito
in the afterlife, fades like words in air.

Poetry came easily when I was
A Helpston lad. Song and sonnets flowed
From my rural pen, and I worked up my rhymes
With the ease of a nightingale singing.
What sweetness then to lift my voice to skies
No cloud could ever blemish, no thunder threaten.
Helpston and its commons was my kingdom,
And I was the bard of all I surveyed.
But I am here, in this Bastille, and all my
Rhyming's gone. Nothing goes with nothing.
And so I try to make my poems lilt
Against the darkling light, a prisoner
Now with no hope of release. They take me
Back to Helpston, my old dreams of freedom.

What if he had escaped, and run away
to London? Perhaps he had help, some old
friend who came to see him, and walked out to
a waiting carriage, where John Clare became
Jack Clarity, Boxer of the Fancy,
a pugilist who when peeled attracted
the admiration and respect of all who
beheld him in the ring. He'd been training
when he was away, shadow boxing in
the airing courts, and now as his coach speeds
back to the capital, Jack Clarity
looks forward to coming up to the Scratch.
But once they count him out the shadows claim
him, and Jack Clarity boxes no more.

He haunts me as I wake, calls himself King
of the Lunatics, tells me this Bastille
has been overthrown, that the doctors
and attendants are all in the cellars
under lock and key. Join me, he says, be
my General. First we take St Andrew's,
then we take McLean's. The nurse comes in to
check us, now the stars are locked away.
We start again. But I've been turned; inside
I'm not the same – I'm his new recruit. First
I'll take St Andrew's. And so I make my
moves, a sleeper who's been activated.
I am his General, he is my King, and
tonight we'll meet once more, set free the moon.

I'll be discharged soon, leave this mad place behind,
its many windows, its Palladian façade,
grounds flat as my mood. I'll not miss the dorms,
the day rooms, or the doctors. At least I'll be
free, not kept here behind gilded bars. And so
I take my leave of St Andrew's, count the hours
till my release, back from the isles I know so
well, that archipelago no sane man sees.
He'll be there, as I walk out the main entrance,
just as he was for a good third of his life.
I'll turn to take one last look, the main building
white against the green grounds, and see him framed in
an upstairs window, looking down at me. Good-
bye he mouths, and for a moment I'm between
two worlds. The door closes, he fades, and I'm gone.

DANCING SLIPPERS

EMILY DEVANE

When, deep inside of you, a beast is growing,
ask yourself this: is it better to fear it, or tame it in some way?
You give it a voice with a wheedling, whining tone
and have it write you a letter, explaining itself.
How pathetic, squatting there inside of you,
trying to multiply without your noticing.

Well, you've noticed it now all right.

You imagine it dancing, with dainty slippered feet,
even though it has none,
because *nodules* aren't the same thing.
When, in spite of the injections of this and of that,
it fails to shrink,
you ask it nicely: *please go.*
But it rolls around laughing,
breaking the needles that try to take a piece of it,
stealing your sleep;
stealing the very heart of you.

The knife is the only answer;
the surgeon wields his instruments expertly,
removing every last bit, leaving nothing but a neat scar.
Now you are no longer connected, you sign a form.
The scientists are interested because of its unusual behaviour,

as if it's an errant child who won't sit still.

You imagine it, like butcher's meat, on a polished white slab, and cannot understand why you feel sorry for it, lying there without its dancing slippers.

OLIVE AT THE GALLERY

SADIE NOTT

He shook her hand as if she was a person, not a mad girl. She was mad, she knew it, or suspected it anyway. You have to be mad to see a psychiatrist, don't you. She smiled at the double meaning in this thought.

'Hello Olive,' said Dr Fry. 'Is that what you'd like me to call you?'

His handshake had taken her off guard and a juggernaut of words slipped from her mouth into the room.

'Liv,' she said. 'No one calls me Olive.'

Her mum always called her Livvie. 'Livvie, love, be an angel and get me some ciggies.' 'Livvie, turn the telly down, it's hurting my ears.'

The kids at school used to call her Olive Oyl.

Olive – what had her parents been thinking?

'I'd wanted to call you Ophelia,' her dad had said years ago, over a Happy Meal that wasn't. 'It sounded beautiful, somehow. Your mum banned it, though. Said it was the name of a crazy girl in some Shakespeare play. So we compromised and went for Olive. It still has the letter O.'

Had she told Dr Fry about all this name business? Sometimes it was hard to know if she'd thought something or had said it out loud.

Liv knew about Ophelia – not the Shakespeare stuff, she hadn't been to that sort of school. But she knew about the *Ophelia* painting. She'd discovered it when she'd typed *suicide*

216

into Google Images. She pressed return and there it was, Ophelia floating in the river, flowers all around her, serene, happy and about to drown. She'd wanted to save it on Pinterest, on the internet pinboard she'd called *Things I Like*. It would have gone well with the other images there – the Tube train all lit up, the Golden Gate Bridge, a volcano in Japan, and a square painted completely black. But the Ophelia picture was too obvious. Like Beachy Head, or Kurt Cobain – the other pictures half of her had wanted to display, and the other half had not.

'Everyone just calls me Liv,' she said to Dr Fry. This version of her name had felt right for a couple of years, but now she couldn't stop thinking about the opposite of living it felt kind of ironic.

Dr Fry went through his checklist questions.

'Have you had thoughts of harming yourself?'

She said nothing, which he took as a yes.

'How often?'

It was impossible to quantify so she gave a stupid answer to Dr Fry's stupid question.

'Forty-two.' The answer to life, the universe and everything.

'What's stopping you from ending your life?'

'What's stopping you?' Liv asked.

Dr Fry smiled. A tricksy smile.

'Take these tablets,' he said, scribbling their name on a green card for Liv to take to the hospital pharmacy. 'And have some time out. I'll write a supporting letter for the university. Go home to Mum.'

Liv could tell he pictured her mum dusting floury hands on her pinny, waiting to welcome Liv home. As if.

In a toilet cubicle Liv popped open the silver foil. She'd never expected the pills would be two-tone. Red and green. *Stop and*

Go, she thought, unsure whether or not to put the tablet in her mouth.

Outside the sky was tank-grey. Liv walked and walked in no particular direction and ended up in Trafalgar Square. She looked up the column's carved ridges, all the way to the top, where Nelson was standing. Nelson or Napoleon, she could never remember which. She imagined herself climbing, spikes on her heels, shinning her way up koala-style. In her mind's eye she clambered onto the high platform and stood, arms outstretched like Jesus looking down over Rio. She saw her imaginary self on the platform, tipping forward, toppling, falling. But she didn't reach the ground.

Perhaps she could find an image of the Rio Jesus, and save it on her *Things I Like* pinboard. Maybe next to the picture of the Golden Gate Bridge. Liv had found that picture when she googled how many storeys high you have to go to definitely die. Google had thought she'd misspelt the word *story*. It brought up an article about a man who jumped from the Golden Gate Bridge and changed his mind halfway down. Somehow he survived and visited schools and colleges telling his story to help stop other people jumping from high places.

A woman was standing in front of one of the glossy black lions. She was watching Liv. Could the woman tell what Liv was thinking? How her thoughts were ricocheting, like a ball of twine, bouncing and unravelling, linking one idea to another, like the silk threads stretched across a dreamcatcher. Half the time Liv felt too visible like this and the rest of the time it was as if she was invisible. The girl who disappeared.

Liv was cold. She could have gone into a café but she would have to speak to someone and didn't trust what might come out of her mouth. Anyway, she hadn't got any money. She'd given away the coins she had to a homeless man sitting with his dog outside the station and then felt guilty about all the homeless people without dogs she hadn't given money to. She looked round and saw the gallery stretched across one side of the square. Somewhere you can be inside. No need to talk to anyone. Warm and free. She went in.

There were circles – Os – in the grills on the floor. Liv wandered through the rooms. People in old-fashioned clothes stared out of the paintings, their eyes following her. A golden O at the pinnacle of a dome pulled her gaze upwards. Letter Os everywhere.

Liv found herself in room forty-two. Her legs ached. She sat. The bench was hard. She could sense the guard behind her. His spectacled eyes. Burning through her skin. Searing two perfect circles onto her back.

She raised her head and on the wall in front of her was Ophelia. *Ophelia among the Flowers* said the notice. It wasn't the picture that was missing from her Pinterest board. This Ophelia was different – she was looking at a huge array of flowers hanging in the air. Blue and blue and blue, and red. White, mauve, orange. Liv decided she would learn the names of flowers. Ophelia had been walking in the misty mountains. She held the flowers in her gaze. And the flowers held Ophelia in their gaze. Ophelia was hazy, almost rubbed out. You might not notice she was in the water. And you'd hardly see the red on her neck. An Ophelia ambiguous enough to sit with Jesus, the Tube train, the volcano, the black square and the bridge in *Things I Like*. An image that said I'm OK as well as I'm not.

Liv wandered downstairs. Some children were going home. Empty chairs. There were a couple of crayons – red and green – and a square of paper left behind. She would steal the crayons.

She liked to steal. Little things, nothing big. She wrote her name, Liv – L-I-V – in thick green crayon on the paper square. An urge, somewhere inside herself, travelled upwards and down one arm and Liv added an E to the paper, a green E after the V. She picked up the red crayon and drew a circle – an O – to join the other letters. Red and green together. O-L-I-V-E. Olive.

She took the paper and crayons and walked towards the exit, past the donations box. She wanted to give something to the gallery. The man with the dog had all her money. She folded the small square of paper in two and posted it through the slot.

Olive walked out of the gallery, down the steps, blinking in the unexpected brightness.

OBJECT

TORY CREYTON

It sits. Unmoved, undusted, unlooked at. In a cave among the shipwreck of discarded tools, the ones not useful enough to have a place, not useless enough to throw away. Bumbled together in a void marked 'maybe'. It sits functionless among silhouettes and shrapnel.

Ornate and silent, it rests. Having opened a door to a room where soft lights flickered and flicked on one by one, if you stopped and looked at them closely enough. And you would, so you could build a lighthouse for the dark.

And the world keeps rippling out around it. It holds a thousand stirrings of unfurling stories to pull into narrative lines. And it was an event. A punctuation, a closing paragraph and new chapter title, carrying characters and lives like portable people.

The lights are on now but we don't know quite where this new home is yet. But it's awake, unslumbered from dance floors and revolving ceilings that were chewed through the night until an alarm clock screamed into the dark WAKE UP.

It doesn't hold the story any more. It sits back, having played its part on stage and now reverently joins the audience on the hinges of the frame. A jigsaw piece that's been clicked into spot for the full picture's tale to keep telling. It holds up the line by taking its position, having brought the spiralling potential melodies of a new opening.

(Object = Library card)

MONTY MODLYN

ALAN McCORMICK

Monty Modlyn hosted a late-night phone-in on LBC in the 1970s. He was warm, cockney-cheeky and consistently upbeat with callers who rang in.

'Monty, I put all the washing in like it said to, and it came out proper mangled. Ruined it was.'

'Oh, sweetie, I'm really sorry to hear that. What's your name by the way, my love?'

'June.'

'June, that's a lovely name, and a lovely month. Now, June, dearest, and I'm not trying to be cheeky, but maybe it's a chance for a new wardrobe?'

'Oh, I don't have money for that. Not since my husband went and everything.'

'Oh, June, I'm so sorry, dear. When did he die?'

'Oh, he's not dead, Monty, he went off with my sister.'

'Ah! Definitely time for a new start, my girl: out with the old and in with the new, as my mum used to say.'

'Your mum was right, Monty, I'll buy a dress in the sales tomorrow. Why not?'

'Yes, why not, my love, and you take care and show a bit of ankle when you can.'

Den, Paul and I were fourteen. It was New Year's Eve, 1975. We were in Paul's bedroom listening to Monty's programme, taking the mickey out of him and the callers, and shutting out the world around us. Even though I giggled inanely, I was secretly seething – how had it come to this? Inwardly I longed for better times, imagining other pupils from school in reverie, dancing and necking the night away.

The numbing comic mediocrity of that night mirrored the years to come in my twenties and thirties after I was diagnosed with myalgic encephalomyelitis (ME). A sentence taken in relative solitary, life happening elsewhere, ceaseless days of drudging melancholy enlivened by snippets of humour and companionship, a life stubbornly endured in the hope of better times to come.

When I first became ill at twenty-six, my friends clubbed together to send me, like an Edwardian lady taking restorative waters, for respite cure at Tyringham Naturopathic Clinic. The residents were moderately wealthy (it wasn't Champneys: here was faded grandeur), often overweight and emotionally fragile, mildly invalided, and occasionally included elusive celebrities seeking a bolthole from the world. A TV star was recovering from relationship upheavals in a suite on the top floor when I was there, and only appeared occasionally at breakfast in a purple chiffon dressing gown and giant sunglasses, to peruse and touch various fruits in a bowl before rejecting them, then disappear up the stairs with a steaming cup of hot lemon water trembling in her hand, her famous red hair aflame and pouring out behind her.

In the ornate gardens, surrounded by statues of Greek gods and marble nymphs, lay the longest man-made pool in Europe. Sun-worshippers sitting around the pool, mainly female, average age sixty plus, were sometimes drawn to the presence of a frail young man in a swimming costume lying by the water but never getting in. I was that young man, and was soon being mothered by various older women, and enjoying the attention. Betty told me about her daughter, who had recently been diagnosed with ME, then also known post-viral syndrome (I never liked that word, 'syndrome'). 'That's what you've got, I stake my life on it!' she said excitedly. 'And what you need to do is give in to it!'

Tyringham was built over powerful ley lines, and attracted shamans, white witches and spiritualists. Betty's friend, a small nervous woman with beetle-black eyes, declared that she was a healer and told me I was a healer too, but that I was too open, and my energies were being drained by negative forces. 'Protect your centre with golden light,' she said, her hand drawing an invisible circle around my bare stomach, 'particularly when your mother is around.'

Not all medics believed ME was a real illness. Fortunately, my GP was more enlightened. He'd read about the condition and when I saw him after Tyringham, he offered the same diagnosis as Betty. The diagnosis, however contentious, would offer some temporary protection and sanctuary. There was a problem, though. I remember an Alan Bennett play shown on television when I was about fifteen. A bourgeois party was taking place in a grand house. A well-coiffed woman strode in and declared with gusto, 'I have cancer!' and, after initial silence, received a smattering of polite applause. Betty was well meaning but also triumphant in her diagnosis, but ME was nothing to crow about. It lacked real legitimacy, no lasting badge of honour would be awarded for fighting it or staying the course, and the controversial diagnosis soon became a curse.

Advice for getting well was so contradictory. Rest or exercise? Fight or give in? Live with the condition or live despite it? Any kind of exercise, even gentle walking, soon exacerbated muscle pains and weakness, but should I carry on and do it anyway?

Later on, medics and therapists suggested carefully graduated exercise as a possible way forward. But for someone whose energy had long gone, and who was impatient and wanted quick results, their strategy was near impossible. In any case, I rapidly found that I could do very little except lie down and fester, and dwell on my symptoms. Even reading was too tiring, my eyesight and brain fogging after a few lines. I was confused, berating myself for not trying hard enough to get well but fiercely hurt and defensive if I was disbelieved or if someone intimated – as a few did – I was faking. OK, bring it on: Pretentious. *Moi*? Paranoid. Who's been talking about me? Hypochondriac. Maybe? But if I were, couldn't I also be ill? Don't know. Well, fuck you, then!

I left my job as a student nurse, and vacated my room in a co-op in New Cross to go back to my parents and their tiny flat in Haywards Heath. My bedroom was only big enough for a single bed and a small CD player. I disappeared into a stupor, lying in bed for maybe twenty-three hours a day for the first six months. Ethereal voiceless music, glorious cascading waves of kora strings, hoots and rumbles of sixties, spaced-out Miles Davis, or deranged celestial whoops and enchanted gobbledegook from the Cocteau Twins' Liz Fraser were a constant, sometimes soothing, occasionally unhinging, companion. My mind would be transported to somewhere else, high, tripping, heat through my temples, my body left for dead on the slab.

I had no choice but to try and sleep my way through, getting up to eat with my parents in the evening, and watch a little television. Dennis Potter's *Singing Detective* took me over and became a totem for my submerged psyche, the convoluted detective plots and blackly comic forties hospital crooning, the anti-hero Marlowe's hot peeling psoriasis skin, his diseased erotic dreams and surreal cinematic suffering, all mingling with my own confused imaginings and disconnection from the real (healthy) world. My parents loved it too (echoing our shared enjoyment of Potter's *Pennies From Heaven* when I was a teenager). We laughed at the incongruity of uptight doctors and nurses dropping bedpans and stethoscopes to suddenly tap dance and lip-synch to Bing Crosby and the Andrews Sisters ('Don't Fence Me In' carrying particular resonance), Dad smiling over at my glassy-eyed infatuation with Marlowe's nurse played by a young, sexy Joanne Whalley.

Listless days in a gloomy half-light were often accompanied by cassettes of books narrated by friends. These included a painfully arch reading of Gertrude Stein's *Blood on the Dining-Room Floor*, and my friend Beatrice's feat of endurance reading, Carson McCullers' *The Member of the Wedding*, in a strange, shaky Southern States drawl, where sometimes she was so tired it became impossible to decipher what she was saying. Words and phrases got lost along the way, but the message came through and I was hooked, twelve-year-old Frankie's story resonating with my own sense of longing and despair. Frankie is bored and trapped by life and becomes obsessed by her brother's wedding and with his bride. Beatrice's drawled narration created a strange atmosphere, another level of recognition and attachment to Frankie's predicament and spirit:

Because she could not break this tightness gathering within her, she would hurry to do something. She would go home and put the coalscuttle on her head like a crazy person, and walk around the kitchen table. She would do anything that suddenly occurred to her – but whatever she did was always wrong ... having done these wrong and silly things, she would stand, sickened and empty, in the kitchen door and say: 'I wish I could tear down this whole town.'

Another friend, Tom, sent a tape of Chinese meditation and breathing exercises, narrated in his deep, resonating actor's voice. From the poem of Fang Sung Kung, Tom spoke evenly and encouragingly:

> With a high pillow I lie on my bed;
> I keep my body comfortable and relaxed.
> I breathe in and out naturally,
> And say the word *quiet* and *relax* silently.
> I think of the word *quiet* as I inhale,
> And the word *relax* as I exhale.

I never got near to the end of any tape before sleep set in, but the familiar voices were welcome, and my friends' acts of kindness made me feel that I wasn't alone and helped keep me going.

I also made tapes for them, endlessly stop-starting cassettes, jamming together 'record' and 'play' buttons, trying to find a feel, a merging flow and theme to the music, carefully nuanced to fit the mood and taste of each friend, tape boxes scattered across my bed, my head zoned in and frazzling. I was moronically obsessive, barely able to talk, let alone take a break for the toilet; nothing mattered more at that moment, and each tape completely exhausted me. Sometimes I'd finish only to find the important final track wouldn't fit (days before digitised music and cue times) so I'd start again, taping over, scribbling again over my cramped spidery writing on the index cover, editing out the guilty overlong track to fit in two shorter ones: Fela Kuti's expansive polemic 'ITT' giving way to Leonard Cohen's 'I'm Your Man', neatly segueing into Al Green's 'Belle'. Damn, J. J. Cale's 'Magnolia' would have worked better. Start again!

Being ill and marking time at home was familiar fare. I'd experienced fevers and pneumonia as a young child in Mombasa, a quiet shuttered room (waiting for my parents to come in and check on me), delirious daytime sleeps held in the safety and relief of cool white sheets, then repeated colds and flus throughout puberty and into my teens.

At school in Sussex, I missed a day a week on average, often Thursdays (double chemistry), occasionally feigning symptoms to encourage sympathy and more time off. I once heated the trusty family thermometer in a mug of tea. The mercury shot fatally off the scale. When I retrieved the thermometer, its end burst and mercury dolloped onto the floor, separating then re-coalescing, then separating again as I tried to scoop it up with a spoon. A line of small silver balls slid under the fridge and I started to panic, fearing mercury was as poisonous as arsenic and as explosive as plutonium.

In the early stages of ME, I contracted pneumonia and was sent to Guy's Hospital. After a week I recovered enough to go onto the ward rooftop terrace. It was like a World War Two TB sanatorium garden, only high up and surrounded by concrete and glass: young men in regulation striped dressing gowns flaked out on deckchairs, basking in the sun, some with eyes closed, no longer moving, as if they were already dead, others chatting and playing cards. I shared a cigarette with a man about my age, sitting on his own. He showed me fine, hard, grey pellets running under his skin and along the veins on his arms and legs.

'I tried to kill myself by swallowing mercury,' he said. 'It didn't work, obviously.' He saw I looked relieved. 'But now they're saying they can't do anything. The drugs to reverse the mercury's flow haven't worked and sooner or later the mercury will collect itself in my heart. And that will be that.'

'Jesus!' I said.

'Exactly,' he replied, with a kind of grin.

The drag on the cigarette made me dizzy and breathless. I gave my pack to him. 'Thanks, and don't worry, it won't be wasted, I'll have plenty of time to finish them,' he said, lighting up another. He added that death would be agony, as his liver was already toxic. Yet he sounded so matter-of-fact, and gave an ironic 'thumbs up' when I left him. His slow, flat voice haunted me for weeks after I was discharged.

When I was a child, Mum had enjoyed my company when I was off school, sometimes colluding in my illness to keep me home. She loved our slow, giggling dances (as did I) when I returned from school for lunch, a frozen Birds Eye TV meal in the oven, Frank Sinatra's 'Cheek to Cheek' circling on the turntable. But when I arrived home from Guy's Hospital, she wasn't there. She'd suffered a breakdown and was recuperating in a small psychiatric hospital in Hove. We visited her in her dormitory, a row of pictures of me, my sister and my nephew arranged on her bedside locker, and while we were there she never stopped crying. But she had close friends in hospital, a strange boarding-school camaraderie, someone to look out for her, and an old woman with long, wild, grey hair came over and hugged me and said she'd been praying for me too. Mum looked on sobbing, and said, 'I love you so much but I'm an awful mother, I should be there for you!'

On her return, she wanted to smother (the extra 's' is mine) me, my illness relegated and merged into her own anxieties, disaster storylines and maternal guilt; the tragedy of the perfect son cut down by a sickness no one understood, and a pitiable mother who was unable to help. After her drugs kicked in, she resurfaced and did her best, an ally of sorts, and we tried to help each other. But Mum's melancholic fateful take on things was dangerous. I tried my best to be practical and positive about my health – it was the early days of my illness, after all – but a heroic yet catastrophic narrative was sometimes hard to resist. I put my own dark comic spin on my predicament, lacing my illness with stories of slapstick medical mishaps and a surreal gallows humour. The comedy of misfortune sometimes devalued things, pulled the rug from what I was going through, and helped cast me as some kind of hapless idiot. But if I was serious and told things how they really were, I worried that I came over as needy and overly intense: one extreme to the other with nothing safe or easily digestible in between.

Mum would wait by the front door of the flat, jumping at it as soon as Dad turned the key to come inside. A catalogue of woe and recrimination would follow, Dad fending her off and walking breathless down the corridor, his energies spent by the time he looked in on me. Once he stopped me in my tracks (just as the plaintive, lonesome whistle was about to blow): 'I'm sorry, I know you're going through it, but I can't listen straight after your mum has had me. I'm tired, but I'll come in later and you can tell me how you are then.' I understood but my eyes smarted with hurt. I'd hear him go into the kitchen where Mum waited with an ensnaring cup of tea, and she was off. After a while came a pained roar: 'For Christ's sake, just shut up!' My own voice quietened in solidarity with his plea for silence.

My sister was worried how Dad would cope with me being ill at the same as dealing with Mum. She said, 'I shouldn't be saying this but' (a kind of introduction that usually warned what was to follow wasn't going to be comfortable) 'I'm really upset about you coming home like this. I know you're ill and everything (everything?) but it's going to be too much for him. It's going to kill him!'

The guilty family story of Dad's heart attacks following a marathon weekend of summer gardening in 1974 still resonated. I remember his flagging energies on that Sunday, regimental lines up and down the garden, the aggravated, guilt-inducing sound of the mower, and his obsessive impatience to get it all done in one go. We determinedly clung on inside, trying to drown things out with the TV ('The Big Match') turned up, feeling bad but also staking our right to relax, to be lazy and not help, justifying inaction with the rationale that it needn't all be done in one go.

Dad didn't die, but after his heart attacks, any time he was late home from work would have Mum wringing her hands and saying, 'He's gone, I can tell, we've just got to get on with it.' Now my sister was worried that my illness and demands would finish him off for good. Life repeats itself, and, like Dad, I have no patience and rush headlong into things, hoping my fragile energies will carry me through. Moving house, I'll frenziedly pack into the small hours for days before, and then have the new house (magically replicating the one before) settled, boxes unpacked and flattened for recycling, pictures hung, kids' toys stacked, books and CDs on shelves, only a couple of days later; and then I let go and collapse.

It's always been my choice to push myself and I've never listened when someone said 'slow down'. Not much changes: I'm writing about past illness while I'm ill with flu, flirting with reality, those loose shadowy sentences and opaque turns of phrase. I've also been nursing my eight-year-old, who's had the same flu, while writing about myself being off school being nursed by my mother.

My first venture out of my parents' flat to an ME sufferers' group was new and yet also horribly familiar: the Sussex village church-hall setting, resourceful flower arrangements ('Can they really be plastic, Vicar?'), Women's Guild posters, Round Table litter initiatives, the generously flowing teapot, Barley Cup (I hate Barley Cup) and Fairtrade instant coffee, homespun shawls for sale for use on frozen, immobile legs. A well-meaning, parochial *Archers* vibe I've always recoiled from. Then the sight of mummified limbs bound in the same cheerfully patterned shawls, sticking out from wheelchairs parked up in the front row, overbearing, anxious parents waiting behind to ride their kids' chariots like Ben Bloody Hur, young women crumpled in the chairs, their deathly pale faces, disarmingly insipid smiles and angry eyes, coiled in on themselves but wanting to shout: 'Understand me, I'm sick, you fuckers!'

Speakers talked about gaining acceptance, applying for disability benefits and where best to buy natural sheepskin pads to prevent bedsores. It was overwhelming, the air full of desperate coping, defeat and hurt, and I wanted to escape. But I listened, my lips slowly separating into the same insipid smile, the hint of a grimace; and next meeting I'd be wheeled in on my own wheelchair.

My rickety collapsible chair was hired from a local charity and was too small. I hated it, and I hated being in it. I felt self-conscious in public, though occasionally I indulged in the mystery and fantasy of a heroic young man (firefighter? Soldier? Or poet?) tragically struck down in his prime.

'Oh, it breaks my heart to see a fit-looking young man like you in a wheelchair.'

'I ain't fit, lady, but thanks for your concern.'

'Oh, you lovely cheeky boy!'

I could stand up unaided and walk a short distance, so the wheelchair was used for journeys over a few hundred metres, to avoid exhaustion and overexerting my muscles. The wheelchair was hard to push and I'd sit rigid, my muscles tensed, my eyes closed (wishing it all away), feeling guilty for making a fuss, always questioning if I should be in it at all: cue the accusatory column ('Monsters Amidst Us') on page seven of the local paper with a picture of a perky, seemingly able-bodied driver climbing out of his Ferrari, which he'd just parked in a disabled parking space. Of course, there were many reasons why his sports car might have qualified for a disabled permit, weren't there?

But tongues like to wag, and if I stood up and miraculously walked from my wheelchair, I confounded expectations. When my friend Beatrice and I arrived on a windy day on Seaford seafront, we couldn't stop laughing, as, first, we attempted to lift the wheelchair out of the boot, and then fold it out and reattach its missing wheels. She pushed off and a front wheel fell away and I tipped forward onto the floor. We were in hysterics. An old couple in a car visibly tutted, and the woman tapped angrily on her passenger side window as if we had transgressed some convention of disabled behaviour and use of mobility equipment. The following week's page-seven headline could have set the letters page on fire.

At my third local ME Association meeting (the second meeting, attended in my new wheelchair, had passed in a fevered blur) I met Adrian. As if attending an old-fashioned introductory agency for the enfeebled, an older woman spotted we were both men and both young, and pushed our chairs together. We smiled shyly at each other, but I detected a welcome energy in his obvious discomfort at being there, a glint of red and anger in his eyes. We ended up talking about music rather than being ill, a mutual way of escaping, and would meet later to swap tapes we'd made for each other, my esoteric tastes for relaxing to kora music and Philip Glass less to his taste than Public Enemy and the wonderful testosterone-filled Soweto beats he made for me. He was new to the game, and I was cast as an unwilling veteran, ready to show him the ropes, but we both preferred to hide from view and neither of us would attend a meeting again.

I hunkered down at home, endlessly sleeping, numbing pain and unwanted thoughts with the prescribed opiate DF118: a low-key medicinal heroin, a soft landing, a warm cave to crawl into, to lie up and wait. Despite its unfortunate effect of bunging me up, it was insidiously addictive and even more soulful than the Valium I used to steal from Mum's handbag when I was a teenager.

I felt so ill and alone in my illness that sometimes I fantasised I might not wake up from a sleep. More often, though, I went to sleep wishing I'd wake up feeling miraculously better. But each day was Groundhog Day and I woke wrung out, a heavy head on the pillow, bones and muscles aching, brain slurring, my vision blurred at the edges.

ME took away my ability to read books. Ironic when I had so much time, but a page would finish me off, words jumbling, my eyes dropping between the lines, white noise, sugar-melt between the letters. Brain scans at St Bart's and St Thomas's would later show that there was neurological damage, reduced blood flow at the brain's stem affecting various cerebral hemispheres and cognitive functions. While brain stamina was reduced and the parts of my brain that took in and utilised information were compromised, the sections of my brain to do with imagination became increasingly stimulated and warped: endless fitful, drooling daydreams and deep REM sleeps full of surreal colour and vibrancy. As soon as I closed my eyes it was like I was tripping, a ready tap of Kool-Aid to turn on and dive into. The escapes were welcome and made up for my inability to take flight in the books still piled beside my bed. They became less taunting and more comforting, the few familiar ones stimulating random flashes of memory, the unread ones offering infinite possibilities and leaps of imagination from their titles alone.

The ME Association magazine clanked through the letterbox each quarter. I eyed it warily: the crude *War Cry* font and cheap paper (before some ME sufferer's celebrity parents raised its profile and turned it all glossy), the black-and-white cover with a young woman in bed, curtains drawn, numerous pill bottles scattered all over her bedside table, defiantly smiling up at the camera from a chasm of pillows. There were some useful advice columns, rallying or pleading letter pages, doctor and therapist trials and regimes, but just flipping through it made me relieved that I couldn't read it properly. Its prosaic drabness, its well-intentioned mantra to gain medical acceptance and its passive-aggressive need to constantly justify and defend the illness filled me with a sinking feeling, drowning in the maudlin hopelessness of it all.

I tried diets suggested in the magazine – the worst and most debilitating being the anti-candida diet (no yeast, no sugar, no wheat, no dairy, no alcohol, no fun) – and I kept to each of them religiously, hoping they'd get me well, but somehow knowing that they wouldn't be enough on their own. In desperation I tried healers, some good, some bad, but nearly all well meaning and doing their best to help. In the right hands, a stranger's light touch over the body was deeply relaxing – skin tingling, breathing slowing down, purple hues through the eyelids. In the wrong hands? Beware the self-proclaimed weekend Reiki Master, because neuroses can also be transmitted through touch!

I learned to compartmentalise my illness, my expression of it, from everyday life. It was safer to unbuckle and let go with a therapist or healer, but less so with people I was close to. If the phone rang, and I was well enough to get up, I'd seek privacy by taking the phone into my room, my reactions initially slow, as if I couldn't remember how to get the words out. Then I'd warm to the task, adrenaline (a sickly, destructive drug in my case) coursing through me so I'd suddenly be wise-cracking, surreally making light of things ('Yes, the wheelchair wheel came off and I practically catapulted into the sea'). My strained laughter echoed how Mum often behaved, switching from the darkest depression with us at home to suddenly screaming with laughter down the phone. Then the light abruptly went out and I was punch-drunk, slumped against the ropes again.

A breakout every few months from the tedium of diets and illness was to really go for it and binge. Vodka! I couldn't tolerate a drink for years, in fact a sip of wine or beer completely exhausted me, but sometimes I would escape to Tom's house in New Cross and drink a Stolichnaya from the freezer in one sitting, my rabid energies unleashed, singing songs at the top of my voice, clowning and yelling it all out.

After a session when several bottles had been drunk, Tom's housemate Ben rallied enough to drive me for my appointment at the London Homeopathic Hospital on Great Ormond Street. Hangovers blissed out everything; no responsibility or need to face up to reality. The car meandered, my nausea turned and rose, and I felt like I was parachuting, enjoying the gravity pull, out of control but somehow safe and not about to die just yet.

In the toilets my piss bubbled and steamed, the cubicle taking on the smell of a doss house. When blood was taken, it spilled apologetically from the side of the needle, watered down and thin, as if from a faulty optic. The phlebotomist shook what frothy pink liquid was left in the tube and said there must be something wrong with the syringe because blood didn't normally look like that! Alcohol, with its false disinhibiting adrenaline, had carried me like a small boat riding excitedly across the waves, to later smash against the rocks and return me waterlogged, retreating into bed for weeks to try and recover, dreaming of the next time.

Beatrice loved visiting me at my parents' flat. My illness, Dad's failing health coupled with Mum's depression, the juxtaposition of a mahogany carved chest, African sculptures and fine Persian rugs crammed into our small flat, spoke to her of faded colonial grandeur, of a family tragically on the wane. Mum came alive when certain people were around and Beatrice was in her thrall as she spun sad tales of her cruel Indian convent, of escapes to the thruppenny seats in the post-war West End. In her later stories, I was cast as the poor gifted son, always destined to be ill. Beatrice smiled fondly at me when Mum said this and then laughed sympathetically when I tried to dilute the atmosphere by making jokes.

Beatrice told me I should write about my illness, the post-colonial malaise that afflicted us. 'That's your story, that's what you should tell,' she said, and here I am, finally well enough, writing it down.

Monty would be proud of me were he still alive, squashing any doubts about baring myself in public:

'Everyone has a story to tell, darling, so why not tell yours?'

'It might not be interesting or relevant to anyone, Monty.'

'Stop with all that, just tell it like it is and let the readers decide, and while you're about it, show a bit of grit, or ankle if there's any to show, people tend to like it.'

ANTAEUS

GARRY VASS

Every day he gets better.
His eyes follow you round the room.
He recognises colours, remembers
the names of the birds,
the duration of his emptiness.
Yesterday,
he realised he couldn't fly.

When he first came here,
we were at a loss. He said
he had X-ray eyes and that
he met the Devil in Safeway's car park.
Presents as depressed. Family gone.
He didn't say where.

He responds to various stimuli:
the patterns on his blanket,
pictures of horses and donkeys,
the music he says
comes from under the floorboards.
We don't encourage him in this.

He's had no visitors, and
reacted violently when
the gardener knocked on the window

to attract my attention to
the profusion of snowdrops in the grounds.
Restraints were called for.

Every day he gets better.
His eyes follow you round the room.
He recognises colours, remembers
the names of the birds,
the duration of his emptiness.
Yesterday,
he realised he couldn't fly.

A CUT TO THE HEART

JOHN MERCER

If you were to ask him, Adam would explain that his contemplative state was brought about by his long consideration of the oak trunk in which he was about to make the first cut. The way a tree is opened determines its future, and the placement and timing of that cut has to be finely judged. He feels a surgeon's responsibility to a venerable patient and a respect for what the wood should become after 100,000 sunrises have ring-locked and preserved its ideal future form – they call this the will of the tree. Adam has been walking around the three-metre trunk for years as it lay in his wood yard. Living with it – as he might say – to discover what inner form lies there. The wood has dried in the moving air, losing weight to the desiccating wind slowly, so as not to disturb the sleeping tensions within which, if roused roughly, will split the wood.

'What shall we make of you?' he murmurs, as he walks the length one more time.

Craftsmen are made from folklore. They sit at the point of transformation and are the agents of change.

Woodworkers like Adam seem older than they are. We can say 'weather-beaten', but let us prefer 'seasoned'. They work patiently with the hand and the eye watching forms ease themselves from the wood and this passivity confers calm, often taken to be a kind of wisdom. Quiet reflection is the juice of his life, and he is served by his leather-strong hands and fingers, taut with wiry sinew with which to hold each moment securely. He is a man who makes obedient decisions.

When he opens oak, turning its book-matched flitches, he does feel himself to be in the middle of a story. He imagines the trace of village life from where the tree stood; shadows from hot summers and tight grain from freezing winds. It is filled with songs from children and birds. Lovers have given it their huddled secrets and the elderly have taken resting moments on the bench to mull the passage of life.

The process of felling and cutting is to appease and release the ghosts with care.

Poor craftsmen with impatient hands cut right in, regardless of the wood-will. Rusty blades meet angry knots and the tree tenses like a wary animal, fearing rough handling; the oak snarls back and, with violent shudders, it splits, refusing to become what it should have been. Some call it sprite-sprung timber.

We give wood character because it is not predictable. We attach metaphors and myths, lest we allow that something bigger is at work. We do not understand life, so we make gods. We know little about nature, so we give her lesser gods and demons who also do not do our bidding. We have swapped our gods for science, but we still touch wood for luck.

It is the year of the felling: age and disease, strong winds and road planning, health and safety have all conspired to doom the tree that has held up the corner of the village green for 300 years. Bent, rusty nails stick out where the council has been putting up posters. Carved deep into the bark is a heart, surrounding

'D+D 1946', and the edges of the bark have rolled forward to form a scar, almost covering the letters. There is a shiny band around the thick lower limb where children have swung on ropes since the tree could bear their weight. The wrought-iron bench, partially embedded in the bark now, sits on a circular path of dusty earth where dogs go round and round just because they can and children hide their eyes in endless games.

On the day. Of a sudden: lorries and hard hats, shouts and cones, tapes and signs and men with chainsaws, confident and big-booted, chugging at the engines, roaring them into life. The foreman arrives. 'He who points' they call him, and he greets a handful of protestors politely pointing them to the council. Then he points to the tree as if to dispel any possible doubt as to why they are there. Lorries strain the chains, guys pull ropes, chainsaws roar and bite at the base of the tree. The carnage is mercifully out of sight behind the tree. Villagers are gathered in a sombre arc a little way off.

And then of that same kind of sudden, the air is filled by silence. The chainsaws are stopped and an arm urges a lorry forwards and a chain clatters into tension and in that silence they see ships' keels and roof beams, floor trusses and boards, wardrobes and chairs, tables and spindles, battens and wedges, shavings and dust bonded in the unity of the form, all falling as one.

Across the road, across the green verge, in an upper-storey window, the shocked faces of Dora and Denis, lightly holding each other's hands, watching as a hole appears and a view they have never seen before opens up. The sky grown bigger.

Either you feel this moment of passing or you don't. Could this have been a good death?

243

*

And now ten years on, the day of cutting. The seasoned timber is rolled onto the bed of the sawmill, chocked and lined up and still; Adam considers that first cut as a jeweller regards the clefting of a diamond.

'Well, what's it to be?' asks the man who will set the blade in motion.

'Give me another minute,' says Adam, sighting along the trunk, one eye squinted, checking where the grain lines up. 'OK. Here.' His hand on the flank like a cattleman reassuring a steer to the slaughter. 'This is the line,' and with red crayon he scores a line of orientation across the end-grain pattern he can read like a fingerprint.

The friends take pry-bars and roll the log into the right position; red line now aligned. The blade shines in the sun then gives a little shimmer as it starts in motion and the lead sawyer pulls the carriage along the bed to begin the cut. Teeth bite into the wood and Adam closes his eyes because all visible things have been set in motion, but there is still everything to hear. The wood cuts well. The blade sings with the sound of sharpness and confidence. Water drips on the blade to keep it cool and the water gathers and soaks the cut surface of the plank, binding the dust to it. A man coughs.

As the cut progresses, the wood tries to close up in the lee of the blade, but the loggers are ready with wedges to keep the wood apart and soon successive flitches are turned open and stacked to the side on sticks to keep the air moving between the flitches. It is like opening a biography.

A crack and a clatter brings everything to a halt. The broken bandsaw blade whisks out of the timber and across the yard like a vicious rattlesnake. Adam will later discover the four parallel cuts on his forearm from a brush with the teeth, but he is too anxious in that moment to notice. They all peer deep into the cut and see the trouble. The gleam of metal.

'It's another one,' says the first man, thumping the bark with his fist. 'Half the trees round here get this. It's the war – they've got shrapnel or bits of Messerschmitts in them.'

'Or Hurricanes,' said another sadly.

'Spitfires maybe?' says another.

'Not round here,' says the oldest, to whom they defer on matters of local history. 'ME 109 most likely. Or flak that got showered everywhere in little pieces. They reckon every tree round here has a little metal in it – either ours or theirs.' He kicks the trunk and looks at Adam. 'So, what shall we do? It's your tree. Another blade will cost £50 and then we may break that too.'

Adam looks at the trunk and says, 'Let's turn it round and saw in from the other end, then we can lift it off the metal.'

'Christ on a bike, that'll take hours.'

'Are we not stout-hearted men?' laughs the oldest as he mounts a fresh blade.

'Arrr – the men of Kent take all the flak,' says the village wit, who pauses and looks around for smiles. 'Well, let's get on with it, but I reckon Adam is buying the beers.'

'It will be worth it,' says Adam. 'The wood is good.'

Either you go on or you stop: the craftsman sees and sees and sees beyond.

They did the cuts, they did the turns and the metal shard slowly revealed itself.

'It's like cutting ham off the bone,' said the man with the pry bar.

The shard, now an upward-pointing finger, was working loose. It's easy to forget that it has its own history, but characterless metal does not carry mystery.

'What is it?'

They gathered round to inspect the metal. Somebody got pliers and pulled it out completely. It was a dull, grey weight with a bright slash where the blade had cut into it. They turned it in their hands, clue-seeking and puzzled. A shape? A mark? A serial number would make it into something definite. Something you could take to a museum and tell stories about – maybe put it on the wall of the pub. After a while, with shrugs, they put it to one side and finished the cutting and as the stacked planks dried, Adam brushed the sawdust from them and discovered the iron stain. He stood back to see the long, purple-brown mark that the metal had leeched into the timber, creating a flame like a memory of its injury, a trace where it had healed, leaving a prized beauty.

'Now what do you want to be?' asked Adam, sitting on a bench, and once more, contemplating.

Either you see choices or you do not.

JEKYLL ADDICTION – HYDE RECOVERY

VICTORIA SHROPSHIRE

Holly was more than a little drunk. She dialled her friend Jeanie and, without saying hello, simply asked, 'Do you want this damn birdhouse?' and fired up the chainsaw.

The plan was to dismantle the four-by-four post on which the copper-roofed mansion for martins sat, casting judgement on the backyard, by sawing it in two-foot increments until it was no more than a stub, planted in cement, a small pine grave marker for her grief.

Earlier that day with Dr Chantrelle, Holly had stated with confidence, 'I'm not leaving my home.'

She had viewed her counsellor with clear eyes and thought about how much money they'd paid him, in addition to Mason's residencies, but the sums wouldn't add in her mind. He'd been their counsellor for over a year, which is enough, she'd thought idly, to pay for two of his kids' orthodontic needs. She had crossed and uncrossed her legs to sit straighter, taken a deep breath, and said, 'I have waited too long. I'm aware.'

Chantrelle had uncrossed his legs and put his notepad aside, then straightened in his chair to match her posture. She interpreted this (rightly) to indicate that this would be their last session.

'You've waited because you love him,' Chantrelle had said. 'It's not wrong for you to love him. Or a version of him. But you should turn to self-care at this point. This river will flow in only one direction, and you can only divert it by so much. He will harm you, if he hasn't already. I suspect he has.'

Holly had listened while spinning the large solitaire on her left hand, the two-carat promise to love and to cherish, feeling the same pinch in the chest that she had felt on her and Mason's wedding day, even as she had repeated the minister's words. This image of their wedding day, her smile thinly covering the exhaustion from the performativity of it all, was the image in her mind now, as she stood with the chainsaw vibrating violently in her hands, sending alarming waves down the backs of her legs.

She could clearly see the adoration in his eyes at the altar, mixed with the complete erasure of the horrible things he'd said to her the night before.

We all drink too much during wedding festivities, she'd told her friends. Especially ones that last for four days and are fuelled primarily by cocaine and bourbon. She had not been naïve. She had also possibly been pregnant. Chantrelle had helped her realise that a baby would not have changed anything; if Holly had been able to carry a baby, Mason would not have stopped being this way, would not cease straddling his cerebral split, would not choose an identity to suit. His passion for her was no match for the hunger that lived in him.

'It doesn't matter how much you give up for him. It will never be enough.'

Chantrelle's words were louder in her ears than the humming Husqvarna. She lifted it to shoulder height, held her breath and connected with the wooden pole, using her left foot to push on its base for balance. Just before its teeth bit, she had a brief vision of blood-spatter. She could lose control of the saw, bleed out in the backyard. Funerals are less messy affairs than divorces.

The last two dresses she'd bought were black. She had wondered around Macy's planning Mason's funeral, because it was one of those weeks when it seemed inevitable he'd kill himself. She'd fingered the fabrics numbly, fantasising about the crime scene. A car accident involving a telephone pole, where no one else got hurt: this was her favourite scenario. She clearly imagined the faces at the graveside. She had already purchased the perfect hat, with a wide brim and a delicate clump of feathers.

'The Jekyll and Hyde routine is too much. I could live with one or the other, but not both,' she'd said, the last time she spoke to Mason's father on the phone.

'He is an addict. You don't get to choose,' Chantrelle had reminded her.

But she did get to choose. She was choosing right now. She was choosing her recovery, not his. She was choosing not to live in fear. She was choosing not to rely on working overtime for avoidance and her dogs for protection. She was choosing a life in which she didn't constantly manage bruises. A life where dinner negotiations didn't dissolve into anyone wielding a Ruger 9 mm.

The chainsaw spat fine flecks of wood into her face; her eyes squinted and her muscles strained to keep the blade running in a smooth, if not level, line. The first cut was the most difficult. She screamed with the strain of it. A loud, visceral noise that made the dogs, watching through the French patio doors, stand and stare with concern. The next pass was easier, the tightness in her shoulders solidifying, fusing with her spine and sending heat down through to her pelvis. The third and final pass with the chainsaw was the easiest, even though her eyes were now streaming with tears and she could barely see. She ground her way through the wood without thought or regret or hesitation, the noise and smell of it a true comfort to her now.

WHAT'S ALL THIS TIME FOR?

FORD DAGENHAM

that
first dry evening
was
righteous but wrong

and long and empty
as anything can ever be

I thought all evening
'what the shit is all this time for?'

it was early autumn
and the cat was on some cheap food
that made his shit stink bad
and I had two bottles
of alcohol-free wine

well they were light and fruity and empty and sad
they laughed at me
and I poured it all away

I lined up herbal teas instead
made them in a big mug like for soup
three four five bags

of Clipper's Organic Sleep Tea

let that lot steep for ages
while I looked at the wall

I sat on the bedspread sipping at the tea

all evening
every evening

and that's as good as it got
for a long long while

LEDGER

MICHAEL LOVEDAY

Happiness? I was trying
     not to feed that traitor.

It's a question of profit
     and loss. I retain the receipts
        from all my conversations.

There's dignity
     in quiet gains. At least
that's how it looks
     from over here.

Don't breathe a word:
     I keep the good days
        hidden under my nails.

RELEASE

GRIEF

ALEXANDER ALI

Two years after my mum died, I had nine and a half years clean at the time, and was at the Monsoon Palace, Udaipur, India, on the second anniversary of her death, December 2014.

The sun set on my grief
There is more now than pain.
Loneliness and emptiness too
The hills, valleys, lake and city
All continue.
As have I, as has grief
Now is enough.
Time to move on. Live again.

THE SPECTRE

DEBORAH MARTIN

Cold hands can hide tiny suns.

When I became sick several years ago, it felt as if my life had been gripped by a pair of cold, unyielding hands. Although my symptoms were frightening, they were by no means the worst part – the worst part was that I had no idea what was wrong with me. Neither did anyone else. Yet I couldn't see at the time that my illness was also a gift, one that would eventually offer warmth and illumination. At the time, I just wanted it to go away.

The year that I got ill, I was a decade out of university. Yet life had stalled for me for many reasons, the recession being the main one, mental health another. I ended up unemployed, living back with my parents and fairly adrift. So when I got offered a marketing role at quite a sober legal organisation, I accepted it, despite my doubts.

Every day I took the train from my suburban home town to a placid office in Glasgow where I edited articles for the organisation's website. And every evening, on the train home, I kept my nose pressed against the window for the entire journey, too distracted by the view to read my book. I'm not sure what I was looking for – some glint of golden light from a secret doorway perhaps, a place where real life pulsed, amber and hot. All I knew was that my own life wasn't real, but just a beige waiting room that I was trapped in. I couldn't remember the last time I'd written a story or a poem, because I was convinced that to be a real writer, you had to have a real life. So until my life became tangible, until I could hold it in my hands and feel its weight and its breathing and its heartbeat, I couldn't write.

Then, in early summer, I became tired in a way that I just couldn't shake. This tiredness wasn't cured by sleep, for my dreams were a bruised, choppy sea that left me worn out. I would go to bed drained and wake up drained, each day passing by in a blur. And before too long, the pain started. A deep ache in my muscles, a stiffness in my joints. It became hard to walk and even harder to climb stairs. Every movement was laborious and often accompanied by dizzy spells. The world seemed to chafe against me, all roughcasting and iron railings.

Worst of all, a grey cloud had settled around my skull, making it difficult to think. It was if my thoughts were tramping, slowly and wearily, through a thick, murky haze. This was the part that really scared me, the fogging of my mind, as it was entirely new to me. I was watching my thoughts from behind a veil: they were like pale moths, beating their wings weakly against muslin curtains.

Sometimes I was so tired that I actually had to command my limbs to respond; I would stare at an outstretched arm and think, *Move*. More than once I had to lift my legs off my bed and place them, one by one, onto the floor. I spent a lot of time in that bed, sometimes crawling beneath the sheets as soon as I got home from work. Yet rest didn't help at all. My body was shutting down; it had lost its operating manual; the lights were dimming. Sleep, that basic function, was beyond me. Sometimes I lay awake all night, close to tears and in a smog of fatigue. Yet the insomnia felt like a symptom of the overall sickness rather than its cause. The cause was a mystery.

The illness had begun imperceptibly. It was as if a drab, dank mist had slowly seeped into my skull, diffusing through my bones, nerves and ligaments. Then one day I realised that my exhaustion had become a constant state. I would try to rest, stretching myself out unmoving for hours on the broken-springed sofa bed of my childhood room, but I never felt refreshed. Until then I'd taken rest for granted; it hadn't occurred to me that there might be some knack to it that could be lost. I was the music-box ballerina whose clockwork had worn down, who could still spin, but sluggishly and to a fragmented tune, gazing at her reflection through a mottled mirror.

When I tried to relax I would find myself in a panic, mind racing, convinced that I was seriously, perhaps terminally ill. With the help of the internet I convinced myself I had all of the worst diseases: a brain tumour, leukaemia, multiple sclerosis, myalgic encephalomyelitis (ME), or perhaps some obscure autoimmune condition that only chose six out of 6 billion, with me being one of them. Up until then, I'd never been a hypochondriac. Perhaps I still wasn't. If the symptoms are real and debilitating, then is it fair to label your fear hysterical? But of course, the fear made my symptoms worse.

My illness had no clear cause, no defined beginning and no sign of an ending. As the months dragged on there were just bad days and worse days; days when I made it to work and days when I didn't; days when I sat at my desk and did nothing, and days when I was fairly productive. When my sick days away from the office started to equal the days spent there, I began to wonder if I would eventually be unable to work. What then? Would I be trapped in my family home for ever, confined to the worn blue sofa bed, staring at the lifeless street outside, a dead weight to everyone around me?

As for my parents, they had their own troubles at the time. There were tensions in their marriage, my mum was struggling with depression, and they were both looking after my younger brother, who has cerebral palsy. I think they wondered what would happen if I ended up incapacitated too – would they have the resources to care for both me and my brother? They were worried about me – they loved me, but their worry often expressed itself as frustration and panic. What was wrong with me? When was I going back to the doctor? When was I getting more tests?

Others in my life just seemed bewildered. When you first develop an unnamed illness, people behave strangely around you. Some just avoid the issue – they'll recite a few platitudes then keep their distance until you're back to normal. Others will assume that you're an attention-seeker, in it for the drama. Still others will want to rescue you, assuming your illness is caused by some deep-seated spiritual flaw.

For instance, after a particularly bad week, I decided to contact my friend Esther, who was at that time training to be a Christian missionary at a church in California. Esther was a person of peaches-and-honey sweetness who resembled a Tommy Hilfiger model merged with a Christmas-tree angel. Next to her I'd always felt lacking, flawed, awkward. Yet she'd always been a good friend, so I sent her an email telling her I was sick, and after a while I got a reply. It was short.

'It's good that God is bringing this up with you: it means you're being raised to a place of wholeness', it said. I reread her email, hoping that I'd missed some words of comfort somewhere. I'd wanted Esther to say, 'That's a nightmare. You must be so scared. I hope you're OK.' Instead I'd got a mini-sermon, a holy diagnosis.

And all the while, I was trying to find answers. I can't remember how many appointments I attended at my GP surgery, how many blood tests they took, how often I sat in the waiting room with its scratchy brown carpet, cheap vinyl chairs and stern poster announcing '36 appointments missed last month' in red felt-tip pen. Whenever I had to call for test results I'd grip the phone tightly, my stomach lurching while the receptionist went off to check, before the inevitable reply of, 'Sorry, the results aren't here yet, try calling back tomorrow.'

In the fog of it all, I can't remember exactly what conditions they tested me for – I'm sure anaemia, thyroid issues and blood disorders were included – but every result came back negative. And with no diagnosis, there could, of course, be no treatment. So I sought alternatives.

That's why, one Monday morning, I found myself sitting in the drab, cramped anteroom of a local church, where I'd come for a weekly faith-healing event. I'd never been to it before, but I hoped that somehow it might calm my fear. I sat between two silent elderly ladies, one with a middle-aged daughter in tow. The daughter was losing her hair, the few remaining reddish-brown strands tied in a thin ponytail, wide pink patches of scalp exposed. I wondered if she'd been losing it for years or if it was a recent thing. Her flat expression, sagging posture and shapeless dress indicated the former. Had she ever been out dancing? Been on a date? Been in love? I felt suffocated by it all, the atmosphere of hopelessness. It was a relief when a door finally swung open and two volunteers walked in, a man and a woman, both grey-haired, wiry and dressed in jeans.

'We're sorry, we might not have time to see you all today', the woman said, surveying us. Four was a crowd there, it seemed.

It was then that I burst into tears. The volunteers quickly ushered me through a door while one of the old ladies tutted at me for skipping the queue. I was taken into a church hall filled with rows of stacked chairs. The three of us sat down in a cramped corner while I apologised for making a scene. I'd come for some miraculous word that I wasn't dying, but now I'd made an annoyance of myself. I was taken aback to see that they were smiling at me kindly. For the first time in months, my panic was met with understanding.

They listened, laid hands on me and prayed. And in acknowledging my right to panic, they set me free to feel calm. This was what had been missing from my GP appointments – a simple act of kindness, of communion. A medicine that wasn't medical.

How different from the young, newly qualified doctor I had seen at my GP surgery. Tall, fidgety and cocksure, he didn't look up when I entered his consulting room, nor did he look at me at all when I sat down across from him. Instead, his eyes stayed fixed on the worn manila folder that had been my medical file since birth and contained a clutch of scribbled notes detailing tonsillitis, skin allergies and iron deficiency. He fired a few rote questions at me.

'You might have to accept the fact that you're depressed,' he declared eventually, still not looking up.

'I don't think so,' I replied. 'I think I would know if I was depressed.'

'Yes, but you still might be,' he said.

It's true that there was a history of depression in my records, one that went back over a decade, so his assumption wasn't outlandish. Yet I knew what depression felt like and this wasn't it. Yes, I was unhappy. Yes, I was frustrated and angry and scared. But I wasn't depressed, for depression was a deadening of self, an absence of feeling. Instead I felt alert, coiled, driven. When I was depressed, my mind said, *I wish I was dead*. Right now, my mind said, *Please, please, please don't let me die*.

So I was not depressed. Or rather, if I was, it was of a different kind than I'd ever experienced, for it had bypassed my mental processes entirely, taking up residence in my bones and joints instead. Was this what he was implying, that my physical symptoms were really just emotional malaise? Yet his manner put paid to the notion that he might be delivering some sage-like insight, for he never once met my eyes. And anyway, wasn't this rather a dated scenario, didn't it have a whiff of the 1980s about it, the doctor telling the seriously fatigued patient that really, it's just psychological? For that reason, I couldn't take him seriously. This didn't mean that he was completely wrong, necessarily. But there is a subtle difference between a real, physical illness that has been triggered by unhappiness and a physical illness that is actually imaginary, that is 'all in your head'. I'm not sure he understood that difference.

On my next visit, for yet another blood test, I saw a different GP. He was a veteran of the practice, originally from the North of England, charming in a world-weary, ruffled sort of way and pretty much everyone's favourite doctor. He hadn't started out that way, though – I'd heard that when he first joined the practice he'd had a reputation for being rude and arrogant, but everything had changed one weekend when he'd gone down to Sheffield for a football match. That had been the day of the Hillsborough disaster, when ninety-six people had been crushed to death. As a doctor, he'd been a first responder to the injured and the experience had changed him, made him softer. Patients tended to feel safe around him.

After he took my blood, I rolled down my sleeve and asked him the question I'd been dreading.

'So, do I actually have ME or chronic fatigue syndrome, or whatever you call it?'

He looked at me from beneath hooded eyes and shrugged in a way that was soothing rather than callous.

'If it's CFS, it's no big deal, we'll manage it,' he said. 'We'll just get you on a programme of light exercise every day until you get better.'

No big deal. We'll manage it. His words, his manner, his use of 'we', all lifted my burden. The fear of this particular diagnosis loosened its grip on me. No big deal.

After that visit, I decided I'd try the exercise idea, even though I still didn't know if I actually had CFS. I knew that putting my body under strain was a risk, but I also sensed that my self-enforced rest, the early nights, the avoidance of activity, could have actually been making me worse. So I started to go on a short run every day, listening to music and pushing through the pain in my limbs. And as my parents lived at the edge of town, I'd sometimes go for strolls into the countryside, marvelling at how quickly suburbia could shift into a deep, hushed green.

More importantly, the void of uncertainty I'd found myself in forced me to acquire a skill I'd never learned. It was a skill I didn't realise other people had, that I didn't even know was necessary to life. That skill was the ability to talk to myself kindly, reassuringly, soothingly. It started one night as I lay in bed, staring up at the ceiling in panic, imagining the worst. I paused, took a deep breath, then told myself:

'You're all right. You're getting better. You're getting stronger. You're healing.' I whispered it over and over, the words a warm balm melting inside of me. In that moment I had wrestled back some control over my illness – not the symptoms themselves, but how I chose to think about them. For although I couldn't tell if stress was the cause of my condition, I knew that stress was

263

definitely making it worse. So from that moment on I vowed to be my own source of comfort. For a long time my head had been crowded with a trio of wretched voices: the critical voice, the anxious voice, the despairing voice. But this new one told me that I was fine, even when I was ill. It told me that I was enough just as I was. It told me that I would heal. Or rather, I told all this to myself. And after that, I cancelled my next set of tests, letting go of the need for answers right then. And I handed in my notice at the job that had been making me so miserable.

Looking back, the most painful part of my illness wasn't the physical or mental symptoms, or even the fear, but actually the regret. I knew that if my condition turned out to be permanent, progressive or terminal, then I had wasted the best part of my life. That's because I'd lived it as a false self, a scared self, an imposter. I had left so many stories and poems unfinished, so many parts of myself abandoned. I was desperate for a second chance.

Thankfully, I got one. Because after a few months, I started to get better, as slowly and imperceptibly as I'd become ill. The pain and exhaustion gradually faded, as did the brain fog. I think a big part of it was when I began to reclaim some of those abandoned parts of myself, the parts of myself that sought enchantment. I found a suitcase of my old dresses in the loft and started wearing them again. I revisited books and films that I'd adored as a child. Music came alive to me once more, and some songs were scarlet threads that I could follow all the way to my heart. I fell back in love with fairy tales.

I learned a little bit more about compassion too. One day, at the beginning of my exercise regime, I went out for a walk and passed an elderly man going in the opposite direction, moving in exactly the same slow, stiff, cautious way that I was. *I finally understand now*, I thought, and I was ashamed at all the times I'd felt impatient at an older person for moving too slowly in front of me. But I also knew that when it came down to it, I didn't really understand at all. I had a chance at recovery but the elderly man did not – his journey was irreversible. Before, I'd taken my health and youth for granted, but I knew that if I got it back I wouldn't do that again.

In the end, I never got a diagnosis and in the end, it didn't matter. Because it turns out that you don't always have to name the foe to defeat it – sometimes being willing to waltz with it is enough. I learned to co-exist with uncertainty for a while.

I can't pretend that my life transformed overnight when I got better, or that I stopped making mistakes, but I can say that I definitely changed. I became a lot less willing to compromise on my dreams and a lot more determined to take myself and my writing seriously. And when the first creeping symptoms of fatigue have occasionally appeared again, I've taken that as my cue to be kinder to myself for a while. After that, the symptoms quickly fade. It's kind of a gift, in its way.

I think that what mattered overall was that I chose faith. Faith that everything was just as it should be. Faith that I would get better. And most importantly, faith that even if I didn't get better, I was still a person of value in the world, that just being alive was enough. In the end, my life itself was the sickness that needed to be healed.

When I first became ill, it was as if some pale, grey ghost had draped herself around me like a damp raincoat. She was both heavy and weightless, and I couldn't seem to cast her off. And who in fact was she, but the angry ghost of myself? The me who had been drowned, again and again, in the bitter waters of my neglect. The me who did not want to spend her days proofreading legal articles in a cramped office, but wanted other things, all of them different, all of them at once. She wanted to wear vintage dresses and scarlet lipstick while working in the offices of a cool arts magazine. She wanted to sip espresso at a pavement café in Paris while writing sparse, elegant poetry. She wanted to sit at a worn oak desk in a woodland cottage, crafting dark fairy tales by candlelight. She wanted nothing at all that I offered her, for I could offer her nothing. And so she had left me and, after a period of aimless drifting, had settled back upon my shoulders, for where else could she go? She was part of me, but she was no longer skin and kin with me. And I, in my lost state, had no idea how far I was from the life that she-and-I wanted. A whisper of distance or an infinite walk? I couldn't tell. And because I couldn't tell, I couldn't move forward.

Of course, at the time, I wasn't able to survey my illness from a serene vantage point and see the spiritual malaise that lay beneath. All I knew was that my body wasn't working, that I was frightened and that I wanted answers. It's only now I can see that the dark and thorny knot at the centre of my sickness was nothing more than me.

Cold hands can hold tiny suns. My illness was a frost that settled upon my life, frigid and unforgiving. But it also forced me to learn to warm myself from within and that's one of the greatest gifts I've ever received.

The ghost of my dream self is still with me, of course. She still haunts me. But these days she's less of a grey spectre, less inclined to sap my spirit. Instead, she's the silver sylph at my shoulder, urging me onward, onward. Urging me to hold my pen tightly and never let go.

VODDY'S CIRCUS

JOHN PEARSON

Here I am again, pushing the week's shopping, standing in the queue at the German Shop. It's cheap – everyone knows it. I look at other people's trolley contents and wonder about life expectancy. The line of people snakes towards the till – past the spirits display.

Now… how does it go? I remember, it's a bleeding circus, Zippo's revenge; all I have to do is look straight ahead. I feel my hands sweat. It's uncomfortable. The cool trolley handle helps. I grip it tightly, blanching my knuckles.

The bottles look like water – 40 per cent Russian names. I can feel my mind swim in this ruddy circus – the checkout lady eyes me with suspicion. She's wearing a black top hat, has thick puce lipstick, a bright red waistcoat and a black, tailed coat. She picks up a whip and points at me. My feet aren't right – too big. I'm wearing giant clown shoes. Vodka bottles on the shelves are clattering and clapping. I need music… quick.

It's in my head. I'm the clown. I'll do anything to keep me from the crowd. The band must play on or the ringmaster will see through me. She's dealing with other acts – lion tamer, juggler and girls riding bareback horses. The 40-percenters are laughing at me; they clink, open their arms to me. Keep the music going. I can feel my hands slipping. The checkout lady smiles – all teeth, eyeshadow – full of happiness. The 40-percenters still wave. *Come back, we love you.* I need more music to bounce around my crappy skull.

My turn at the checkout. Her eyes flash, as if asking me, *Have you forgotten something?* I'm standing there in big, bouncy clothes with fluffy cannonballs for buttons. I reach into my pocket and pull out money like a flurry of petulant petals fluttering onto the checkout conveyor belt.

At last I can walk out of the ring. *Have a nice day!* I wish I had a hooter on my trolley as I stomp towards the exit. The music recedes into an echoing distance as the theatrical curtain of the automatic doors swishes open. The 40-percenters' cries are far away now. I turn and bow: *I thank you.*

THE WORD

KATE BROWN

The word bounces and giggles. She watches it walk across the surface of the kettle. She has never been so scared of it before, so certain it's intent on causing her harm. With an effort that hurts her temples and both sides of her head, she blinks. The word vanishes.

She stares at the kettle, surprised, challenging the letters to come back. They don't. Instead, her reflection; the chair she's sitting on, her elongated face, crossed legs, one slightly elephantine. She adjusts the leg so the curve of the kettle reduces it to normal size. She can't do anything about her face.

The stack of empty wine bottles in the corner. She starts to count. Hardly believes it, feels sick, flicks a strand of hair out of her eyes. This movement hurts just as much as blinking did. She's off her guard for only a moment, but that's long enough. The word is back.

This time it stretches out across the draining board towards the kitchen sink. She can't read what it says, but she knows it's laughing at her. It's wiggling its hips. It is, dare she think it, sexy. She bows her head and turns her attention to the scrambling detail of the patterned lino floor. By disappearing inside herself, perhaps she can confuse the word, make it think that it isn't important to her.

She's got its very nature wrong. The word is an attention-seeker. It snakes down from the draining board, across the floor and up her leg. It oozes multiplying letters, taunting her. Now she can read it. Now the word has become words.

You should have known better.

She looks at the wall, burning with shame.

She should have known better.

The tickling feeling round her ankles subsides. She starts to sweat; a good sign. When she is absolutely sure she is alone, she takes a breath and relaxes the fingers she's been clenching into fists.

Once, when her hangover was finally in retreat, she tried to write down every letter that had ever persecuted her. It was simple, really: they always formed the same words, the same accusation. She hoped that, by listing the letters, by putting them on view, she could exclude them from her heart.

NOTES ON DARKNESS

ELLEN HARDY

March 2017

The house is quiet; perhaps you can catch a dream yelp from one of the dogs if you strain your ears. It's an old house, with its own ancient orchestra of creaks and settlings. After 400 years, the floorboards hold the memories of so many footsteps it seems hardly disruptive to think you hear a tread on the landing, even long after the last of the day's goodbyes.

This isn't a specific memory. It could be a weekend, or I could be working from home. Perhaps my partner has just popped to the shops. Anyway, there's no one else here. This is a positive pleasure – I like being alone, perhaps too much sometimes. In this non-specific memory I've remembered something I need to get from upstairs and am focused on it, perhaps turning over an idea about work with another part of my brain. Up the uneven but neatly carpeted stairs towards the bedroom, then I pause and put my hand on the brass door handle. The shift happens in an instant, and though by now I recognise it for what it is, I find it is possible to completely disbelieve your rational self. So although I try my best, my heart fills with frightened blood and hot sweat pricks at the small of my back. Somehow I am convinced that on the other side of the door, a horror awaits. Not any old monster under the bed, but a specific vision: a rope slung over a high beam and a garrotted body strung beneath it, slowly turning.

I wait by the closed door, trying to push the vision away. But *don't be ridiculous* has no meaning here. I throw the door open and rush in, scanning the room rapidly from corner to ceiling. It is, of course, empty – the duvet covers twisted in familiar disarray. I sit on the bed and let the horror fade; like a dizzy spell it will pass quickly, and afterwards I will feel strangely normal. I know this, but I still feel suddenly exhausted. I want to call my brother, but things are different now. I don't need to worry about him twenty-four hours a day. So why am I sitting here, trying to excise the vision of a hanged man from my head?

June 2015

The bus from Inverness is almost always empty. You might see a spiky teenage couple or a woman struggling with a pram, occasionally a lost tourist. Once a narrow-eyed skinhead with a spiderweb face tattoo, reeking of beer. Today the driver mutters something incomprehensible at me as I pay in cash and I smile vaguely, hoping it didn't require a real response. I find myself on rocky ground here, linguistically; as I sidle past groups of men in town I sometimes play 'Scottish or Polish?' in my head, attentive to the outer edges of their consonants and syllables, but am often stumped for the answer until I move closer and catch an entire word or phrase. After nearly six months living by Loch Ewe on the north-west coast, John says the Inverness accent is ugly, harsh – but I can't tell the difference. I haven't spent enough time in the Highlands.

The bus lumbers from central Inverness to housing estate to industrial backwater with an unhealthy electronic wheeze. By the time it's climbing the hill beyond the city I have stopped worrying whether it will make it around the next bend and am preparing myself for the day ahead. I get out of the bus at the hospital – nodding cautiously at the driver – and walk down the gentle curve of tarmac to the well-spaced one-storey buildings. The wards sit at the end of long corridors that stem from a silent central entrance hall, a light-filled linoleum space that also has a gym, a therapy kitchen and the consultants' offices. From above, the complex must look like the illustration of a chemical compound.

I walk through the entrance hall and turn left along the corridor to John's ward. It's only been a few days, but the staff know my face and they buzz me through. Through the swing doors I pause, taking in new faces in the armchairs facing the TV that's fixed to the wall somewhere to the right of my head. Hardly anyone here looks or acts mad, at least not straight away, but there is something vegetable in the collapsed quality of those puffy pyjama-clad forms, as if they've been upended in their chairs from plastic shopping bags.

I spot John through the glass, sitting at the battered picnic bench in the middle of the courtyard. He's talking to Arch, another resident, and the sight of their two red heads together makes my chest hurt. I take a breath and head for the door to the courtyard, open it. I miss John's smile because I'm concentrating on Arch, who lurches to his feet and barrels towards me with his arms outstretched. He has very dark brown eyes that almost hide the pupil, and I'm slightly mesmerised by his blank face as he bears down on me. But he only wants a hug – and a cigarette. I'm smoking again, hard.

'Getting on all right with Arch, then?' I say to John, as we head towards his room to collect his things.

'Honestly, he's the nicest guy in here,' he replies.

'Do you know what he's got?' I ask, not bothering to try and phrase the question properly. John doesn't, so why should anyone else?

'Schizophrenia, I think. He mentioned something. He seems all right on his meds, but he's a regular.'

We sign out of the ward; John is my responsibility until 5 p.m. My eyes linger, as ever, on the wound at his throat. The metal staples are gone, but it's still an angry raised welt from ear to ear. It's hard to imagine it will ever fade.

'The staff are really confused by you,' John says, chuckling. 'Apparently most people here hardly ever get visitors.'

I wonder about this, later, after John has been discharged and returned home to the south. When I'm sleeping on a mattress outside his room, or hovering just beyond his line of vision while he works or walks or stares into space. When he's howling with pain that has no physical cause. His crisis was short and sharp; our lives changed for ever, but we are lucky. My mind skirts other possibilities – the hospital regulars, the under-equipped, the abandoned. Those who do not recover. It's hard not to think, *There but for the grace of God.*

September 2016

We squint at the sycamore, debating its last hours on earth.

'Are you sure it won't fall on the house?'

'I think I can manage that.'

'I know you can, I just – look. If you have to hit something, aim for the vegetables, OK?'

'Got it.'

'Are we sure it's late enough in the season?'

'I don't have to do it this weekend.'

'No. No. It'll be fine. Thank you, really.'

'It'll make a big difference.'

'Yes. So much more light!'

It's a young tree, a self-sown sapling that has suddenly started to loom large and inappropriate by the low wall of the back garden. When you step back and consider it, its size is meaningful. Its branches have a ballerina's reach, far beyond expectations. It is as if it has heard of other sycamores, standing graceful and globe-shaped in open English fields, and is determined to reach its fullest expression. It has to go.

John hefts his chainsaw – bought specially for the occasion – and starts to trim away some of the smaller branches. I watch for a while as the mess of obliterated greenery starts to build up on the ground, and I can smell sap. Then I retreat to the kitchen and start taking things out of bags and putting them in the fridge; olives, cheese, Prosecco. It's only been eighteen months since the hospital, and every time John visits I find myself putting together a celebration. I am celebrating, although I do not say it, the fact that he is still alive.

The tone of the chainsaw changes from snap to grind; I know that John is slicing a wedge from the nearside of the trunk, pacing around it, slicing again, waiting for it to reach tipping point, seeing which way it will fall. There's a silence, then I hear a shout. I run back outside to see John gesturing wildly and yelling. 'Push it away! Push it away!' The tree is swaying, fatally unbalanced, its leaves fluttering to the rhythm of a deep internal rupture. I clamber up on the low wall and put my entire weight against the trunk, levering myself off the stone because I know the strength of my arms alone is inconsequential. I lean in, away from the house, inhaling fresh-cut wood and bruised leaves, the gritty bark rigid against my unprotected hands. The sycamore groans once, and falls – not cleanly, wrenching slightly on its trajectory towards the grass, but away from the house. John and I whoop and howl as it goes. The change is instantaneous – as it tips over it tears open a new square of sky and the whole garden seems to breathe more freely.

This new expanse is a pleasure only until the tree hits the ground. As the top branches whiplash off the grass, a bird blasts upwards from the fallen sycamore with an outraged clatter of wings – pale grey, taupe, a flash of something dark. A collared dove. I know them well enough from the garden, there are several pairs who croon to each other from the rampant ivy and – yes – the self-sown sycamore. But it's the middle of September now, the tail end of a long, hot summer. There shouldn't have been anything nesting there at all.

John has already moved on to stripping the tree down further, his professional efficiency. You can see why estate managers love him, even if he is incapable of performing the same trick for himself. Sometimes it seems perverse, to be so universally admired and so utterly lacking in self-belief. But that's the way it works, isn't it? I move towards the branches that held the dove, half hurrying, half holding back. There should be a word for this feeling – there probably is, in Japanese or German. I have the definition ready: the faint hope that your fears are not going to be confirmed, barely competing with your absolute certainty that they are. There's the nest – a loose, dry fretwork of twigs and leaves, more of an assemblage than a structure – and beneath it, inevitably, the chicks. There are two of them and they are, I see straight away, hopeless – wrinkled, eyeless pink lumps with the graceless outlines of an inverted elbow, smeared with a patchy coating of greasy yellow hair. They remind me of foetuses, and dinosaurs – I can see the bulbous blue shadow of their organs through their skin. Nevertheless I swoop on them, only picking up the faint peeping sound they're making as I gather them unresisting into my palm.

'Look,' I say to John. He comes closer and his eyes soften, but he turns almost immediately back to his task. I am the one making this a problem. But I choose to insist. 'Would she come back to them, do you think? If I put them somewhere safe?'

John looks around, only giving me half his attention. He will not get upset about this. And why should he? Doves are common. It will be the third nesting of the year. To say that worse things happen would be too obvious.

'I don't know, Lizzie. You could give it a go.'

That's all the encouragement I need. I pick up the remains of the nest and chivvy the chicks back in. I find a lidless piece of Tupperware in a drawer and put the nest in it, then cast around for a suitable spot, eventually settling on a sheltered fork in the apple tree and wedging it firmly, imagining it's obvious enough for the mother dove to find. Then I go back inside and start calling bird sanctuaries. I find myself ridiculous – all this fuss for a couple of pigeons – but from the familiar ache in my diaphragm, I also know that I don't have a choice.

By early evening, the garden is quiet. John has cleared away the remains of the sycamore, divided the trunk into logs and stacked them in the shed to dry out for fires the following winter. It's one of those warm, rose-blushed late summer evenings, edging into autumnal chill as the sky darkens. Standing at the sink, beginning to think about closing the door into the garden, I can hear the mother dove outside. She has spent the afternoon flying back and forth across the garden, not calling, merely bereft. John has noticed my misery and even put a gardening glove over the chicks to try and keep them warm, but I am by no means sure this is helpful. Do doves have a sense of smell? I shake my head and close the door, pour Prosecco. John is upstairs, cleaning up after the garden, so I sit and take a mouthful of wine. Everything is briefly quiet. Then I hear it – a high, reedy screaming, the sound of baby doves calling out as the colder air starts to numb them away to shrivelled skin and toothpick bones. From far away, it seems, I can see the Prosecco bubbles mincing their way up the sides of the misted glass in my hand, can firmly instruct myself to connect this observation with the whine and hiss, but I seem to have developed a kaleidoscopic internal filter – turning, turning and fracturing everything into screaming.

October 2017

It's well known that some languages have expressions that are unique to them: the smell after the rain, for example, or the feeling of pleasure at someone else's misfortune, are not ideas that have precise equivalent terms in English. Eskimos, children quickly learn, have over a hundred different words for snow. *Kummerspeck* in German describes the difficult reality of weight gained during times of sorrow – or, if you're going to be deliciously literal, *grief bacon*. The Japanese have *bakku-shan* – a woman who is attractive from behind, but a sorry disappointment when viewed from the front – while Arabic gives us *ya'aburnee* – the wish to die before your beloved, because you cannot stand the idea of living without them. The final nod must go again to German, that most elegantly muscular language with its relentless composite words. *Backpfeifengesicht*, perhaps appropriately unsightly on the page, describes a face badly in need of a fist.

After my brother tried to kill himself and very nearly succeeded, I was presented with a surprising new conceptual lack. It wasn't one I had ever thought of before, let alone expected to live so acutely. How could I express – in English of all things, a language belonging to a culture so exquisitely ill at ease with emotion – the fact that I appeared to be grieving for someone who was still alive? Who would believe such a thing?

No two suicidal depressions are the same. This uncertainty places an almost unbearable strain on those responsible for someone whose psychological state is, has been or might soon become a danger to their own lives. In the very thick woods of a mental health crisis, the advice from professional organisations can seem so non-specific as to be insulting. *Are you concerned about a friend or family member?* ask leaflets in subdued colours. *Are they more than usually withdrawn? Are they sleeping more?* You who are propelled into the centre of a battlefield, searching around desperately for some body armour and a really effective tank, are offered the therapeutic equivalent of a nice cup of tea and a chat.

In our intensely medicalised society, we learn that there is a specific and identifiable physiological root to every ailment, and that more often than not there is a sophisticated medical intervention that can alleviate or cure the problem with a reasonable degree of success. The chemistry is understood. But when the brain of a loved one turns on itself, this miraculous certainty disappears. You are not prepared for the fact that there is no quick release. The bandage does not come off in ten days. The course of medication is a stab in the dark. The symptoms may or may not come and go at intervals of weeks, months or years. The diagnosis, prognosis and treatment are, to all intents and purposes, unknown. The only thing you can be completely sure of is that the person you once knew, the one you could rely on unthinkingly to remain in one piece from day to day, no longer exists.

Two and a half years after John's attempted suicide and hospitalisation, I still search his face for the telltale grey tinge and desperate eyes that show he is struggling. Far too often, that's exactly what I find. His medication mostly allows him to function, but the illness that overtook him that day may linger for ever. I am no longer anxious or grieving in quite the same way, but alert, as I always will be, for signs that the darkness may win again.

BOTTLE GIRL

LOIS L. HAMBLETON

Your mother thought
perhaps of nightshade you had sipped,
or drained a leaden mug full of the Devil's piss.
Yes, that was you, my dearest girl,
my useless eyes were forced to view
a sad demise of me and you.

A veiled lady shook your arm
Forgive me now I mean no harm,
a drop for you and some for Him
and nothing more will hurt within.
Strange your way has always been
but I will make what's seen, unseen.

The nurse removes the detox tube.
Your speech, unslurred, departing
fumes release a sweeter breath.

Two years, now passed, of course I watch,
though you are joyful in your new-found bliss.
And I, reprieved, relieved that you,
once mine and murmuring fair
of childishness, no longer dwell
within that foetid rot, the bile,
withdrawal's bright-green vomit cup.

The endless bottles stacking up.

The times you tried so hard to stop.

I see you now with steady gait, relief,
the pride that holds your body straight.
That veiled lady you no longer see,
unholy mother, gone, dispelled in me.

Don't fear the chinking, clinking sound
as bottles still are all around...

Sing now of freedom.

BETTER

LAURA PEARSON

One day you will wake up and it won't be the first thing you think about. You might notice the weather, or speak to your partner, or reach for your infant child. You might do all three before you remember. That will be a good day. You will be telling your illness that it isn't the most important thing, after its lengthy dominance.

That day you might feel something other than bitterness when you look at your ravaged body. You might feel something closer to pride. Or just acceptance. Acceptance would do. When you get out of bed, you might be stiff and weak, but you'll be stronger for standing. Remember that everything takes time. Every step is a small triumph. Reward yourself for surviving, for living.

One day you won't remember the names of the people who treated you and the critical dates of your illness. You'll feel sorry about that, at first, but then you'll realise that it means you've come pretty far. It means it's behind you, getting smaller. And while it will never be completely out of sight, it will reduce to a speck, and a speck is nothing to be frightened of. No one was ever defeated by a speck.

It's possible that you'll have to go through it all again. Not now, but at some point. Thinking about it makes you feel tired, but if you have to do it, you'll do it. You did it this time when you thought you couldn't. You have no idea what you're capable of. Try not to think about it. It's a waste of your energy, and it might never happen. If it does, think about it then. Save your energy for fighting.

In the darkest part of the night, when you stand beside your child's bed and you can hardly breathe for the weight of the love you're carrying, be still. This is what you did it all for. You deserve this. If your child snuffles and turns, seems likely to wake, reach out your hand and place it gently on her forehead. She will settle. You are all she needs to feel safe.

And on the days when you cry like the world is ending, don't try to stop. You've been through something difficult, and your body and your mind are still adjusting. Let them adjust. Give them all the time it takes. Remember that you are better. Not in the sense of being fully recovered, but in the sense of being better than yesterday, better than the day before.

LAST ORDERS LADIES AND GENTLEMEN, PLEASE

JOHN PEARSON

So, you've gone then?
At last I've licked
your limpet-like grip
from my lost life.
I've no regrets.
Though I was frightened
I knew you had to go.
Beckoned and banished, sent
to an open sore of a grave
full of mildewed, midden-made fermentation
frothing with false faithfulness
and ice-cold fire.

You, canker-close friend,
now divorced and deported,
you leave a vacuum
which I fill to the brim with relief –
I have prised the rusty shackles
of your evil grip.
Though you may still play
with my woeful, weak mind
I have new supreme strength
to sever the jaundiced umbilical noose

you once used to make me swallow
your sallow, snake-like charm.

MATT'S SONG

HELEN RYE

Somewhere in the mess of space, the hidden languages of cells, the human race, there's a song sung over you, and you are more than this. You are more than the sum of the veins collapsed, of the shame the morning after, of all those times he beat you. You are more than a guy in a wet sleeping bag in the car-park stairwell, a kid in a stranger's bed because there's nowhere else to go, more than the things you did and those words they said to you. You, you child of stars and the universe, are more than a woman dumped bleeding out of the car with none of the money he owes you, than the one with the tablets to keep down the voices that say such painful things, than the thoughts that burn acid tracks inside your head and will not leave you.

You are the phoenix that, now fallen, will rise again to fledge outrageous feathers out of dirt and ash, the butterfly whose fragile wings grow veins of tempered steel, a fighter, survivor, the rage of rivers at flood, the quiet, tender shoot that, growing slow and dogged, unspectacular, shatters through concrete and tar and turns its leaves defiantly to unimagined sun. You're a fucking unsung superstar and you can do this thing; you can take this moment and lay it down end to end with the next, and then another and another. And the bright skies and moonlit nights and sunny days and rainbows may be other people's dreams, but there's a little shine of that ahead for you too, somewhere, sometime, and then you'll get to make your own. I promise you. I promise. Because there's a song sung over you, and you are more than this.

MIRACLE OF SOBRIETY

MAGGIE SAWKINS

You bow before
the empty glass
that was made
to be filled
with liquid lightning
and cannot consider
water as replenishment
for your thirst,
so the empty glass
remains more
redundant
than the umpteen
empties
in the back yard
as the soul goes
running on empty
to the sanctity
of the altar
of wine
and the goblet
half-full
with ruby lightning
the goblet that can
with a single sip
of its miraculous

contents
quench the thirst
of one without thirst
and set on fire
the thirst of another.

YOUR REACTION TO *THE SOPRANOS* FINALE (I'VE BEEN TRYING TO REMEMBER OUR LAST CONVERSATION)

JAMES O'LEARY

You thought more should have been revealed: you felt cheated by the ambiguity. You were found dead in Stephen's Green. I no longer crave answers from endings.

ACKNOWLEDGEMENTS

Thank you, Hackney Recovery Service, WDP and St Mungo's for allowing us to go in and teach creative writing to your service users. Particular thanks to Alex Gostwick, who was so supportive throughout with regular supervisions and sitting in on all sessions. When Alex left, Flavia Marlin stepped into his place and was instrumental in letting us continue our teaching there.

Huge thanks to the Arts Council for giving us two grants, without which none of this would have been possible. ACE's support allowed us to continue teaching at the recovery service when we were no longer able to teach on a voluntary basis, and funded our nationwide callout for submissions. Our funds also went towards the artistic production of this book and various events. Thank you again Alex, for helping with the applications, Tory Creyton too. Thanks to Tom Mallender both for teaching poetry sessions to the service users, and for your advice on ACE applications. We are very grateful to poet Ruth Valentine for stepping in to help choose the poetry for the anthology with her discerning literary eye.

Thank you, Spread the Word, for your publicity support in 'spreading the word', and to Dominique de Light for a fruitful phone conversation that helped support our vision for the future.

Thank you to those who enabled us to host our successful events, particularly Francesca Baker for excellent events management, and to all those who volunteered to stand at the door and help put away chairs! Thanks to Housmans for the use of your bookshop, and St Margaret's House, Bethnal Green.

Thank you also to all our readers and panel members: Rob True, Susannah Vernon-Hunt, Astra Bloom, Tory Creyton, John Pearson, Michele Kirsch and Sadie Nott. Thank you to all our contributors for your patience and commitment to the project, and particular thanks to Sadie Nott for your brilliant idea of compiling a reading list. Thanks also to John Pearson for contributing one of your artworks.

Lastly, a special thanks to our friends and family, for your continued support and generous pledges to help make this dream a reality.

WRITERS

Alexander Ali, thirty-nine, married, father, Devon dweller via London, and English-Pakistani heritage. Dog owner, nature lover – been continuously stepping up to life on life's terms, one day at a time, since 2003. Grateful for a life beyond anything he could comprehend as a busted, broken manchild.

Julia Bell is a writer of novels, poems, screenplays and essays. She is also the course director of the MA in creative writing at Birkbeck, University of London. Her first novel, *Massive*, dealt with issues of food and drug addiction and she is interested in the usefulness of creative-writing practice as a tool for improving well-being. Her latest long-form essay, *Radical Attention* (Peninsula Press, 2020), also deals with the addictive nature of some aspects of digital culture. You can find out more about her work at www.juliabell.net.

Astra Bloom's writing kept her going during debilitating illness, bringing her joy, relief and healing. In 2015 she won the Bare Fiction Poetry prize. She has also come second in the Brighton Short Story Prize, and won the Brighton Flash Fiction Prize. Other shortlists and commendations include: the Bridport Prize, the *London Magazine* Essay prize, the *Mslexia* Novel Award, and the Bristol, Sunderland and Waterstones Prizes. Her poetry is printed in journals including *Under the Radar* and *Magma*. Her memoir features in *Common People*, an anthology of working-class writing.

Kate Brown is a filmmaker and writer. She has spent many years trying to figure out how life works without using any substance to hand to create an alternative reality. She's concluded that writing is the answer. Her films *Julie & Herman* and *Absolutely Positive* have been shown at film festivals and on television in Europe and the USA. She also made a short documentary for BBC *Newsnight* in 2016 about access to hepatitis C treatment. Her short stories have been published widely. Her first novel, *The Women of Versailles*, was published by Seren Books in 2017. Kate lives in Berlin and was recently awarded a 2020 work stipend for non-German literature by the Berlin Senate Department for Culture and Europe. She is using the time to write her second novel.

Gary Bryan was a member of the creative-writing group at Hackney Recovery Service/St Mungo's. He is an ex-intravenous drug user – IVDU. In December 2017 he nearly died and needed emergency open-heart surgery because of a bacterial infection caused by drug use. It was a massive turning point in his life and he's now over three years free of heroin, crack and cocaine. Writing has helped him to process what happened because, as it turns out, nearly dying saved his life. Despite struggling with a number of health problems as a result of his past drug use, he is studying for a degree in horticulture and hopes to work in community gardens aimed at helping other people with mental health and addiction problems. Gary believes strongly that addictions are coping mechanisms for past trauma and pain: a normal response for some people who can't cope with everyday life.

Eileen Carnell is a teacher and university lecturer with an interest – politically, professionally and personally – in many aspects of health, especially mental heath. Understanding the power of learning to bring about change, she has supported classroom groups of young people and their teachers to examine ways of focusing on issues to do with people's relationships with food. At a personal level Eileen has attended counselling and therapy sessions, both in groups and individually, to support recovery in her own and other people's lives. She feels it is important to keep older people's issues on the agenda, as so often eating disorders and body image are considered to be the concern of young people only. Eileen believes that writing and personal reflection are key to recovery.

Alan McCormick lives with his family in Wicklow, Ireland. His experience of long-term illness has helped shape his writing: an outsider's view, always rooting for the underdog. He's been writer-in-residence for the stroke charity InterAct Stroke Support. His fiction has won prizes and is widely published, including in Salt's *Best British Short Stories*, *Cōnfingō*, the *Sunday Express Magazine*, and online at *3:AM* and *époque*. His story collection *Dogsbodies and Scumsters* was longlisted for the 2012 Edge Hill Prize.

He has just completed a memoir, *Holes*, and his second story collection, *Wild in the Country*. See more at www.dogsbodiesandscumsters.wordpress.com.

Tory Creyton believes that addiction takes up a huge amount of wasted time. Through a series of fortunate incidents something new came along at the right moment, something as simple as reading and writing. It offered a completely different way to explore difficult 'things'. Writing makes it possible to put the formless into form. Then you can sculpt it into something calm, or messy or stupid or sad, or anything you want.

Francesca Baker is a creative and curious individual with a love of words. She sees recovery as something to work towards, encompassing all aspects of life – mental, physical, social and spiritual. As Virginia Woolf said, 'my head is a hive of words that won't settle'. So she puts them to use, exploring the world and then writing about it. Her day job is journalism, copywriting and marketing – more words, then – and her business is called And So She Thinks. You can follow her on social media @andsoshethinks.

Ford Dagenham's childhood anxiety led to teenage depression and adult alcoholism. His discovery of alcohol in quantity was a eureka moment, and he felt free enough to develop a poetry habit and was published on several now defunct poetry websites. His chapbook *A Canvey Island of the Mind* was published by Blackheath Books somewhere in his thirties while working for the NHS. Two decades and a dozen ignored breakdowns after his teenage eureka moment he got himself outside of the booze (and associated pick-me-ups and put-me-downs) due to an escalation in his depression and a massive decrease in buzz. In the light of sobriety he fully noticed his depression, anxiety and drinking, and how it had informed his writing and life for years. He has since had his poetry published by Poems-For-All and in *C-O-N*, *Razur Cuts*, *Glove* and *Paper & Ink* magazines. He was most recently published in the chapbook *Judas-hole* by Tangerine Press and in the Grist anthology *I You He She It*, published by Huddersfield University. When he's not writing, he's most likely photographing toys or the sky. You can visit him at hatchbacksonfire.blogspot.com, where he posts new work daily.

Claire Dean's short stories have been widely published, and also included several times in *Best British Short Stories*, an annual anthology. Her collection *The Museum of Shadows and Reflections* came out in 2016. Claire struggled with alcohol dependency for several years. Recovery has meant trying to recover from the reasons why she was drinking. It's ongoing, still scary, but worth it.

In June 2016, two months after moving to Yorkshire, **Emily Devane** was diagnosed with breast cancer. Finding solace in picking up a pen, she wrote in hospital beds and waiting rooms. Words became a way to process her darkest thoughts – and to escape them – during her treatment and recovery. Emily has since won awards for her short fiction, including a Northern Writers' Award, a Word Factory apprenticeship and the Bath Flash Fiction Award. She teaches creative writing and is an editor at *FlashBack Fiction*, an online journal for historical flash fiction. This is her first published poem.

John O'Donoghue was diagnosed with 'manic depression', as it was then called, as a teenager back in the 1970s. He was sectioned five times and spent time in a therapeutic community, a large hostel for homeless men, squats, the streets, and Pentonville Prison, where he was remanded when unwell. His life turned round when a worker in a halfway house helped him apply to university. He now lives in Brighton with his wife and four children and is a lecturer in creative writing. His memoir

Sectioned: A Life Interrupted (John Murray, 2009) was awarded Mind Book of the Year 2010.

Jamie Guiney is a literary fiction writer from Northern Ireland. His debut short-story collection, *The Wooden Hill* (published by époque press), was shortlisted under Best Short Story Collection in the 2019 Saboteur Awards. Jamie's short stories have been published internationally and he has been nominated twice for the Pushcart Prize. In 2010 he suffered a debilitating virus. The road to recovery was long, ending with Jamie and his wife walking 580 miles across Spain on the Camino de Santiago in 2013.

Lois L. Hambleton is a retired further-education lecturer from Birmingham. She completed an honours-level creative-writing module at university as part of her degree studies and used literature resources to aid her teaching within inner-city rehabilitation units. She found that adults suffering and recovering from mental ill health and addiction issues always responded well to poetry-reading groups and creative-writing sessions. When her own daughter became addicted to alcohol about seven years ago, the impact upon the family was devastating. The frightening events that led to her eventual collapse, hospitalisation and detox will never be forgotten. She is over five years into recovery now and all her family are very proud of her.

J. L. Hall is a Scottish writer living in Edinburgh. Her essays, travel writing, life-writing and short fiction have been published in print and online, including in the *24 Stories, Tempest, Wanderlust* and A. M. Heath/TLC *Free Reads* anthologies, plus the forthcoming Patrician Press short fiction collection, as well as on Booksbywomen.com and Imustbeoff.com, and in *The Mechanics' Institute Review*. She has been the winner and finalist in several international and national writing prizes. J. L. Hall lives with PTSD and believes that writing creatively but safely about fictional and real trauma can be healing. She is also a creative-writing teacher and mentor, exploring place, nature and well-being.

Polly Hall has been published in various anthologies and online e-zines. She finds the natural world especially healing and a great source of inspiration. Find out more about her novel, *The Taxidermist's Lover*, and other writing projects at www.pollyhall. co.uk or @PollyHallWriter on Twitter.

Ellen Hardy worked in digital media in Beirut, London and Paris before returning home to Oxfordshire in 2016 and studying for the MA in creative writing part-time at Birkbeck, University of London. She graduated in 2018 with distinction and in October 2019 joined UEA as a CHASE-funded postgraduate researcher in creative critical writing. Her fiction has been published in a number of anthologies, most recently the *Brick Lane Bookshop Short Story Prize*, and she has been shortlisted for the Myriad Editions First Drafts prize.

Nada Holland was under contract with the Dutch publisher De Arbeiderspers, and a reporter and cultural critic for leading Dutch newspaper *NRC* in the US, before completing a UEA/ *Guardian* Fiction Masterclass with Gillian Slovo and a Gold Dust mentorship programme with Jill Dawson. Her work has appeared in the *Asia Literary Review* and John Bird's *Chapter Catcher* and she was recently longlisted for the Lucy Cavendish, *Mslexia* and Bridport novel awards. Her debut novel *Motherborn* was published by Lendal Press in February 2021.

Kerry Hudson was born in Aberdeen. Her first novel, *Tony Hogan Bought Me An Ice-Cream Float Before He Stole My Ma* was published in 2012 by Chatto & Windus and was the winner of the Scottish First Book Award while also being shortlisted for the Southbank Sky Arts Literature Award, *Guardian* First Book Award, Green Carnation Prize, Author's Club First Novel Prize and the Polari First Book Award. Kerry's second novel, *Thirst* was published in 2014 by Chatto & Windus and won France's most prestigious award for foreign fiction, the Prix Femina Étranger. It was also shortlisted for the European Premio Strega in Italy. Her most recent book is *Lowborn*, a non-fiction exploration of the legacy of poverty. *Lowborn* was a Radio 4 Book of the Week and was longlisted for the Gordon Burn Prize and the Portico Prize and shortlisted in the National Book Token, Books Are My Bag Reader's Awards and as a Saltire Scottish Non-Fiction Book of the Year.

Stephanie Hutton is a consultant clinical psychologist and writer who works with people in recovery from psychological and medical trauma. Her immediate family lives with the consequences of heroin addiction. She has been shortlisted for awards including the Bristol Short Story Prize and Bridport Prize, and won Best Novella in the Saboteur Awards.

Anthony James was born in South Wales in 1956. Between the ages of three and seventeen, he suffered violent abuse by a brother nine years older; in his mid teens he began to drink alcohol to excess. Nevertheless, his poems, short stories, reviews and essays were published in a large number of journals. He graduated with honours in English at Swansea University as a mature student in 1991. Anthony's own experience of violent abuse led him to a lifelong sympathy with feminism and the liberation of women. His books *The Happy Passion: A Personal View of Jacob Bronowski* and *Amputated Souls: The Psychiatric Assault on Liberty* were published by ia (Imprint Academic) in 2011 and 2013. In May 2013, he was hospitalised because of liver disease caused by excessive drinking, which was expected to prove fatal. However, he recovered and began work on *Orwell's Faded Lion: The Moral Atmosphere of Britain 1945–2015*, published in 2015. He is currently working on a volume of memoirs called *Victim of My Own Arrogance* and a series of short stories reflecting life in contemporary Britain.

Angela Jameson is nearing completion of her first novel and has a few other projects on the back burner, including scripts for radio and screen. She likes to explore the hidden fault lines we all have, which become raw and exposed at moments of weakness and pressure. 'More in Common', her story in this anthology, reflects how the human flaws that lead to addiction aren't always the sole domain of the addict. She writes at www.angelajamesonwrites.com and tweets as @writerlyanj.

Ruby D. Jones was born in the South Wales Valleys during the 1984 Miners' Strike. She now lives in Cardiff and works as a freelance non-fiction editor. Her writing has appeared in the *Guardian*, *Mslexia*, *The Mechanics' Institute Review*, *Hippocampus*, *The Moth* and others. In 2019 she was awarded an Arts Council grant, won the Queen Mary *Wasafiri* New

Writing Prize (life-writing category) and was placed in the Center for Women Writers' International Literary Awards and the Fish Short Memoir Prize. She is currently working on an essay collection on the themes of addiction, desire and the body. She tweets, sporadically, @RubyJonesWrites.

Nicola Jones is a white, working-class, queer, femme woman. She is in recovery for bulimia, binge drinking, trauma and bereavement by suicide. She has written stories and kept a journal since she could first string sentences together. Her creative writing is sporadic but imperative. She works with the LGBTQI+ community, running queer youth groups, and is also a sexual health outreach worker delivering sex and relationships education to young people.

Peter Jordan is a recovering alcoholic. His debut short-story collection *Calls to Distant Places* won the Eyelands Short Fiction Prize 2019. You will find him on Twitter at @pm_jordan.

Adam Kelly Morton was born and raised in Montreal, Canada, where he now resides with his wife and four children. Since beginning his recovery on 28 January 2008, Adam has worked extensively as an acting teacher, freelance writer, filmmaker and actor. His writing has appeared in Spelk Fiction, The Junction, *The Fiction Pool, Cabinet of Heed, Talking Soup* and *Open Pen*, among others. He is working towards an MA in creative writing (distance learning) at Teesside University.

Angie Kenny is a writer and teacher living in Las Vegas. Although the setting for her story 'Protect Me From What I Want' is Los Angeles, Angie's relationship with recovery and the main characters began twenty years ago in New York City. Addiction takes many forms. But sometimes the only way to help those you enable is to set them free.

Michele Kirsch has been making up or embellishing true stories most of her life. After a thirty-year career in journalism, she started writing her memoir *Clean: A story of addiction, recovery and the removal of stubborn stains*. Published by Short Books in 2019 to great critical acclaim, it went on to win the Royal Society of Literature's Christopher Bland Prize for a first book from an author over fifty. Interweaving the story of recovery from a long addiction to prescription drugs with stories about cleaning flats in east London, the memoir touched a nerve not only for those with experience of addiction and recovery, but also those who like nothing better than a gleaming skirting board. She is currently working on a second book, set in foetid, murderous, mid-1970s New York City.

James O'Leary is a poet from Cork. His chapbook *There Are Monsters in This House* was published by Southword Editions in 2018. He was selected for the Poetry Ireland Introductions Series in 2017 and his poems have been broadcast on RTÉ radio. He has written and directed several short plays and his poetry-films have been screened at festivals in Ireland, Scotland and Canada.

Michael Loveday began writing aged twenty-nine, when his 'midlife crisis' arrived a little early. Writing (journalling, poetry, life-writing, essays, fiction) has been crucial to his recovery and well-being ever since. His flash fiction novella *Three Men on the Edge*, about three men struggling with life and relationships in the London suburbs, is published by V. Press (2018) and was shortlisted for the 2019 Saboteur Award for Best Novella.

Scott Manley Hadley is satire editor at *Queen Mob's Teahouse*, an online literary journal. His publications include the poetry collection *Bad Boy Poet* (Open Pen, 2018) and the chapbook *My Father, From a Distance* (Selcouth Station Press, 2019). He was highly commended in the Forward Prizes for Poetry 2019 and he blogs at TriumphoftheNow.com.

Deborah Martin is a writer living in Glasgow. She was a finalist in the Fish Short Memoir Prize 2018, a co-winner of the FrightFest screenplay idea competition 2017 and a finalist in Poetry Rivals 2016. Her short stories, poems and essays have appeared in various collections. She has also written and performed in two stage works: *Broadcast* and *Rise*. Her writing has featured in video art, on radio and on podcasts. She has an MA in creative writing from Birkbeck, University of London and is currently working on a short-story collection.

John Mercer talks about creativity as a spark that can ignite a range of materials. These materials might be wood, words, sounds or paints, all of which can be used in the realisation of an idea. As a multidisciplinary artist, he is constantly looking at what it means to recover things – sometimes from memory, by recycling, or from ideas in old notebooks and bringing out histories. For example, every piece of wood used by a sculptor or cabinetmaker already has a story within it. A writer is acutely aware of the interconnectedness of all these things.

Andy Moore was one of the original members of the St Mungo's creative writing group, alongside Susannah Vernon-Hunt. 'Down and Down', one of two poems by him included in this anthology, emerged from the group.

Robin Mukherjee has written for television, radio, film and theatre. His most recent film, *Lore*, was critically acclaimed worldwide, winning many awards. His original drama *Combat Kids* was nominated for a BAFTA. He is currently adapting Paul Scott's (Booker Prize-winning) novel *Staying On* for cinema, supported by the BFI, and *No Destination*, by Satish Kumar, also supported by the BFI. His book *The Art of Screenplays: A Writer's Guide* is published by Kamera Press, and his novel *Hillstation* by Oldcastle Books. He is Course Director of MA Screenwriting at Bath Spa University.

Sadie Nott began creative writing in 2014. She has won a Creative Future Literary Award. The opening of her coming-of-age novel was selected to feature in the TLC Free Reads anthology and was shortlisted in the York Festival of Writing, DHA Open Day and Retreat West competitions. Her short stories have appeared in LossLit, The Book of Godless Verse, *The Selkie* and Liar's League. Her fiction is informed by her own history of psychological troubles. The writing process of exploration, elaboration and communication often makes her feel better at the end of the day than she did at the beginning of it, which is recovery at its simplest.

John Pearson, an amateur artist, writer and poet, is a member of Havelock Writing Group, Portsmouth Poetry Society, Havant Poets and participates in many city-based projects, including writing for Portsmouth's radio soap, *Conway Street*. John has been published in *South* and was highly commended in the Carers UK poetry competition with a very tender poem about caring for his mother. 'Last Orders Ladies and Gentlemen, Please', included in this anthology, was written during the early stages of alcohol recovery as a cathartic piece to help him express his relationship with alcohol and subsequent sobriety. Now 1,600 days sober, John is working on his first pamphlet collection.

Laura Pearson is a writer who lives in Leicestershire with her husband and two young children. She is the author of three novels. In 2016, she was diagnosed with breast cancer while pregnant with her second child. She's now recovering, one word at a time.

Helen Rye has won the Bath Flash Fiction Award, the Reflex flash fiction contest and third place in the Bristol Short-Story Prize. She is an editor at *SmokeLong Quarterly* and at the literary journal *Lighthouse*. She worked for ten years in homelessness and addiction/recovery. Her immediate family has been affected by addiction and loss.

A legal professional, **T. K. Saeed** took a break from writing technical documents to complete a course in creative writing. She has used creative expression as a means to heal from themes of depression and addiction in her own life.

Lane Shipsey is a writer in recovery from the accident of being a woman.

Maggie Sawkins has been writing poetry since the age of nine. She lives in Portsmouth where she delivers creative writing projects in community and healthcare settings. Her live literature production *Zones of Avoidance*, inspired by her personal and professional involvement with people in recovery from substance misuse, won the 2013 Ted Hughes Award for New Work in Poetry. www.zonesofavoidance.wordpress.com

Dr Victoria Shropshire is a derelict debutante, with a vulgar yet devoted following primarily composed of her best friend Autumn, her brother, and her father-out-law. (There might be a few others.) A writer and researcher, whose expertise focuses on the impact of inherited narratives on identity (re) construction, she is currently working to publish her debut novel, a fictionalised memoir in which a derelict debutante struggling with a chronic illness is rescued by Dobermanns and drag queens. Her own drag persona, Miss Hap, has not been seen for decades, but might make resurgence in order to boost book sales. (Times are tough, after all.) A cancer survivor with a wicked sense of humour and a truck-stop vernacular, Victoria is a lover of dogs, cigars, books, beaches, jigsaw puzzles, Netflix, and all things halloween. Her pet peeves are seahorse birdbaths, cypress clocks and velvet paintings of Elvis. She is always looking for new disciples at www.derelictdebutante.com.

Rob True was born in 1971. Unable to read or write very well, he left school with no qualifications. His wife taught him how to use paragraphs and punctuation when he was forty and he began writing stories, which have been published in *The Arsonist Magazine*, *Open Pen* magazine, *Low Light Magazine*, *Occulum*, on the Burning House Press website, and in *Litro* magazine. His book *Gospel of Aberration* is published by Burning House Press. @RobTrueStories on Twitter.

Garry Vass spent nearly twenty years as an academic, teacher and researcher. At the same time, he was addicted to drugs and alcohol – self-medicating anxiety and depression. After several crises, he changed direction and entered recovery. Garry credits the continuation of this recovery to writing and reading poetry.

Susannah Vernon-Hunt started taking heroin in her early twenties. This, and most other drugs, tracked her for the next thirty years. Sometimes she managed to stop and have fragments of a kind of life, but never for long. Then, after a stint in rehab, she put down everything for some years. She was happy, and her family greatly relieved. Deceptively, alcohol trickled back into her life, and in the blink of an eye, full-blown alcoholism. She found herself more desperate than ever before, but found her way to WDP, a charity helping people affected by substance misuse, affiliated with Hackney Recovery Service. With a brilliant counsellor, and Lily Dunn's exciting creative writing course, which inspired this book, she moved out of shame and isolation, and began her journey, back into life. She continues to keep up with the writing group at Hackney Recovery Service.

At the age of twenty-five, an urge to write gave **Annie Vincent** a reason to stop drinking. Initially documenting a troubled past, she is now writing a full-length work of non-fiction focused on the morally dubious things we do to get by in life, even when we seem to know better. She lives in London and works in social housing. Twenty-five years later, this is her first published story.

Katie Watson is a writer based in Liverpool and has worked in the charitable sector for over eight years. She is also studying to become a psychotherapist. In 2018 she was selected for a scholarship to train as a writing guide for Write Your Self, a global writing movement aimed at supporting women to reclaim their stories after experiencing trauma. In the same year, her poem 'There is a Problem in My Home' was published in *The Bell Jar*, an anthology of writing based on mental health. In 2017 her poem 'Toast' came runner-up in the annual *Mslexia* Women's Poetry Competition, and she also performed her work at the Edinburgh Fringe Festival as part of *That's What She Said*, a spoken word event run by For Books' Sake. Her work focuses on themes such as mental health, identity, feminism and LGBTQ+ experiences, and she is currently working on a novella.

Unbound is the world's first crowdfunding publisher, established in 2011.

We believe that wonderful things can happen when you clear a path for people who share a passion. That's why we've built a platform that brings together readers and authors to crowdfund books they believe in – and give fresh ideas that don't fit the traditional mould the chance they deserve.

This book is in your hands because readers made it possible. Everyone who pledged their support is listed below. Join them by visiting unbound.com and supporting a book today.

Annabel Abbs
Jools Abrams-Humphries
Timothy Ades
Farah Ahamed
Liz Ainsworth
Kathryn Aldridge-Morris
Abi Allanson
Kim Allen
Lulu Allison
Sheila Allsopp
Deborah Alma
Marie Alvarado

Edie Anderson
Sophie Anderson
Anya
Hope Atlas
Hannah Austin
Lisette Auton
Lucy Avery
Karen Badenoch
Neil Baker
Thereza Baker
Caroline Bald
Matthew Barr

Sue Barsby
Atty Bax
Val Bayliss-Brideaux
Sara Beadle
Victoria Beecher
Ruth Behan
Jean Bell
Kirsteen Bell
Denise Bennett
Susmita Bhattacharya
Andrew Bishop
Mark Blackburn
Sophie Blacksell Jones
Marti Blair
David Bleicher
Astra Bloom
Catalina Botello
Casey Bottono
Lucie Bowins
Samantha Boyce
Stephanie Boyd
Penny Boyland
Lia Brazier
Robin Brodhurst
Ann Brolan
Andrew Brooker
Rebecca Brooker
Iain Broome
Sandesh Brown
Christian Brunschen
Danny Brunton

Charlotte Lottie Bryan
Julie Bull
Stuart Burleigh
Anna Burtt
Sebastian Buser
SJ Butler
Caroline Butterwick
Patrick Byrd
Elen Caldecott
Marion Caldwell
Pete Caldwell
Chaucer Cameron
Louisa Campbell
Rosie Eleanor Canning
Ted Carmichael
Eileen Carnell
Clare Carr
Jenny Cattier
Mavis Chow
Alix Christie
Geraldine Clarkson
Rachael Clyne
Peter Coles
Lorna Collins
Jennie Condell
Trevor Coote
Ruby Corah
Isabel Costello
Charles Couzens
Ruby Cowling
Lisa Craig

Tim Craig

Richard Craven

Dr Vanessa Crawford

Lesley Creyton

Julia Croyden

Erika Cule

Eva Culhane

Elaine Curtis

Emma Cuthbert

Tara Darby

Rupert Dastur

Patricia Davies

Susan Davies

Marisa J Davis

Kat Day

Rachael de Moravia

Graham Dean

Tom Dean

Victoria Delahunty

Wendy Dossett

Christopher M Drew

Jessica Duchen

Lucy Duncan

Rachael Dunlop

Ben Dunn

Caroline Dunn

Jane Dunn Ostler

Kathryn Eastman

Sharon Eckman

Viv Edwards

Jennie Ensor

David Eskinazi

Carrie Etter

Cath Evans

Daisy Evans

Frances Evans

Jo Evans

M. J. Fahy

Elizabeth Fakhr

Mia Farlane & Kristen Phillips

Karen Feldwick

Oliver Feldwick

Abi Fellows

Victoria Field

Nathan Filer

Lucy Finn-Smith

Joyia Fitch

Julie Fitzgerald

Kylie Fitzpatrick

Rob Fletcher

Pat Foran

Caroline Fox

Holly Fox

Eddy Francis

Philippa R. Francis

Ruth Franklin

Lisa Fransson

Nicky Freeling

Kim French

Melissa Fu

Symington Gail

Frances Gapper

Di Gardiner
Kieran Garland
Stuart Gee
F. Ghiandai
Daniele Gibney
Barbara Gilbert
GMarkC
Miranda Gold
Sophie Goldsworthy
Jackie Gorman
Anita Goveas
Melanie Grant
Michelle Gray
Nick Gray
Courtney Greatorix
Theo Greenblatt
Susan Greenhill
Jo Gregory
Lottie Gregory
Oliver Gregory
Kitty Grew
Rory Grew
Jennifer Guttenplan
Sarah Guy
Julian Gyll-Murray
Caroline Hadley
Ian Hagues
Jacki Hall
Emily Hambleton
Lorna Hambleton
Richard Hamblyn

Ian Hamilton
Thomas Hand
Jack Harber
Katharine Harding
Lisa Harris
Shelley Hastings
Sophie Haydock
Anwen Hayward
Niazy Hazeldine
Simon Heath
Sarah Hegarty
Alison Helm
Alice Hemming
Lianne Herbert
Kirsten Hesketh
Lisa Heslop
Paloma Hillman
Susan Hodgkinson
Julian Hoffman
Sandy Hogarth
Gemma Holden
Nada Holland
Lorraine Hooper
Mark Hornby
Kate Horstead
Victoria Hulatt
Sue Ibrahim
Sangeetha Iengar
Tania Inowlocki
Keri Jackson
Kellie Jackson & the Word

Away community
Sarah Jacobs
Anthony James
Heidi James-Dunbar
Angela Jameson
Carolyn Jess-Cooke
Daina Joblin-Hall
Alice Jolly
Chris Jones
Gaynor Jones
Sarah Jones
Angie Jorgen
Laura Juett
Martyna Kamińska
Sharon Kearney
Rachel Keen
E.J. Kelly
Chrys Kelson
Kate Kemp
Christopher Kenworthy
Aaron Keogh
Indu Khurana
Dan Kieran
Campbell Killick
Michele Kirsch
Korin Knight
Sarah Knowles
Teresa Kupfer
Reuben Lane
Andrew Leach
Tom Lee

Janet Lees
Kath Lewis
Pippa Lewis
Sandy Lieberson
Yin F Lim
Amy Liptrot
Toby Litt
Adam Lock
Kate Lockwood Jefford
Jane Lomas
Joe Louis De Canonville
Michael Loveday
Robert Loveday
Nina Lucking
Rosemary Mac Cabe
S D Mackay
Paige MacKenzie
Fiona Mackintosh
Andrea Malizia
Adam Marek
Alison Martin
Anna Mazzola
Ali McGrane
Amanda McLachlan
Mark McLaughlin
Otis & Lewis McLaughlin
Donna McLean
Catherine McNamara
Barbara Joan Meier
Annette Mercer
John Mercer

Marian Mills
Alex Mitchell
John Mitchinson
Damhnait Monaghan
Linda Monckton
Mary Monro
Patrick Morris
Richard Morriss
Sarah Mosedale
Jim Muirhead
Robin Mukherjee
The Munster Literature
    Centre
Kate Murdoch
Kim Murdock
Karin Murray
Peter Muyshondt
Carlo Navato
Lara Newson
Sophie Nicholls
Joanna Nissel
Nova Nolan
Samantha O'Reilly
Dominic O'Shea
Sylvia O'Sullivan
Louise O'Neill
Phil Olsen
Nicholas Ostler
Jane Ostler-Barnett
Elizabeth Ottosson
Cheryl Pappas

Ian Parr
Dave Parry
Colette Paul
Jane Pearce
Esme Pears
Heather Pearson
John Pearson
Rosie Pearson
Eleri Pengelly
Penny Pepper
Ann Perrin
Cathy Pitt
Steve Platt
Justin Pollard
Tamara Pollock
Steve Pont
Clare Pooley
Briony Pope
Sue Powell
June Prunty
Mel Pryor
Alexa Radcliffe-Hart
Vlad Railian
Kerry-Jo Reilly
Victoria Richards
Anna Richardson
Mihai Risnoveanu
Jane Roberts
Johanna Robinson
Benjamin Rolfe
C.D. Rose

Miranda Roszkowski
James & Monica Rowe
Lydia Ruffles
Cathy Runciman
John D Rutter
Joshua Ryan
Kerry Ryan
Tamim Sadikali
Tanya Savio
Shannon Savvas
Maggie Sawkins
Anneke Scott
Sheila Scott
Tanya Shadrick
Dhruti Shah
H Shah
Neema Shah
Jacqueline Sharp
Anna Shelton
Jeanette Sheppard
Victoria Shropshire
Jerrie Ann Shropshire
   Edgerton
Diane Shugart
Jo L. Siegel
Julia Silk
Eleanor Simmons
Mish Singh
Rachael Smart
Elaine Grace Smith
Jillian E. Smith

Kay Smith
Eamon Somers
Zoe Somerville
Mandeep Soor
Ruby Speechley
Nicola Spurr
Chris Stammers
Sharon Stammers
Helena Stephens
Gillian Stern
Paul Stevens
Fiona Stewart
Kay Stratton
Jane Street
Anne Summerfield
Judy Sutton
Kate Swindlehurst
Christopher Tait
Helen Taylor
Jean Taylor
Neil Taylor
Richard Taylor
Sion Tetlow
Rosie Thapa
Andy Thesen
Bev Thomas
Issy Thompson
Liz Thompson
Steve Thompson
Mike Scott Thomson
Patricia Thorburn-Muirhead

Isabel Tomlin

Wendy Toole

Kerstin Twachtmann

Sophie van Llewyn

Eva Verde

George Vernon-Hunt

James Vernon-Hunt

Jonathan Vernon-Hunt

Victoria Vernon-Hunt

Jo W

Brian Wagstaff

Judi Walsh

Caroline Ward Vine

Ellie Warmington

Zoe Weston

Barbara Wheatley

Hannah Whelan

Rachel White

Jan Wigley

Andrew Wille

Judith Williams

Tiffany Williams

Anna Wilson

Christina Wilson

Margot Wilson

Alison Woodhouse

Charlotte Woodward

Millicent Woolls

Georgina Wright

Duncan Wu

Sofka Zinovieff